THE FLANDERS CASE

by
David R Ewens

Grosvenor House
Publishing Limited

This book is published by
Grosvenor House Publishing Ltd
28-30 High Street, Guildford, Surrey, GU1 3EL.
www.grosvenorhousepublishing.co.uk

A CIP record for this book
is available from the British Library

ISBN 978-1-78148-591-0

About the author

David R Ewens is as familiar with the history, landscape and communities of Ypres and West Flanders as he is with Kent, where he lives and writes.

1

Frank Sterling got up from his desk and wandered over to the sash window that overlooked the small market square. Business was not brisk that late afternoon in early September. As he looked down, he saw a young woman negotiating the door of the small Spar supermarket just opposite, struggling with her wispy hair, a pushchair and its mardy contents, a grizzling toddler. Down on the same side as his office, there was a small queue in front of the cash machine – people topping up their money for the week. In Jack's Café a few doors down from the supermarket, one or two old folk were finishing their tea as things were packing up. A few leaves whirled half-heartedly in little flurries in sheltered parts of the square. They blew in, settled, and then no breath of wind was enough to get them out again.

A small cloud that had momentarily hidden the early autumn sun scudded quickly on, releasing a burst of beautiful, sharp sunshine onto the sparkling, eye-catchingly green sward of the churchyard, and glinting off a bauble on the belt of the young girl sitting huddled with her boyfriend on Sterling's favourite bench. The grey and green of the market place and churchyard was a perfect counterpoint to the delicate blue of the sky.

Soon it would be the time of day he looked forward to most, that bit at dusk just before night really took over from day and the contrast between the black of the roofs and the leached light of the sky was at its starkest. He wondered if that was the time he liked best because of the sudden evening coolness and the smoky smell of autumn, or because his first pint at the Cinque Ports Arms beckoned. It was a close call.

His office wasn't big, but he had made it comfortable. From the door down in Market Street next to the library, a narrow flight of stairs led to the first floor and the office door. Inside, the desk opposite was old and cheap, but large enough, with a telephone on the right and a computer in the middle. The computer was one of the latest, and his main concession to technology. Everything else was in its place – paper for the printer, pens, pencils and notebooks – all the tools of his trade. Someone had once suggested he was borderline OCD. He couldn't argue with that. To the right of the desk, the two-drawer filing cabinet had a long way to go before it would ever be filled up with case files. But he didn't mind that. He had plenty of time.

In quiet periods, as an antidote to boredom, Sterling worked the lever of his high-backed chair, gas pressure letting him move smoothly up and down. There was a chair for clients in front of the desk and against the wall by the filing cabinet was a sofa for their associates, if there were any. The editor's lamp on the desk with its green shade and faux-gold stem convinced him he might be on the way to success.

He kept the walls white for optimism's sake. There were pictures of hop farms and scenes from the Stour and Medway – not many, just enough to avoid a completely bare look. If the radiator under the window (connected in some mysterious way to the library below) stopped functioning, a two-bar electric fire supplied enough supplementary heat to make it almost cosy on cold winter days. A globe on a little table in the corner between the desk and the window was a reminder of the world beyond Sandley.

Some ancient quirk had caused the office and the stairs that led to it to be inserted into the building as a kind of afterthought, as if the local government powers-that-be had decided the library's resources would not fill it all, and that separate premises would generate extra revenue. They were right about that, and it was Sterling who was providing it through his lease. There was a room behind his, with access by a separate flight from the ground floor, which held local archives.

He was about to turn away from the window when he noticed the black BMW and its tinted windows pull deftly into the only spare parking space in the narrow roadway. I never have that kind of luck, he reflected. His eyes flicked automatically to the number plate. It was new but not personalised, so there were no clues there.

The woman who emerged from the car was fully aware of the eyes that turned in her direction from all around the square, from the man waiting for his money at the cash machine to the woman coming out of the dress shop on the corner. Sterling put her in her early thirties, a bit younger than him. The neckline of her black dress was low, at least from his viewpoint, and the hem was just short enough at the bottom to indicate class, but not vulgarity. Her pale skin contrasted with the sheen of her long, almost-black hair and the sparkling rubies at her ears. Describing her as slim overlooked the fullness of her figure. The woman from the dress shop seemed exasperated at the display, as if a sister was letting the side down. The man at the cash till lingered for a longer viewing. His look was sly and appreciative.

Sterling thought of Andy Nolan, always for some long-forgotten reason referred to by his full name and never just as "Andy" or "Nolan". In the many long hours they had spent together in police patrol cars and pubs, back in their early days on the force, Andy Nolan had thought up a classification system for men and women. A man's man liked the company of other men, spent time in rugby club bars, drank beer and talked about sport. A woman's man preferred the company of women, listening to them and taking an interest in them, discussing hair, fashion and soaps. It was easily possible, in his classification, to be a gay man, for example, and still be a woman's man. A woman's woman might spend her working days as an investment banker amid the banter of an all-male office, but prefer to spend non-working time with other women. Then there was the whole Pandora's Box of the man's woman.

There were faults in Andy Nolan's system, and blurs between all the categories. Back then, they were callow, overconfident young men with no inkling of how little they knew of people and life, and guilty of all kinds of dubious, sexist, assumptions. But in that first glance at the figure below, Sterling had no doubt about which category she fitted into.

She looked around her as she slammed the car door with a gentle clunk. She clearly knew what she was looking for as she focused on the library and the small doorway just next to it. Sterling pulled his head back, the habit of long hours of surveillance, as her eyes moved from the sign above the doorway below to his window. It seemed he was going to get a visit. He looked around the office with a new eye. Everything was more or less in its place, but the sunlight highlighted one or two patinas of dust on various surfaces, which he quickly wiped down. He had just stationed himself in his chair and reactivated the computer screen when there was a brisk knock on the door.

'Come in,' he said, not shouting, but projecting his voice so that he knew it would clearly be heard, and through she came, preceded by the scent of what he thought might have been Samsara.

'Mr Sterling?' she asked, displaying the same confidence and self-awareness as when she'd emerged from the car.

'That's right,' he replied, half-rising from his desk and trying to look as if he had been engrossed in something important, rather than daydreaming by the window.

'And you are….?'

'Gloria Etchingham, Mr Sterling', she said, as her eyes, a clear light blue, took in the surroundings.

He offered his hand from over the desk and received a distant, light handshake from slender fingers – one of those less than hearty affairs involving finger and thumb grasping finger and thumb, rather than whole palms. He could see a small mole above her left breast that acted as a kind of optical lure. He tried hard not to stare. He indicated her seat and sank back into his own. He steepled his fingers as he leaned back, realised immediately that it looked pretentious and shifted his hands down to his lap. There was a pause.

'So, Ms Etchingham….' he began, leaning forward, 'how can I help?'

'Mrs Etchingham', she said firmly. 'Mr Sterling, my problem is rather delicate. Before we get too much further, I need to know more about your credentials, and most importantly, of course, your ability to be discreet.'

That's blunt, he thought, but it usually happened at some point. He spread his hands on his desk, palms upward.

'Well, I'm in the Association of Private Investigators, and I am a former policeman. I expect I could get some endorsements from former clients. But actually trust develops, in my experience, from how we get to know each other in the initial interview. As for discretion, well, that is guaranteed from the moment you engage me.' Sterling smiled and tried to rustle up a sense of being solid and reassuring.

The trouble was that the API was a casual, slack organisation far more interested in subscriptions than regulation; being an ex-policeman might be more a danger signal than a source of confidence; and he had no former clients, or indeed any clients at all, to endorse him.

But something worked, either in Sterling's manner, or in what he'd said, shifting things for the woman in front of him. Now she leaned forward with a sudden intimacy that caused a flush to creep up from his neck to his face. A small smile replaced the previous frown.

'It's not a police matter,' she said. 'All I need is a small operation – someone with a bit of determination and imagination. Someone with a never-say-die attitude.'

Some of the elements she identified applied to Sterling and some didn't. He did not believe his attitude could be described as never-say-die, but his operation was certainly small. Whatever assumptions she was making, it was not the time to hold back.

'OK, Mrs Etchingham. I think I'm your man. What's the problem?'

'I recently lost my husband,' she said. 'You may have read about it in the papers. He disappeared three months ago. The police found his blood in our garage, but they never found his body.'

'He loved me, Mr. Sterling, so if he was still alive, I'm sure he would have contacted me. If he'd been kidnapped, I would have got some kind of ransom note. I've heard nothing. I think he's dead. There's no other explanation.' Her eyes pooled momentarily with tears. When she had recovered a little, she continued. 'He ran a clothing import company very successfully for many years, and one or two other things. He was a little bit older than me, but we got along well. I miss him.'

'I'm sorry that things are so difficult for you, Mrs Etchingham', said Sterling. 'It's particularly hard when things are unresolved. I have actually read about the case, and I know the police haven't made much progress, but I also know that I simply haven't the resources to match what they can do. I'm not sure they'd welcome outside interference, either. Imagine the reception I'd get trying to muscle in.'

'Oh it's not that, Mr Sterling. I'm not confident about the police, especially after all this time. But there are some things that haven't been sorted out. It's not just about Keith's disappearance, or money issues and things like that. After all, whether he is alive or dead, I haven't been left destitute.'

She was silent for a moment, whilst Sterling thought, no, destitution must be a long way away, taking into account the customised BMW outside, the expensive perfume and the sophisticated dress.

'I think something happened in Keith's family that really bothered him, and he wanted to find out more about it. It was a question of honour. Now he's gone, I want to know the truth.' She sniffed and got out a small, embroidered handkerchief to dab at her eyes. 'That way,' she said, 'I can put everything behind me and start to move on. Keith would have wanted me to. So I decided to go through all his papers from scratch.'

'And what can I do that the police can't, Mrs. Etchingham?'

'I want you to provide the discreet service that you promised when I first came through that door. I think what I've found could be important, but I can't make head or tail of it.'

She moved to her handbag and got out a sheet of her husband's company notepaper. She clasped it instinctively to her chest. Her eyes met the detective's. Then she made her decision and pushed the paper across the desk. He leaned forward. Excitement brought a sudden tightness around his ribcage.

'Find out what this means, Mr. Sterling.'

He looked at the sheet. Apart from the name, address and details of the company, only a few letters and numbers were printed in a bold, masculine hand in the middle of the page.

CFC EF 9174 II.G.14

Mrs. Etchingham's eyes shone. Sterling could not tell if it was because they had just brimmed with tears, or because she was excited. 'That's my husband's writing. I'm sure it means something – but what?'

'I'm sure I can find out,' he said. 'But couldn't you do this yourself? Anyone with access to a computer would probably be able to find out something. I'm not sure why you've come to me.'

She looked down at the desktop. 'I've never really needed computers. I left school at 16, Mr. Sterling, and Keith and I got together not long after that. He used to say that I had different talents.' Her eyes met his with a sly smile. 'He didn't trust computers himself, either. He did everything by telephone in the early days before he built his companies up, and when he was really successful, he got other people to do the computer work.'

Sterling offered no more objections. If the woman wanted to hire him, that was fine by him. Nothing else was occupying him. If it meant more meetings with her, that might be a bonus.

'You'll need to know my terms,' he said, giving her his daily rate. 'There will be expenses, too, and of course, VAT. I think we should start off with two days and a review at the end of that. I can start tomorrow. If I don't find anything, and honestly, Mrs Etchingham, I can offer no guarantees, at least you'll get a full report about what I've been up to. I may need to run something by one or two trusted associates, but of course they will only know a fraction of what you've told me.'

Her face fell, but Sterling knew he couldn't do everything on his own. He took a few more details, and then the interview was coming to a close.

'It's good to have met you, Mrs. Etchingham,' he said as he rose from his desk.

'You must call me Gloria, please', she said softly.

Sterling did not in general believe that an investigator should get too close to a client and vice-versa, and he certainly did not believe in being on first-name terms. In this case, he believed first-name terms after just a

30-minute interview had the potential to make things go very badly.

'And I'm Frank,' said a voice he barely recognised.

'I look forward to an update at the end of Thursday … Frank.'

The click of her heels down the narrow staircase and along the passageway to the door below felt lighthearted, almost relieved. Sterling moved involuntarily to the window to peer down. She knew that's what he'd do. As she unlocked the car and opened the door she looked up with a small smile. Her hand came up in a tiny, shy, jerky, shoulder-high, open-palmed wave – just for him. Then she was gone.

A song came from nowhere into his head from the popular music of a previous generation, the music he was locked into. It was the David Bowie version of "Sorrow" that he remembered, not the Merseybeats'.

The girl in the song was a blonde and Gloria Etchingham was a brunette, but there was plenty of sorrow she could cause. If Sterling had known how much, he might have grasped the opportunity she put in front of him with less careless speed.

2

Sterling stayed at the window after the BMW moved off. A small, rational part of him sensed that Gloria Etchingham had put on a performance which he had been drawn into, and that he had been played. So he needed to be cautious. But a larger, more naïve part felt flattered and important, as if there was a spark between them, and she'd specially selected him for a crucial task.

As he looked out, something in the churchyard near where the courting couple had been half an hour before caught his policeman's eye. A thin young man in a dark leather jacket was leaning coolly on one of the headstones. Sterling just had a chance to note the John Lennon gold-rimmed spectacles, the pale face and the narrow head; brown hair cropped short on top. Maybe the man sensed Sterling's gaze. A minute later, he was gone, drawing back around the church and then striding down towards Holy Ghost Alley. It was too late to follow, so Sterling returned to his chair, picked up the sheet of paper, leaned back, put his feet up on the desk and scanned the jumble of letters and numbers. A few moments later, he tipped forward and started the computer.

After an hour of searching for the meaning of Keith Etchingham's code and reading news reports of his disappearance, he was little further forward. He looked at his watch. He had been due in the pub 20 minutes ago. He turned the computer off, slipped on his overcoat and made his own descent, though less daintily than Gloria Etchingham, down the stairs and into the square. It was time for that pint. He could mull things over and seek further inspiration in the pub.

He followed the footsteps of the thin man into St Peter's Street and Holy Ghost Alley. The alley started off as a kind of tunnel cut between two houses, and was then hemmed in by the brick walls of little Edwardian villas that enclosed small back yards. It was claustrophobic until you burst into the wide high street up from the quay.

Sterling's local was a few yards up on the seaward side. He'd had a fondness for the Cinque Ports Arms since his first-ever pint of beer here before a cricket match against Sandley School. His team had arrived early and the teachers had let them wander into town. He didn't play well that afternoon. He couldn't hold his drink as well as he'd learned to in his mid-thirties.

Now his first watering hole was his favourite. The landlord had changed since those sunny, youthful days, of course. The current incumbent, Mike Strange, had been "something in the security services" before his battered retreat to Sandley. He and his wife Becky had taken over the pub three years before, after a traumatic experience in the Middle East. Mike was still prone to "episodes", and his hands shook occasionally as he pulled pints. Sterling had never known a person to move more swiftly or silently. He still gave a start every time Mike materialised to remove empty glasses and crisp packets.

Now he was at the bar – a short, wiry man of about 40 with a sallow complexion and brown eyes. His dark, close-cropped hair was flecked with grey. Although he dressed casually, he was dapper, from the light desert boots on his feet to the immaculately ironed jeans and the sharp creases of his Oxford shirts. He rarely spoke, and when he did, he said little.

Sterling thought of the time he had met Becky in town. Over coffee, he had tried to find out more about him. 'Ah, Mike,' she had replied, wistfully. 'Well, he's certainly not like you. He reckons that you could start a party in an empty aircraft hangar, and that you'll talk to anyone. Look at you now, having coffee with me. He's much more introverted. He likes and admires you for all the things he's not. But he's very loyal and trustworthy, and he's afraid of nothing. You might find that out one day.'

At the bar, Mike raised his eyebrows as Sterling approached. After a moment, a pint of Spitfire appeared. Mike gestured with the side of his head towards the little sofa in the corner by the fire. Sipping the top off the pint, Sterling wandered over. Jack Cook, approaching fifty, large-framed and going to seed, was in from the café. He was a cheerful and generous drinking buddy, witty and louche enough that you could forgive his casual, virtually compulsive untrustworthiness – especially where there was money to be made.

With him was Angela Wilson, the librarian. Her slender black fingers drummed the tabletop. She was impatient for news. Her Sandley friends still didn't know why she had left the metropolis for their hick little country town. The burglary at the house she'd just moved into had been Sterling's last case in the police. 'I didn't get out of London for this,' he remembered her saying after the court hearing had sent the young housebreaker down for six months. In the lonely turmoil of Sterling's life then, his wife gone, his job gone, he sensed a kindred spirit.

'You were just unlucky. What happened to you wasn't typical. It's nice down here, actually. I'll show you,' he'd said in the coffee shop near the courthouse. And he had, in trips to the coast and walks round the town, whilst she developed his talent for crosswords, and, with her witty and wide-ranging discourses, helped him to plug the gaps in his education. Because of her, there was less to regret about his careless inattention at school.

'So, Frank, what's new?' said Jack.

The question was inevitable. Everyone in the Square had seen the comings and goings (or rather, the coming and going) from Sterling's office. He had been considered a promising police officer in the local force – allegedly alert, bright and hard working – but with a number of flaws. One of them surfaced now.

'You mean the building inspector's visit?' Sterling said flippantly. 'Very routine, Jack. Nothing at all to write home about. Everything just as it should be.'

Angela smiled widely. 'Yeah, right.'

On the sofa with his pint, Sterling made an announcement. 'Well, lady and gentlemen' (Mike had appeared silently at his elbow, making him start as usual), 'I've got myself a case.'

Since they were all, in their different ways, in ruts – the library, the pub, the café – they took a borrowed pleasure in Sterling's attempt to be different. They willed him to succeed.

'Of course, client-investigator confidentiality prevents me from being able to divulge more details,' he said, the police-speak borrowed from many a tortured encounter between police spokespersons and the press, 'but I am able to report that I am both excited and intrigued. 'And,' turning to Angela, 'I may need help with a little research.'

The banter continued into the evening. The group moved on to other things. But towards the end, with a couple more pints having slipped smoothly down in the way of the first, and the crossword set out companionably in front of them, Angela and Sterling drifted back to the subject of the Etchingham visit.

'I imagine she made a pretty big impression on you, Frank,' Angela said. 'A woman like that.'

'Did you see her?'

'Saw her. Smelled her perfume at the bottom of the stairs. Saw the car.'

'Well, she was very attractive.' It seemed pointless denying the undeniable.

'How about the case? Is it going to be interesting? And just as important, is it going to be safe?'

'Yeah, both, I think.'

'You know what you're like. Just don't get into any muddles like the ones you've got into in the past.'

Their eyes slipped down awkwardly to the final clue in the paper in front of them:

Sounds like quiet filth, idiot (7), with only four letters missing - S_H_ _ _K.

They were silent. Sterling reflected on the "muddles" that had done for his marriage, and with them the pain and dislocation. A natural tendency to pessimism had not helped.

At around ten, it was natural for everyone to drink up and leave the cosiness of the pub for the cosiness (or otherwise) of their homes. At the door, Sterling looked back and nodded at Mike, mouthing his thanks, and as always, Mike was ready to acknowledge them. The journey home was a gentle stroll down No Name Street, over the road, through the arch of the Guildhall, across the Cattle Market and into his house just beneath the grassy embankment, the street lamps orange-capped sentinels as he padded on his way. He felt good – a case, some much-needed income, the company of friends.

A little final celebration was all he needed now, so he put on some West Coast balladry. The knock at the door a few minutes later caught him at a moment of mellowness. Sterling could be naïve, especially after a couple of pints, and when he heard the knock on the door, he opened it in hope, rather than fear. But caution was what should have guided him. The door, barely ajar, was shoved sharply right in his face, banging his forehead.

Sterling was five foot eleven, and his assailant was shorter, but he seized the advantage straight away, and never gave it up. A punch landed right on Sterling's collarbone just as his hands were feeling his forehead. Another landed in his stomach, doubling him over, and he found himself on his hands and knees in his own hallway, not quite knowing whether he was gasping or retching. A balaclava-covered head bent to his right ear, the mouth a mean little 'O'. Sterling could smell the damp wool and feel the spittle of his attacker on his ear. At the same time, he heard the heart-soaring guitar riff at the end of "Ship of Fools". He wondered if some sort of prescience had influenced his choice. Equally ludicrously, hope flashed through his addled brain that future enjoyment of that riff would not be ruined by the current association.

'That job you took today,' said the 'O' in the balaclava. 'You know what I'm talking about. Leave it alone. Carry on, and it'll be much worse than this.'

He aimed a final kick at Sterling's rib cage, which connected with what must for him have been a very satisfying crunch, and then slipped back into the night. Before curling into a ball by the radiator to analyse which bit was hurt the most, which bit might be broken, and whether any blood was staining his much-liked hall carpet, Sterling thought it sensible to crawl over to shut the front door. He didn't want his attacker to come back thinking that he had not quite finished the job.

Sterling was no stranger to beatings, administering and receiving. He'd been in plenty of police vans at closing time on New Year's Eve and other flashpoints, and he had participated in his fair share of rucks. So although he didn't relish violence, not like some of the other men, and, he reflected, women, cooped up for half an evening and raring to get out and crack a few heads, he did feel that he knew about it. And the thing about the going over that he'd just received was that, although it hurt, his experience told him that it had been administered just a tad half-heartedly. A kick in the balls as a coup de grace would have been far more powerful a message than the kick in the ribs. And why not a punch on the nose to generate a bit more blood and drama? It had all been a bit tentative.

"Ship of Fools" had long finished by the time Sterling lurched into his armchair, with this and other thoughts flooding through his mind. He knew his weaknesses, but there was something else. Setbacks, bullying, intimidation – they just made him more stubborn and determined. He knew in that moment that he'd be seeing this case right through to the end, despite the throb in his forehead, the wince of pain in his ribs that every tiny shift brought, and the tenderness in his stomach. In that same moment, the answer to the last unsolved clue popped into his head: *schmuck*. Of course. Someone must have been trying to tell him something.

3

It would have been a glorious morning. The sun rose from the bank behind the house and flooded the back garden, as neat and well clipped as a good bourgeois garden should be, and with golden colour. But Sterling was still smarting from his carelessness and the bruises on his forehead, shoulder and ribcage. His stomach felt tender as he rubbed it gently. The only visible part of him that had taken damage was his forehead, and there was a slight but unmistakable swelling right in the middle of it. He'd need to explain that away to the sharp-eyed Angela, and maybe Jack, if he went down to the café for a mid-morning refresher. But he still had the case and he needed to move on to the next stage. He limped back along the way he'd come the night before, the sun on his back this time, and the paper Gloria Etchingham had given him tucked next to the wallet in his jacket. It was barely 8:30 when he climbed the narrow stairs to his office, put the kettle on for a second, post-breakfast cup of tea and set the computer humming.

Once again, he set the sheet in the middle of the desk. It still gave up as few clues as when he had first looked at it. CFC stood for chlorofluorocarbons – those gases once used in deodorants and now abandoned because of their impact on the ozone layer. In the bathroom of his father's house was an old map of the UK and all the old counties, produced for distribution to clients by a CFC manufacturer based in Watford or somewhere close, presumably to grease the wheels of any deals that were going. That company must be nowhere now. He was digressing again. He added 'prone to distraction' and 'tendency to wander off-task' to his list of foibles and character defects.

The letters and numbers on the sheet drew him back. He didn't think CFC had anything to do with gases. What about EF and the numbers? Nothing leapt laterally into his head. He supposed that the 'II's were Roman numerals, rather than the small 'l's or large 'i's of the alphabet. He considered whether the dot between the 'II' and the 'G' was significant.

He wondered how investigators managed before computers and search engines. They would have spent time in libraries amongst the books and microfiches. He was even lucky there. If Google couldn't help and his progress up here foundered, there was always Angela downstairs, with her cryptic crossword mind, her tenacity and, not least, that intimidating first-class degree in History and the master's degree in Information Science – and not from the University of Tiddlyham, either. His mind drifted from Angela to Gloria Etchingham. Everything had happened quickly yesterday. He should have been more focused on finding out more about her, her husband, and the circumstances of his disappearance – not on that little mole. He had allowed himself to be diverted. But if he didn't have any luck, it wouldn't be an ordeal to give Gloria a ring – in the interests of the investigation, of course.

He should have persisted a bit longer on his own, but he could not ignore the top-class researcher at the bottom of the stairs. He was on someone else's time, too, so that was a good reason for a short cut. And another cup of tea would be most welcome. He clattered downstairs and into the library.

Although Angela had not long opened up, it was already busy with some of her regulars – pensioners, mostly, reading the newspapers and having a warm. She was at the front desk, her brow furrowed in concentration over her mail. Then a small queue developed as customers came with queries. Sterling sat at the table opposite the desk and waited. He knew that although Angela had been born and brought up in London, her family were from Trinidad. She was tall, only an inch or two shorter than Sterling, and with her high cheekbones and slender frame, it was easy to imagine that she descended from West African royalty. Her fine wrists and neck were, as usual, adorned with delicate silver bracelets and necklace. Although she often favoured black trouser suits and white blouses, it must have been a special day, as she was in a black skirt and red top – the colours, as he now knew, of Trinidad and Tobago.

Sandley was a conservative place and non-white faces were a rarity. Sterling remembered the stir when Angela first arrived, the muttering about take-overs and inundation, and then how short-lived it had all been. She greeted all the customers with the same easy charm and friendly smile – patient with their questions and quick if necessary to offer extra help. Under Angela's influence, the sub-library was a genuine community centre.

He had been leaning back on two legs of the chair, watching. The leaning back was a habit he could not shake off, like a recidivist former smoker. As the last query was dealt with, he tipped back just that small fraction too far. Testing the boundaries was part of the same habit. To stop himself from toppling onto his back, he grabbed the table. He managed not to fall over, but there was a clatter and screech as his knee smacked into the table. Everything was quiet after the sudden movement. He shuffled in the chair as Angela and the rest of the library looked over at the source of the commotion. When she was free, he limped over.

'Smashing up my library, Frank?' She looked more closely at him. 'What have you done to your head?'

'Sorry about that.' He glossed over the reference to his head. 'I thought you might like to participate in a bit of detection, Angela.'

'So you're stuck already, then.' A little dual-purpose smile played across her face – a reaction both to the racket and the detection, or lack of it.

'Well, time is of the essence.' He offered the scrap of paper. 'I've looked at one or two things on Google, but nothing came up of much use. It's got to be a code of some kind.'

'Genius....' murmured Angela, but her eyes lit up. 'Do you want to hang about, or do you want to leave it with me?'

Knowing Sterling and his business, she guessed that he was not exactly pressed for time or juggling a range of commitments and responsibilities. 'Come on, let's have another go on the computer.'

A short, hunched, elderly man came to the counter to hand back some books, his old-fashioned courtesy meeting Angela's warm, modern professionalism.

'I can be all yours for a bit now – the mighty resources of the county council are at your beck and call.'

Sterling liked the idea that there was a large organisation behind him. On Angela's computer at the desk, the search engine's home page already invited action on the screen.

'Well, let's try CFC first – break it up a bit', said Angela.

They had no joy with that – all Chelsea football club and Sunday soccer in North Essex. It didn't look as though they were going to get anywhere by lazy, modern, technological methods. As Angela's restless fingers skipped over the keyboard, Sterling's attention wandered. By a quirk similar to the one that had inserted his office separately on the first floor, these premises were graced with stained glass windows – not of ecclesiastical quality; more 1930s semi-detached front door glass panels – but shards of early morning sunlight glinted over the surface of the workstation. There were no motes of dust, he noticed. Angela managed her domain tightly. He reflected that he hadn't really asked Gloria Etchingham much about the paper. He had been too busy on other things. He saw eventually that Angela's red-tipped fingers had fallen still.

'Leave it with me for a bit, dream-boy. You might consider giving your client' (Sterling detected that same sardonic undercurrent) 'a ring and getting a bit more background about this code – if that's what it is. It seems to me that what you've got to go on is pretty flimsy. Actually, the whole thing is flimsy. And maybe dangerous. You didn't say how you got that bump.'

He shrugged and let her get back to her other work. But he knew she was right, too – right about everything. It was quarter to ten, a decent, late enough time to give Mrs Etchingham a ring – and he was convinced that she'd be reassured about his energy and commitment if he wanted an update. Back upstairs in the office, a fly buzzed against the window, the tap-tap getting fainter and more futile with lack of progress. A paper clip had made a jagged scratch on the right of his desk, just by the green-shaded editor's lamp. He punched in Gloria Etchingham's number, expecting to remember them in the coming weeks. He was about to hang up after six rings when a sleep-drugged voice drifted along the wires.

'Hello?'

'Mrs Etchingham, Frank Sterling. I hope it's not too early. I'm working on your case and making progress, but maybe you can help me some more with a couple of things.'

'Hang on a moment.' There was a scraping sound. 'OK, I'm back.'

'It won't take long. That paper – with the letters and numbers on it. You said it was among your husband's papers. Can you tell me any more about those?'

'Keith had loads of papers,' she said, 'Business, family, horseracing – and he was quite well organised. The police went through them all. The tax people would have if they'd been able to get their grasping hands on them. I found them amongst his family stuff. He dabbled a bit in family history – subscribed to a website. But he didn't really share that with me. Actually' – Sterling could detect a wistful, sad little note in her voice – 'there were parts of his life I knew nothing about. He was interested in the wars. Some of his family were killed in the First World War – in Belgium or France. That scrap of paper was in that section. Why didn't you ask me this yesterday, Frank?'

Yes, why not? he thought. Because he was concentrating on the wrong things. But he blustered.

'Well, in things like this, you sometimes don't know what you need to know until you need to know it, if you see what I mean. And I thought I might have enough information already. I'll probably need to get back to you at other points, as well. When you have a chance to check, you might like to try and find out which family history website your husband subscribed to. There's another thing....' He was remembering that mean little balaclava-covered mouth and the kick in the ribs. It was quiet at the other end of the telephone. 'Did anyone know what you were asking me to do?'

'No. I never tell anyone my business. Why?'

'Well, I don't think it's anything much, but I got a bit of a warning yesterday. It probably isn't even connected with this case. Don't worry about it. I'll get back to you if I need to.'

At the end of the call, Sterling noticed that the buzzing of the fly had stopped, and he could see why. It was struggling helplessly in a spider's web in the left hand corner by the window – and getting weaker. He couldn't see a spider, but the end looked inevitable.

So, Keith Etchingham had been interested in his family history – and the First World War. Maybe there was something promising there. Those letters and numbers could be some kind of record. He was already thinking that it would have been good to have paid a bit more attention in history at school. He switched on the computer and flexed his fingers. If you were interested in your relatives around the First World War, where would you start looking? If they were male relatives, and they went off to fight, the Services would have some sort of record. It was time for another search. The trouble was that he didn't have a name – just a jumble of letters and numbers. He started with the Royal Navy and through that, found himself in the National Archives.

Half an hour passed in interesting but random and irrelevant fact-finding. He knew more about the Battle of Jutland. He knew that Nelson had been 12 when he joined the Navy – and considered the best officer that ever served. He knew that many records had been destroyed by Luftwaffe bombing in 1940, and that Samuel Pepys had worked for the Navy Board after the English Civil War. But he was no closer to solving his clue. He wondered why he had chosen the Navy to begin with. The odds, surely, were with the Army.

The British Army website didn't seem too promising. There was plenty about joining and plenty about Afghanistan, but nothing about records, or records of war dead. Sterling got sidetracked again, this time by pages on the Victoria Cross. It was fascinating, but not getting him further forward. He idled down through a list of 'frequently asked questions'. It was deaths that Gloria Etchingham had referred to – some of her husband's family killed in the First World War. And here was a question, in, of all places, the Royal Military Police section. His finger on the mouse trembled very slightly.

'My ancestor died during a campaign. Can I find information about him?'

Maybe there was something here. He followed the link. On the website was a "Debt of Honour" database. He wondered how common the name 'Etchingham' was. He keyed in the information he had – the name and the Great War. If this was just a diversion, it wasn't unpleasant research. The webpage came up quickly, and he wasn't deluged with Etchinghams – there were just three in the records.

And then he found something. 'Now we're motoring,' he whispered to himself – the phrase Andy Nolan used at the beginning of any joyrider pursuit. But when he came to think a little more, all he had done was to solve the riddle. The reference he'd spotted was to somewhere in Belgium, but did it have any significance? He looked up at the clock on the wall. The minute hand was obscured by the crack at five minutes past the hour. It was time for coffee and some more thinking.

He clattered back down the stairs and into the library. Now that he thought he'd cracked the riddle himself, he wanted to stop Angela from wasting her time. He did not want to get on the wrong side of her – not that she was the type to bear grudges. Fortunately, it didn't look as though she had made much progress. She seemed to be grappling with a particularly complex enquiry from another one of her elderly regulars. Sterling shuffled from foot to foot as he waited. He wanted to pop down and see Jack and get that coffee. A moment or two later, the pensioner moved slowly off to the bookshelves, and he was at the front of the queue.

'Angela, I think I've found something. I did manage to speak to Gloria Etchingham and that gave me a lead.' He could hear the apologetic tone in his voice, and his open palms reached out to her.

She rolled her eyes, but she was smiling, too. 'Good job I got diverted, then. What have you found out?'

'The reference is to somewhere in Belgium. I'm going to see Jack and ask if I can borrow one of his cars. I'll see you later.'

It was busy in the cafe. The mid-morning crowd was in. Serious inroads were being made into the carrot cake, and indeed all the cakes Jack baked so diligently for every morning rush. It should have been a traditional small town coffee shop that Jack ran, full of genteel pensioners with time on their hands. Jack did have that clientele, but the tables were also populated with professionals. There was a centre for mentally ill people in Stour Street, and there was a fair sprinkling of those in the café, as well. A couple of community support wardens were taking the community part of their job descriptions more seriously than the support part – lingering over coffee and cake.

Throughout the cafe was the steamy aroma of fresh coffee and a smell of baking. Someone had made elves' footprints, where you press the sides of your fists in a walking pattern on the window and add toes with thumb and forefinger, on the misted window next to the door, fading fast. A waitress produced a milky coffee. This was Sandley. There was no such thing as latte here. Sterling smiled his thanks, but she'd already moved on to the next person in the queue.

Jack joined him at his tiny table, wiping his large, pale hands on his apron. His red face made his eyebrows seem all the more sandy. There was a gap in the right one. He always seemed to get scorched with fat, or suffer from other culinary hazards.

'How's progress with the Great Detective?'

Sterling liked Jack, and he'd known him for years, but he was a gossip, and there was talk of other vices. Jack's question made the ex-policeman in him cautious. Some of his cases in the force had gone horribly wrong. He looked into his coffee. A whirl of steam emerged from the froth and joined the fug. He tried to see the exact moment of transition.

'I might be making a bit of progress, Jack. Not really sure yet. But I've got a favour to ask. Can I borrow one of your motors for a few days?'

Jack had a garage with some bangers that he worked on when he wasn't baking. He was restless, whereas Sterling got so deep into relaxation he couldn't get out.

'You can have the Peugeot if you want. I tuned it recently. It's running well. Where are you going?'

'I think I may need to go over the water for a few days. I've got one or two things to check out.'

'France, eh? This is quite a nice little job you've got, Frankie-boy.'

It was Belgium Sterling was heading for – a place just few kilometres east of a town called Ypres. But he let Jack think France. This was Sterling's case, and he didn't want to share it with anyone, not even Angela, and certainly not Jack. He finished his coffee. He'd go over tomorrow, and if he was going to do that, he'd need to make arrangements – book ferries and a hotel.

Where was Ypres, anyway? He was proud to be a Little Englander because he was content in his little town and community. Besides, the Greens were right. He saw no reason for the wilful overuse of finite resources spent on travel. But part of him was uneasy because there was a big world out there and he lacked curiosity about it. There was something else – something in Jack's manner he couldn't quite put his finger on.

The waitress was cleaning tables when Sterling left. As the weak sunlight eased through the steamy window he could see the glistening, just-wiped surfaces and the dry bits she had missed.

Back in the office, it was straightforward to check locations and book a ferry from Dover to Calais. The hotel was easy too. But he shook his head at all the equipment he allegedly needed to drive legally in Europe – the fire extinguisher, the luminescent warning triangle, the breathalyser kit, the headlight shades, the spare bulbs, the first aid kits, the GB sticker, and some things that were even more obscure. He'd been a policeman, so he knew the reality. He could ignore all that. Jack wouldn't be supplying it, anyway. He wondered where his passport was.

In the pub later on, word had got out about the car and the journey. Sterling had Jack's gossip to thank for that. He knew that Angela would have been discreet. Things were going to be different for a few days – and not very welcome for such a home bird. He took comfort in his pint.

The pub emptied, and he thought he'd better go home and pack. As he made for the door, Angela touched his arm.

'Take care, Frank', she said. 'I've just trained you up on the crosswords and that. Big investment. I wouldn't want to have wasted my time.'

Sterling did take care on the way home. He didn't want any encounters like the one the evening before. He kept wide on the pavements and cast his eyes left and right, up and around. Someone might have malice in mind, but he was ready to avoid a complete ambush, and ready for a rumble, as Andy Nolan would have said. In the soft September air, with just enough of an autumn chill to make him turn up the collar of his jacket, the wind soughed around the trees and rooftops and bats whirred and swooped in the night sky.

His footsteps quickened as he approached the front door, but he could see nothing that looked like a threat. Key, lock, open, in – he didn't linger. When the door was shut, he stood still in the hallway, his head slightly tipped as he tried to make out any sound. He saw the scrap of paper amongst the junk mail, crumpled as though it had been picked from a bin and hurriedly smoothed. "LEAVE IT" was crudely printed.

Sterling knew what he had to leave, but he also knew that he couldn't. It wasn't because of the flimsy professional code of the Association of Private Investigators, or the sacrosanct interests of his client. It wasn't because he loved danger, since he could be as squeamish and timid as anyone else. He just couldn't tolerate being told what to do and what not to do. That was why he couldn't stay in the police, and that was why he was going to Belgium in the morning. Still, he trawled back through the day. How did the people making the threats know what he was doing? His safety depended on finding out, or at least making sure nothing more leaked out.

Packing didn't take long – that was one thing he had learned to be good at. On the stereo, Bob Dylan had finished too.

Almost the last clue Angela and Sterling solved this evening had flummoxed them for a little while.

'Nine back into old sports car and ate a Great War memorial' (5, 4).

At the time, he hadn't made much of the answer they had worked out. He wasn't one for signs and portents. Those Roman historians Angela had spoken of in one of her mini-lectures, writing about three-headed calves and other grotesque omens before great battles, left him unmoved. But in the middle of all his subsequent travails in Belgium, and at the Menin Gate itself, his mind drifted back to that evening in the pub and he thought that maybe there was something in that mumbo-jumbo, after all.

4

Even as he was dreaming that night, Sterling was speculating about what Angela might say in another of her roles – that of dream interpreter. His father was telling him what he'd always said – count the days you're going to be away and then count out your shirts, socks and underpants. Go through what you have to do in the morning and pack your toilet bag accordingly. His voice was kind and warm, as it always was, and although he was there in his dream, Sterling was missing him.

The scene changed to the exam hall at school. His best friend Nicky Moran was next to him, fiddling with his pencil-sharpener. Then Gloria Etchingham was on top of him, wearing very little, her breasts looming over his face. There was that little mole on the left one. Her smile was mysterious and generous at the same time.

Crossword clues flashed through his head. Angela was shaking her head sadly. In front of him was the mean little 'O' in the balaclava … and the first punch coming in freeze frames into his face. He woke with a start. Between a small gap in the curtains, a small ray of sunshine made a yellow slat on the back of a woman in the picture of a hop-picking scene in late 19th century Kent.

It wasn't late, but he didn't have time to linger, either. A quick breakfast and a cup of tea and he was on his way with his grip to Jack Cook's. The ferry was at 10, half an hour away, and he'd arranged to meet Jack at his garage at quarter to nine. The sweet smell of honeysuckle carrying on the soft breeze greeted him as he walked down Tannery Lane. Green paint peeled off the garage door. A little knot was missing from the wooden lintel over it. He looked automatically right and left down the lane, the habit of training. Only a young man with his daughter and her packed lunch emerged from a neighbouring back yard. The My Little Pony case gleamed pinkly, garishly, in the early morning sunshine.

Sterling knocked softly on the inset door, and when Jack's general assistant, Mickey, opened up, he stepped over and through. He longed to tell Mickey that his pudding basin haircut had gone out of fashion circa 1844, that those baggy jeans were never ever in fashion, and the cow's lick across his forehead completed the unfavourable look. But Jack told Sterling that Mickey was amazingly popular with the girls in the shop and elsewhere. He said that Mickey had The Look – which Jack defined as a cocky smile, an irrepressible confidence and cheeky eyes. If Mickey didn't click with one girl, he apparently wasn't afraid to try another. Sterling could tell Jack was envious.

'Mickey,' Sterling said.

'Mr. Sterling.'

'Jack about?'

'In a bit, Mr. Sterling, probably, but he's given me the keys, just in case.'

Sterling looked into the garage. There was a workbench and tools scattered around. A soap dispenser promised effective cleansing from swarf. Lined up were three cars – an old Jaguar, an even older Lotus in British Racing Green – drab and ugly, in Sterling's view, and a decrepit little dark green Peugeot 106. He knew which he was getting.

'Jack told me to tell you it will run OK. You'll need to fill it up. It doesn't like fifth much. I don't think there's anything else.'

Jack didn't appear, so Sterling thought it best to get going. He'd seen TV programme once in which the narrator said that the philosopher Immanuel Kant barely left Konigsberg in his entire life. Maybe he felt a lurch any time he strayed too far. Sterling always felt a lurch when he left Sandley – the market square, the familiar pubs and shops, even the cash machine down the lane next to the surgery. He was a private eye without a car and travel-phobic. It was a joke, really, and he couldn't even claim to be producing a rebuttal of the *Critique of Pure Reason*.

It wasn't a smooth drive down to the ferry at Dover. The Peugeot rattled and occasionally shuddered if he took it above 55, and Mickey was right about getting into fifth. There was a nasty grinding sound every time Sterling tried. The car had been built at a time when power steering was an optional extra. This was a completely basic model, with even the head rests long discarded. The spongy feel around corners was positively alarming. Even as he edged in good time down the Jubilee Way, the road that swept down from the cliffs in a long curve right to the terminal, avoiding the town altogether, he wasn't relaxed. He'd noticed the silver Ford never more than three cars behind, right from the Eastry turn-off. But, he thought, it was broad daylight. What could possibly happen to him now?

The White Cliffs weren't so white close up. In the watery late summer light, they had a kind of grey pallor. Herring gulls wheeled and glided over clumps of tough vegetation clinging on to fissures in the chalk. Looking hard, Sterling could see the cliff paths. He and his father used to come out with all the other picnickers on Sunday afternoons with their little fold-out tables and striped metal and plastic chairs, eating sandwiches and drinking tea and beer as the Channel glittered, and ferries in endless procession docked in and departed from the port below. In those days, all Sterling wanted was to be on a ferry somewhere exotic and romantic – the Riviera, the Adriatic, or maybe Scandinavia. It was the opposite now. Now he'd rather be up on the clifftop with his father, listening to his stories. He'd been a customs man, and a good one. Over many years, he'd come first in the unofficial league table for spotting contraband.

Leaving England isn't difficult – it's getting back in that's harder. The bored douanier in the customs block could barely bring himself to look at Sterling's passport. Somehow his moustache looked as tired and bored as he did. At least the girl at the ticket booth had something to do as she keyed the Peugeot's registration number into her computer. Her look asked 'How far do you think you're going to get with that?' as her appraising eyes ran up and down the car's battered lines.

Sterling joined line 137 to become part of the queue for the ferry. In the car in front, a young couple was bickering. The woman looked resolutely out of her passenger window. Even in profile, Sterling could see her pout. Exasperation squeezed the man's shoulders. Sterling felt glad to be alone. To his left, a man and a couple of boys were having a desultory kickabout, holding their hamburgers in greasy paper and taking opportunistic bites as the ball thudded gently back and forth. The air had a salt tang and a whiff of diesel as Sterling wrestled with the window handle. Why do people want to go on holiday – the packing, the ten-hour drives or the ten-hour plane rides, cloistered in the end with people they'd probably hate? It wasn't exactly homesickness he felt at that moment – more a yearning not to be going away.

He looked hard, but there was no silver Ford in the vehicle decks – just the cars and vans of holiday makers, a few coaches and lorries bound for destinations across Europe. He followed the last passengers through the metal doors and joined the crowd clanging up the stairs to the brazen lure of duty free shops, restaurants, bars and one-armed bandits, whose lights winked like particularly forward street-walkers on a wet night. He didn't need any perfume and he could buy his booze in the pub. He was set on coffee and the paper, and a quiet spot away from the little schools of children darting this way and that, as if hitched together with invisible rope. He wondered why they weren't in school, and wished they were.

He reviewed his progress. He had a capricious and beautiful client. His thoughts gravitated back to the first interview. He had a scrap of paper with a code he thought he'd cracked. He had received two warnings and a still sore shoulder after a late-night beating. It wasn't much to go on, and that was why he had found himself on a ferry to Calais with a clapped-out car in the decks below. At least it wasn't a divorce case.

He got up and stretched. The atmosphere in the rest area was close, and the tinkle of the slot machines and the restless meanderings of his fellow passengers were making him tense. It was time for a bit of air. He picked up his holdall and wandered to the back of the boat, finding the door to the outside passenger area. There were little pools of water on the green metal decking and little spots of rust pitted the railings. He could barely see England's coastline in the haze. The sea was calm and a rich blue for September. The churn of the ferry's screw made a wake that was thick and foamy, but gradually absorbed back into the sea in a long tail. He hunched his shoulders, pulled up the collar of his jacket and leant his forearms on the rail. The breeze was cool, but the sun warm in his face. No one else was out here. He began to think that maybe it wasn't so bad being away for a day or two. He got out his mobile telephone to check for messages.

Sterling's guard was down, but years in the police had heightened his senses, and he became aware that it wasn't just him standing there, with the wake stretching into the distance, the seagulls hovering on the air currents and the tankers dotted on the channel horizon. He was half turning as the blow came, and it was the turn that saved him.

His telephone spiralled from his grasp into the sea. A powerful surge of pain shot down from his shoulder blade, but that was better than a blow to the back of his head. Then he was in a desperate, scuffling, wrestling embrace. His opponent was large. Sterling's face was buried in his collarbone. He was pinned to the railings and his back was arching over and into the sea. Any further and he was going to tilt and tip over, no doubt bashing his head on the stern as he went. What a miserable way to go, and for what? A strong, gloved hand was in his face, pushing it relentlessly back. Another hand was prising his arms loose from the large bulk in front of him. There wasn't long to go as resignation spread over him, loosening his limbs.

The door opened. One moment, Sterling was in a death struggle. The next, those same schools of children that earlier he'd wished crossly away now darted across the deck. Now they were at the railing on the left, now at the railing on the right. Their shrieks and giggles mixed with the harassed warnings of their teachers. Sterling's attacker had slipped away in the noise and disorder while he leaned over the rail and retched above the wide-eyed gazes of his now-silent saviours.

It was easy to pass off his illness to the concerned teachers as sea sickness and not a reaction of shock and relief at his unexpected reprieve. It was more difficult to work out the reasons for a second assault in just a couple of days. This one had been as serious as the other one had been casual. Just now, he had no answers. But he knew that this was no game. He had wanted the case and he wanted to solve it, but he wanted to stay alive, too.

For the rest of the journey, he stayed inside and made sure he had plenty of people around. He found an aircraft-style seat in one of the compartments opposite the duty free shop and planned his route from Calais to Ypres. Cross-country would be best. He did not want to be followed, and thought he could slip away into Calais and buy some time and safety. Opposite, a grey-haired man took a sip of his brandy from a cheap glass. His wife had a glass of wine. The man raised his glass in a silent toast. Sterling caught the scent of cheap perfume as a pink-haired teenaged girl sulked past with her hooded boyfriend. There was a continual wall of noise from the ship's turbines, the queues in the bars and coffee shops, and a restless bustle of movement throughout the ship. Sterling was very comforted.

It was comforting, too, to join the sea of people making their way below decks to their cars. Get in amongst them and all you had to do was drift until you came to the right door at the bottom of the right flight of stairs. Sterling checked the Peugeot and found nothing that might be of concern – but how would he know? A bored deckhand in orange overalls and a hard hat gestured urgently. Sterling was holding up the line. He started the car and blinked as he emerged from the darkness of the hold.

He hadn't been to France since he was a kid. He hadn't been anywhere. A notice reading "Tenez a droit" reminded him to drive on the right side of the road as he left the docks area and looked for the sign to take him away from the motorway and into Calais. He felt better on the road to Cassel. He checked his mirrors frequently, but no one was following.

The landscape was empty under the bright French sky. It was canal country, and as he crossed the bridges, the canals stretched out in wide silvery threads. Villages and towns passed in steady procession as he reflected again on the case. Gloria wanted him to break it, so she wouldn't object to this journey. But someone in England had wanted to stop him, and someone in the Channel wanted to kill him. So not everyone wanted the same thing. By the time he reached Steenvoorde on the Belgian border, he reckoned he had two enemies from the two separate assaults. Near Vlamertinge, he saw two men unloading tools from a van outside a market garden. Two elderly women were walking among the plants and flowers, each holding baskets with their selections. He knew that Ypres must be close.

Sterling came in through an industrialised retail estate. A new Alfa Romeo sports car welcomed him from a raised dais outside a huge glass and steel structure with other shiny automobile temptations – if you were of a type to be tempted. Less fancy units stretched up concrete roadways. Outside a warehouse a sit-on tractor-mower was perched on top of long metal pole.

Here, abroad reminded him of England – the commercial side of Canterbury or the space between Margate and Ramsgate – but as soon as he got to the town square, Europe took over again. A huge medieval building stood in the top corner and stretched halfway down. If it had not been for the case, he might have wanted to explore. But then he thought that if there had been no case in the first place, he wouldn't have been winkled out of England.

He parked in the square and found the hotel on foot. In the cool, wood-panelled interior, the receptionist welcomed him with a small smile.

'You can have a room overlooking the marketplace if you want, Mr Sterling.'

'Thank you,' he said. 'I'd like that.' He needed to find out who had come with him to Ypres.

The room was clean and comfortable. Two single beds were set out at right angles to and either side of the window. On the opposite wall next to the door was a wardrobe with some hangers. A small desk and table lamp fitted snugly under the window. There was a small picture on the wall, maybe the room's only decoration. It looked like a van Gogh – maybe the peach blossom at Arles. In the top corner between the door and the wardrobe, a small television hung down from a Heath Robinson contraption attached to the ceiling. It was slightly lopsided, as if someone had climbed on a chair to adjust the picture and knocked it all out of true. A door led off to a small bathroom.

Sterling sat on one of the beds and ran his hands through his hair. He could feel a dull ache from the blow on his shoulder. The duvet was thin, but he could double up with the duvet from the other bed if he was cold. He realised he was hungry. If he had the wit to put things in phases, phase one of the case was over. But he was never much of a one for phases, and anyway, he had the wrong sort of wit.

Although he was hungry, detecting had to come before foraging. He settled in the chair at the desk and looked out of the window. It was nearly 7 o'clock. The hall dominated the square in its medieval finery. He remembered vaguely that Ypres had been blasted apart in the First World War and rebuilt in its original image. He could see the Peugeot in the middle of the square near the bus terminal, which was set artfully next to the car parking amongst the cobblestones.

Day was being transformed into night as he looked on. In the cafés around the square, lights came on and he could see the dull orange glow of outside heaters under the awnings. The pale half-moon hovered in the blue evening as the sun's light bled away. In the gloaming, knots of people waited for buses to sweep them off – this one to Menen, that one to Komen, another to Roeselare – all in a steady rhythm. Sterling began to notice that many places in this region had alternative spellings. For English people, "Menen" was surely the "Menin" of the crossword clue. A large, shaven-headed young man in just a T-shirt and trousers waddled on the pavement beneath his window. The fabric of the T-shirt kept catching in the folds of flesh on his back.

Sterling had never minded the night-long vigils in the patrol car with Andy Nolan. There was always something to see or something to keep you awake, and Andy Nolan was never short of a joke or a story, or a classification system, for that matter. But those days were long gone now, and he felt alone.

As he watched on, the cafés filled up, and then he noticed a new movement. Towards eight o'clock, streams of people – school children, old people, people wearing medals, people in berets, people in uniforms – began streaming in small and large groups up towards the right of the hotel, and out of sight into a street leading off the square. A couple of very young teenaged boys, one with hair shaped in a Mohican and the other with blonde gelled-up spikes, and both in bomber jackets, surreptitiously hunched together to light up beneath him. Their group forged on ahead, with harassed adults who must have been teachers at the front and rear. The receptionist could explain about all that later on.

For the next few minutes, nothing much happened. Sterling scanned the square in sweeps from left to right, chin now cupped in his hands, elbows on the desk. His belly rumbled. He was just short of telling himself that no one had followed him to Ypres. Then he noticed a figure enter the square from a street to the right of the hotel – tall and thin, in a leather jacket – too far away for further detail. He shifted in his seat. Those were not the clothes of a Belgian, and his direction of travel was not with those flocks of others. Something in his gait and manner was familiar. He walked towards the Peugeot, but didn't stop.

He gave it a quick sideways glance, and then moved off towards the other end of the hall.

Sterling knew who it was. The man who looked like John Lennon had followed him from Sandley. As Sterling was turning away, he caught another movement below and to his right. Two men in dark casual jackets and fawn trousers emerged from the night's lengthening shadows, and then another two, not far away. They were tall and well turned out; their hair short, light brown and neat. Brown, highly polished shoes reflected in the last of the evening light. They could almost have been in uniform. For a second, Sterling could not think who they reminded him of. Then he had it – these were the Seventh Day Adventists who sometimes come knocking on suburban doors – or people uncannily like them. Hard eyes stared into the distance beyond the hall. Sterling had much to think about. He could do it while he had some dinner.

Au Miroir was the café he chose. It looked the liveliest, and he could survey the square from the opposite angle to the hotel while he was mingling amongst the local drinkers. He took a corner seat at the window. Clearly, the spaghetti bolognaise he ordered had come from two huge vats in the kitchen, but he needed fuel and the beer was good. He was missing England already – the Spitfire and the crossword, the comforts of home – but at least he could examine the reputation of Belgian brewing. And he had made progress with a case that was perhaps more important than he had realised. He knew he had to be careful, but ensconced at that cosy corner table and lulled by all the medieval beauty in front of him, he underestimated, by some distance, the danger he faced over the coming days.

5

The young receptionist with shiny red hair also managed the breakfast buffet. Sterling observed her bustling about in this different role, her freckled face flushed in the room's warmth, before reflecting back on his latest nagging dream. He had been making notes from a physics textbook in some kind of classroom laboratory. John Lennon, his round glasses flashing in an angry face, had been telling him that research could not be pure research anymore. You had to publish papers and chase after funding. When he disappeared, a woman in a white coat came in and asked Sterling what he was doing.

'I've just started a Physics PhD,' he said. 'I'm making a few notes'.

'Where are you getting your funding from?' she asked.

Sterling said that it was all paid for, but she said that couldn't be right, until she saw the confirmation among his notes. He followed her into the corridor.

'I'm a bit worried about all this,' he said. 'I can't understand the textbook, even though I'm making notes, and I'm doing this PhD, but I haven't even got a GCSE in Physics.'

Angela often provided unexpected insights into Sterling's dreams. This time, he thought he knew what she'd say. You're out of your depth, Frank, and the case is too complicated for you. And you might not get paid.

The restaurant smelled of bacon, kept in a large metal container. The lid slid back to reveal a mass of stuck-together meat that achieved the miracle of being burnt and undercooked at the same time. The girl had clearly seen too many breakfasts to notice anymore. In silent islands around the room, fellow guests picked their way desultorily through their food. A child in the corner with blond curls banged his spoon arhythmically on his plate. A baked bean was propelled onto the floor. His father did nothing. His mother, blond hair escaping from a clasp, looked boredly out of the window. Sterling imagined swiftly walking over, removing spoon from hand, throwing plate against wall and cuffing the kid, in smooth unhurried movements. The 'plink... plink, plink' rattled tinnily in his head.

'Miss...?' he called out to the waitress-receptionist. If he was going to stay a few days, it would be good to know her name.

'Christina,' she smiled.

'OK. Thank you. Christina, why did I see streams of people heading out to the right of the square last night?'

She looked at him. 'Aren't you here for your war dead? At 8 o'clock, everyone – except we Flemish – goes to the Menin Gate to pay their respects and hear the Last Post. That's why the British come. The Ypres fire brigade sends trumpeters – every day since it all began in 1926.'

The Menin Gate. He remembered the crossword clue again. It made him miss the pub, and in a more obscure way, England itself. Maybe he'd go along, to get some background, though he was more intent on solving Gloria's little mystery.

The square had had a soft magic in yesterday's evening glow, supplemented by the lights as they went on in all its hotels and cafes. In the morning light, it sparkled in a new way. He had noticed that the hall in the square was now a museum. Lennon was out there somewhere waiting for him, and those others. But where he was going he wanted no company. He guessed that the In Flanders Fields Museum would have a map to show him where his destination was, and give him a way to keep his own company.

Inside, the air was cool and the light supplied by muted spotlights. A man with a seemingly permanent frown lodged between his eyes briskly took his money and pointed to an interactive map.

'You'll find what you're looking for on that.'

And he did – it was in a lane off the Armentières road, about four miles east of Ypres. He made a note and ensured that there was no record of his search. The tourist guide had a good map of the town and the surrounding district. He was lucky to find the information so quickly, as he had not been organised enough when he left England. He lingered at the entrance to the museum beyond the ticket office, engrossed for a minute or two in the story of a Berlin student conscripted to the Ypres front in 1916 in an interactive display.

He didn't have to wait long. At the other end of the entrance area, Lennon had slipped in. A small queue had developed at the ticket booth. Sterling moved quickly into the museum and out of sight. Maybe in other circumstances, the displays and stories would have occupied him all day. Angela would have loved this. But he hurried on, room by room, in an urgent rush to the exit.

He was in the street moments later, heading for the car. For a furious moment, he thought it wouldn't start. Then a blue plume of exhaust spurted into the crisp air and he lurched away, rattling over the cobbles into the road and heading towards what he identified as the Lille Gate out of the town in the direction of Armentières. He glanced in the mirror and just saw his stalker pitching into the street. Lennon knew that Sterling had slipped away from him. He stood still, put his hands into the pockets of his leather jacket and watched him go. 'Yes', Sterling breathed as he rattled up Rijselsestraat to the other end of the town. As he puttered along he realised, in a small eureka moment, that Rijsel must be the Dutch name for Lille.

It wasn't hard to find Chester Farm Cemetery. The war dead were buried all over West Flanders and beyond, and the signposts to the cemeteries, in white lettering against a sombre brown, came up every few hundred metres. Sterling turned left off the Armentières road into flat well-cultivated farmland. Flemish and Dutch people had come to Sandley in the 17th century to escape persecution. Their Low Countries brickwork and architecture was everywhere in his hometown. Everything was different here, but curiously the same.

The cemetery shimmered in the Flanders light. Sterling needed his coat, but he also needed his sunglasses as he stepped from the car in the lay-by onto the springy deep green turf. He drew up for a moment at the gate of the cemetery, enclosed in its perfect brick and white stone rectangle. He could see a tractor a few fields away, and two men in work boots talking and pointing at something beyond. The rows of pristine headstones extended out symmetrically before Sterling. He breathed deeply to calm himself. He'd remembered to bring the reference Gloria had given him. He squatted at the headstone near the back of the cemetery furthest from the gate and the road. All the details were here – Etchingham, Frederick (EF), Private 9174, row II.G.14. Sterling learnt further that the young man had been in the 4th Battalion of the Middlesex Regiment and killed on 10 October 1917, three years after the start of the war. He was 'Remembered with honour'.

Sterling wasn't sure why tears sprang into his eyes in that immaculately kept piece of ground deep in the Flanders countryside. It had all happened nearly a hundred years ago. But Frederick Etchingham had been ten years younger than Sterling when he died, and the landscape then had not been the calm and peaceful setting it was now, with the wind whispering softly through the nearby trees and the shadows wavering under the sky.

The turf around the headstone looked undisturbed. So did the flowerbed full of hardy annuals in which the headstone stood in perfect relation to all the others. Sterling had been to many crime scenes and walked in line with many other police officers searching for clues and murder weapons. There were archived film reports to prove it. He could tell that nothing had been left in this little corner of Belgium even as he scrabbled through the soil with his fingers, feeling a weight of blasphemy and the reproach of his ancestors. He stood up and stretched. It was disappointing. What had seemed so clear-cut in the office in Sandley was murkier here. He drifted back to the car. If there was nothing here, he'd been wasting his time. In the car, he put his hands on the wheel and reflected. He did not much relish the conversation he'd have with Gloria Etchingham.

As he prepared to go, he thought that perhaps he'd been too hasty, and that he should sign the book of remembrance, if there was one. It would be a form of penance for scrabbling about in the soil. Just inside the gate of the cemetery was a small square metal door set into the stone, with a handle perfectly shaped for a half-closed fist. It looked standard enough to be in every Commonwealth cemetery in southern Belgium and northern France. The book was there. Sterling leafed through the comments, which were overwhelmingly poignant: 'Rest in peace', 'Never forgotten', 'Very peaceful', 'Thank you'; 'We will remember'.

With the book was a register. Sterling wondered why he had been so fixated on the headstone. He turned immediately to Frederick Etchingham. He quivered slightly with the feeling that comes when you know you are on the right track. There it was – a small rectangular card sellotaped under Etchingham's details. He peeled it off and slipped it into his pocket – but not before he had memorised the neatly printed letters.

He took a last look at Chester Farm Cemetery. He did not think he'd be returning. Some of the side wall towards the left had been knocked or fallen down. A little warning tape in yellow and black fluttered in the breeze. He hoped someone would come along and repair it soon. The souls of the dead in the cemetery deserved that.

The bright bricks and stones and white cross receded in his mirror as he drove back to the main road. But something else caught his eye – and it looked uncannily like a silver Ford. He was still excited by his discovery, but now he was anxious as well. Somehow Lennon, if it was him, had managed to follow him after all those manoeuvres at the museum. The question was, how could he stop him next time?

As he drove back into town on the bridge over the moat, he thought he had the answer when he saw a young cyclist. It wasn't that he was riding with no hands on the handlebars, even on the cobbles, or that in one easy, confident movement he swept off his pullover and draped it round his neck. It was that he appeared to be going the wrong way down a one-way street.

At the hotel, Christina had turned back into the hotel receptionist. Sterling wondered when she did not have to work. He leaned sideways with an elbow on the counter and clasped his hands.

'Christina, don't you ever have time to rest?' She looked up from the computer screen. He noticed her green eyes. Small earrings and a ring on her right finger were little green islands on her pale skin.

'Well, Mr Sterling, this is a family place. We all have to work here to make it worthwhile. Have you had a good morning?'

'Not bad. I'm going to need to make a telephone call back to England. Can I do that from my room?'

'Yes, Mr Sterling, all the instructions are by the phone, but it's expensive.' She looked at him for a moment; eyebrows raised a little, one just a little higher than the other. 'Don't you have a mobile telephone? Everyone has a mobile these days.'

'I lost mine on the way over.' Sterling winced as he rubbed his shoulder and thought of the struggle on the ferry. I'm also going to need to get on the internet. Any advice on that?'

She thought for a moment and made a decision. 'I have a laptop behind the counter. If you don't need to be online for long, you can come and use that'.

'Lovely offer, Christina. I'll come back when I need to do that.'

He turned around from the second stair up towards his room.

'One last thing, Christina … What does *Uitgezonderd* mean?'

When he heard the answer, he resumed the trudge upwards. The idea was promising. He might need it if he could solve the next part of the riddle. He sat at the desk and looked over the square. It was getting towards lunchtime and Ypres townsfolk were filling up the cafes, interspersed with groups of British and Commonwealth visitors. At the café below, a couple of doors from the hotel, a plump Flemish man and his wife were attacking what Sterling now knew was one of the Ypres staples, spaghetti bolognaise, and drinking what looked like the cherryade he had been fond of when he was a kid. But surely it wasn't that. It was something else to check with Christina.

Even Sterling could follow the instructions for external calls. He pushed the buttons. There were more clicks and bleeps than usual, but then came the familiar English dialling tone. Efficient and cool as ever, Angela picked up after three rings.

'Sandley Library. How can I help?'

'Angela, it's Frank.'

'Frank, how's it going? Any progress?'

He was glad to hear her voice. Angela was like all his other friends. She could tease. She could laugh at his outlandish dreams. But when it all got to a certain point, he could rely on her for anything. Another of those times had come around again.

'Yes, good progress – if progress means fighting off someone on the ferry, losing my mobile and getting followed by five people at the last count. And, probably most important of all, finding something from that reference we researched.'

'Frank, when you say "fight off", what exactly are we talking about here?'

'Angie, I'll tell you about it later, but most of the tools of my trade I can't get access to here. I really mean my computer. If I read out what I found at Chester Farm, can you do a bit more digging for me?'

'Read away. I'll have some time to look this afternoon.'

Once more, Sterling gave silent thanks for his own personal researcher. 'Here we go: Pop TH SaD Exec P. It's pretty obscure. But I have confidence in you.'

'More than I have in myself, maybe. Take care now, Frank. It sounds as though things are getting dangerous.'

He hung up. Angela was right, and what was disturbing him was how Lennon seemed to know where he was and where he was going - in fact, he seemed to know every aspect of his business. The less Lennon knew, the safer Sterling felt. If Angela found anything out and it involved another journey, he wanted to do it without anyone else being involved. He lay on the bed, hands behind his head, staring at the opposite wall. His idea just needed thinking through.

A few minutes later, it was time to cement his friendship with Christina. Being a private investigator meant long hours of boredom, sordid secrets and an uncertain income. But attractive hoteliers were a bonus.

'Mr Sterling – again', said the hotelier in question. There was a sardonic smile to go with the raised eyebrow. He felt himself beginning to be smitten.

'Christina, I'm going to be here a few nights, I'm sure. Please call me Frank. What I need this time is a bicycle hire shop. I think I'm going to get a bike and pedal around a bit.'

Clearly, she did not take him for a cyclist, but she directed him to a place in Diksmuidsestraat, one of the streets opposite the hotel. It was 1:30. The shop was not likely to be open till two or later. He decided to join the townsfolk at Au Miroir for a croque monsieur, which he learned was a toasted ham and cheese sandwich, and maybe some cherryade.

The croque tasted good. He got the cherryade by pointing to a glass that a man was drinking from a few tables away on the terrace. It was a kind of strawberry beer. He would not repeat the experience, and felt a pang for a pint of his local brew. But homesickness was not high on his list of worries. As his eyes scanned the square from behind his sunglasses, there was Lennon on a bench outside the Town Hall, and there were the other men, still dressed like Seventh Day Adventists, window shopping opposite the Grote Markt, doubtless looking for jackets with a continental cut. Lennon looked like Lennon – skinny in a black leather jacket, slouching a little. But the others … Sterling could see how they filled their jackets and slacks. They had muscles, and their bull necks signalled trouble and violence. Somehow, he couldn't finish his croque anymore, and the bitter taste in his mouth didn't come from the Früli beer.

6

It was 2:15 when Sterling left Au Miroir for the bicycle shop on Diksmuidsestraat. It was in a district of other small shops, away from the tourist traps and clothes shops of the Grote Markt. Here, the locals had much of what they needed for daily life – a pizzeria for a quick lunch, a dry cleaner's, a delicatessen. On the corner of Diksmuidsestraat and Oude Houtmarktstraat, a street cleaner finished smoking a roll-up and flicked it in the gutter, scooping it up adeptly in one smooth movement with his litter pick-up stick and slipping it in the waste receptacle. Sterling reckoned he did it that way because it was quicker than putting it directly in the bin.

He looked up above the display of mainly 'sit-up-and-beg' bicycles in the shop window. 'Cycles de Groot' said the sign. If Sterling had worked out from estate agent's boards that 'Te koop' meant 'for sale', he assumed that 'Te huur' meant 'for hire', and here bikes were for hire. As he entered the shop, a bell tinkled towards the back. The smell of rubber and lubricant and other bicycle mysteries once again triggered memories of childhood. The narrow shop frontage was deceiving. Two rows of bicycles for every type or combination of user stretched long metres back into the store with a central aisle in the middle leading to a counter at the end. One row was led by a little pink number with stabilisers – 'My First Bike'. From a doorway next to the counter, a tall man with swept back curly dark hair and a bandit's moustache emerged, wiping his large, oil-grimed hands with a paper towel.

He tilted his head back a fraction. It was more economical than saying 'Can I help you?' but his dark eyes did not seem unfriendly. Sterling asked if he could speak English and this time, there was a downward nod.

'I need to hire a bicycle,' said Sterling, strangely losing confidence for a moment.

The man looked slowly past him up one row and back down the other. 'You've come to the right place, then. But I'm sure you won't mind me saying that you don't look much like a cyclist to me.'

Sterling wondered how both Christina and this man knew he rarely cycled, but like Christina, he seemed a person he could deal with. 'Well, I'm not,' he said. 'On the other hand, I'm not going on a gut-wrenching, sweat-drenching training tour of the Flanders battlefields. I just need something I can potter about on around Ypres, with a lock in case I want to go into a shop or a museum or something.'

'OK, I think I've got something for you.' From a corner full of hire cycles, he wheeled out a sturdy, black, man's bicycle with high handlebars and cross bar. 'If you want to sit on it, I'll adjust it for your height. It's got mudguards.' Almost to himself, he muttered, 'I just don't understand bikes without mudguards. Who wants a wet stripe up their back when it rains? God....' To Sterling, he said 'The deposit is 150 euros and it's 20 euros a day.' They completed the transaction.

'Where are you staying?'

Sterling paused and stood up straight.

'Come on, why so sensitive? I just don't want you cycling off with my expensive hire bike.'

They looked at the bike. It was functional and clean, with a newly oiled chain, but old and black, and had a battered air. They looked at each other. Then they laughed.

'Hotel Sultan.' Sterling knew why he felt prickly, but he needn't have made it so obvious.

'Well, business is slow today', said De Groot, 'and you look like a man who has some interesting stories.' He was weighing things up, as Christina had over the laptop, and made a decision of his own. 'Why don't you come out back for a coffee?'

Sterling didn't think Angela would get back to him for a while, and Lennon and the others would be hanging around waiting somewhere for him. Why not?

The front of De Groot's shop was immaculate. His new bicycles gleamed and enticed. His hire section was very respectable. Everything was orderly and neat. Through the blue curtain into the back, the workshop rivalled the front part. To the left of the square room, two bicycle stands had bikes currently being repaired clamped on them. The workbenches that served the stands were laid out with instruments like the benches of an operating theatre. Ledgers and files lined the shelves above in perfect order. In the corner opposite the curtain, a desk faced the outer shop, with a high-backed office chair and a lamp. The surface of the desk was empty except for a large black telephone, a biro, immaculately lined up in parallel to the edge and blue in-tray and out-tray, one on top of the other. From the window, Sterling could see into a little cobbled courtyard with a small tree. There had been a sharp rain shower, but now droplets of water sparkled in the afternoon sun.

From a tiny fridge next to one of the workbenches, De Groot got some milk, and from a cupboard over a small sink he got down two delicately enamelled cups and saucers. Coffee came from a Kona jug. From a transistor radio on the windowsill, Jim Morrison sang in a rich deep voice full of challenge and mystery.

'What were you saying about mudguards?' Sterling said, curiously.

'Oh, you know, modern cyclists. They don't want to go on roads. They want to go on tracks and in the mud. Without mudguards. If they do want to go on roads, they still don't want mudguards. It's as if they want to get as wet and dirty as possible – to be closer to nature or rubbish like that. It makes me mad. There's no good reason for it. You can put them on easily. They aren't heavy. You can get them in different colours if you really want. They don't make bikes more difficult to park. They don't cost much. They don't splash up mud and water in the faces of cyclists coming along behind.'

'You've clearly thought deeply about mudguards, Mr. De Groot.'

'Yes, maybe a bit too much.' De Groot knew that he was being teased. 'I'll be mother,' he continued.

'I'll be mother?' said Sterling. 'Your English is really good. The English of the English. It makes me feel right at home. Jim Morrison and the Doors too. Whereas all I know is how to say "*Dank u*".'

They shared another smile as they settled opposite each other in two old brown leather armchairs, newly upholstered. Sterling wondered if the obsessive neatness and tidiness of his new acquaintance exceeded even his own. There was no stray oil in this workshop-cum-office, and he didn't think he could have managed that.

'Funny accent, though,' said De Groot, with a mischievous look from under his eyebrows as he sipped from his cup. He was saying what Sterling was thinking but too polite to come out with – that the perfect colloquial English was delivered with a strange Dutch intonation.

'Touché,' Sterling murmured. 'How did you learn it?'

'I did some at school of course. We all did. And then I was a racing cyclist years ago, and there were some British guys in a kind of multinational team. They were good lads, and English was the most common language, so I picked up the slang from them. We got a taste for West Coast rock from the Americans on the team. Racing was hard, but there were good times, as well – in the bars and clubs where we toured.'

He eyes lost their focus for a moment, and then turned back to Sterling. 'I wouldn't worry about not speaking Dutch. Why should anyone bother? There are only a few million of us, and here in Ypres at any one time, there are probably more English speakers – in the central areas, anyway. We like it when you say "*Dank u*" to us, but we all speak English to some degree.' Abruptly, he changed the subject. 'You don't look like a cemeteries and battlefields geek, and you're not a tourist. Why are you here?'

Sterling shrugged. 'I'm looking into a couple of things.' He sipped his coffee and glanced out of the window. He thought of Lennon and the other men mooching around outside, and could feel his face clouding over and his muscles clenching. A cloud obscured the sun and darkened the courtyard and the office. 'I wonder … Do you have a map of Ypres I can borrow?'

'Not for nothing am I a signed-up member of Ypres Town Tourist Board.' De Groot's tone lightened. Either he was not very curious, or he knew how to bide his time. He returned to his armchair from the shop with a detailed map of central Ypres and spread it out in front. 'What do you need to know?'

'I don't know... Nothing specific – except – what about buses and trains, cycle paths, general stuff about Ypres?'

'Cycle shop owner, cycle renter, amateur historian, tourist guide. I can tell you all you need to know.'

Forty minutes later, Sterling did know as much as he needed to about Ypres, from its total destruction in the First World War and faithfully produced rebuilding to the nightly Last Post ceremony at the Menin Gate. Vauban, Louis XIV's chief military engineer, had supervised the 17th century fortifications, and they still existed in the eastern part of the town. Sterling knew how to get to the railway station, and the bus station was incorporated into the main square. De Groot reminded him to cycle on the right. Their coffee was finished. The bike was ready. It was time to go.

'Thanks, Mr De Groot', said Sterling as he wheeled the bike through the front door of the shop.

'Everyone calls me Martin. You can, as well.'

'Good of you. I'm Frank'.

'Happy cycling, Frank. Let me know how you get on.'

When Sterling looked back, De Groot was still at the door. It looked as though he was shaking his head, but Sterling couldn't be sure.

He wheeled the bike the few hundred metres back to the hotel. It was not yet time for bone-rattling rides on the cobbles. Christina did not raise her eyebrow when he asked her where he could lock up his new bicycle. She was getting used to his little ways. She just walked him through the space at the back of the hotel and pressed a code into the keypad lock of a small shed in the yard. She cupped a theatrical hand to his ear and whispered. 'One-nine-one-four – 1914 - are the buttons you need – easy to remember.' Her breath felt warm on the side of his face, and her fingers brushed his hair.

Back in the foyer, he had some time before he'd call Angela. He needed to think and plan, and he needed not to be diverted. From the reception desk, he felt green eyes looking as he went back upstairs to his room.

He knew he'd dozed off because he had that fuzzy afternoon taste in his mouth. A siesta feels good, but he was always groggy waking up. His watch said half past five. He cursed himself till he remembered that it was half past four in England, and Angela would still be in the library. He just had to remember Christina's instructions for using the phone. He knew he'd been successful when he heard Angela's voice.

'How did you get on?' he asked.

'Hi Angela. Have you had a good afternoon? Busy? How's the weather over in Sandley?' Angela caught the urgency in Sterling's voice, but her tone suggested that some courtesy would still be welcome.

'Sorry, Angie. It's just that I'm stuck without your input. I'm making a bit of progress in one direction, but knowing what those letters refer to is going to really make a difference.' He made a mental note that progress was managing to hire a bicycle.

'I'm finding it a little hard to justify my role as your auxiliary researcher.' She sighed. 'Anyway, I'm really sorry, but I haven't got that far. It's been a lot harder than

I thought it was going to be. I'm going to take it home and have another go after I've had something to eat this evening.'

Sterling could barely hide his disappointment. 'Did you get anything at all?'

'Frank, I really am doing my best, and I've got my day job. But I'm thinking that SaD might be a phrase on its own, because there's a comma after it. Pop could be anything, but not likely to be a fizzy drink or 'father'. I'll have to carry on looking at that. 'TH' must be an abbreviation for something. 'Exec', likewise – 'Executive' – that might be plausible. As for 'P', well, honestly, that could be anything. I've been thinking about context, Frank – is it going to be the same theme as what you've already found out, or something completely different? What do you think?'

Sterling was thinking that now he had to trust his friend. She wasn't going to push him. That wasn't her way. But if she was going to make progress for him, she had to know what he knew – not everything, of course, because it was his case – but enough to really help. He told her the key things – that he'd been to Chester Farm Cemetery, that he'd found the current information there, and that he thought the 'theme' was connected with the First World War.

'I reckon that I'm being directed to another location, and it's probably around here. I can't do any more tonight. Can I call you in the morning? If you've got something for me then I'll be able to follow it up.'

After he'd set Angela her homework, Sterling looked out over the square as the shadows lengthened. Its proper name in Dutch was the *Grote Markt*, De Groot had said, and the hall dominating it was the Cloth Hall, or *Lakenhal*. He couldn't see his stalkers, but he knew they were close. He learned the phrase on the scrap of paper exactly as it was written, and found a crack in the floorboard under a rug and slipped the paper in.

Perhaps he was being over-cautious, but he felt safer. He felt safe so long as he was always ahead of the game. When that changed, he was vulnerable. When he thought about how he'd been attacked over the last few days, he felt a sheen of sweat on his forehead. Then he shivered. The letters stayed in the front of his mind. But no matter how much he thought about them, they still made no sense. A walk might clear his head, and he knew where he would go.

Outside in the warm evening, he caught the tang of frying oil from the *frituur* a few doors down from Hotel Sultan. A dark-skinned girl, her ponytail slipped through the space at the back of her red-and-white-striped baseball-cap, doled out chips from the serving booth with bored efficiency. A small cluster of English schoolchildren milled around. One of them, surely aged no more than 14, was pulling bravely on a cigarette as his eyes watered, and he spluttered. Sterling longed to tell him it wasn't worth it, remembering the pain of trying to stop. Smokers who stop are never non-smokers. They are just ex-smokers, and can fall from grace at any time.

On the pavements, the locals were tucking into their Früli beers, Hommelbiers and spaghetti bolognese. On one terrace table, an old woman read the paper as her tiny white dog yapped at passing rivals in the square. As the evening drew on, it seemed that an invisible pied piper was drawing one group of people to the east of the Grote Markt and leaving another completely alone. The language of the zombie-group was English.

The people enjoying their terrace suppers were Flemish. Sterling joined the stream of zombies.

It wasn't a long walk, but as they got closer to the Menin Gate down Meensestraat, he began to think of the Sunday school story he'd listened to so raptly about Jesus and the moneychangers in the temple. On either side of the street, hawkers peddled souvenirs of the Flanders battlefields, mixed up with booths selling sweatshirts and hats – and anything suitable for long days trekking around the cemeteries under the still-warm sun. In the doorway of an outfitter's shop, closed much earlier in the day, a young man with a wispy moustache and a furtive air offered charcoal sketches of imagined Great War scenes – a Tommy on guard at a trench, hunched over a cigarette, tin hat and helmet obscuring his face; a pair of worn-out horses hauling a small artillery gun in a mire of mud, bullied on by a soldier in shirt sleeves.

A girl, clearly local, pressed a pamphlet into Sterling's hand – Captain Casey's battlefield tours. He shoved it into his pocket. At the end of the street, a policewoman in navy uniform and plain Glengarry-style forage cap and traffic torch barred the way through the great memorial arch across to what looked like a suburb on the other side. It was a quarter to eight, and Sterling knew that the Last Post began at eight o'clock, but already people were milling around. He stayed on the fringes. The arch was made of white slabs of Portland stone, plain except for the thousands of names of the fallen on every visible surface and from everywhere in the world. His eye was drawn to the nearest panel. In the 40th Pathans, the bugler Zamon Ali was inscribed with his comrades. Sterling wondered by what path he'd come to die on a battlefield in Europe far from his Indian home.

He scanned the other panels for Etchinghams and Sterlings, but had no luck. Even if he'd found an Etchingham, how would it have helped? He could not see Lennon or the other men, but felt sure they were close.

At exactly eight o'clock, the buglers of the Ypres fire service marched into view. The crowd stopped milling, even the youngest teenagers, and fell quiet. Sterling had not come to Ypres to immerse himself in long-past wars. He was sure that many of the young men in the Ypres Salient and all the way down almost to Switzerland had thought little of patriotism, honour or sacrifice for their country. The brutality and efficiency of war would have knocked that quickly out of them. But he felt a surge of emotion as the sad notes of the Last Post rang out under the Menin Gate arch.

After a small group laid a wreath and the super-annuated buglers had shuffled off, presumably to their suppers and Schnapps in nearby terraces, he climbed the steps of the memorial onto the adjacent embankment. The last faint blue was fading from the sky as night took over. Looking up, he could see the faint forked tails and scythe-shaped wings of swifts high in the darkening air. He thought he could hear them, too, their screams and screeches filtering down as they took their insect supper on the wing. And, as a gloomy reminder that he was not alone or free, there was Lennon leaning casually against a panel at the bottom of the stairs Sterling had just climbed up. As the chill of the night sharpened, he shivered and went in search of supper of his own.

7

The zombie-streams had disappeared to the hotels and hostels. The pedlars and hawkers had packed up their goods and retreated for another day. The chocolatiers in Meensestraat and the Grote Markt were finally putting down their shutters after a last flurry of business. A bus inspector in a peaked cap leaned at a bus stop and took drags of a cigarette surreptitiously cupped in the palm of his hand, held by thumb and forefinger. He flicked it away as a bus pulled up. The passengers were in for an unpleasant surprise if they were riding without tickets. The lights and lamps of Au Miroir beckoned once more. Sterling stationed himself at a table looking out to the square, beyond the knots of locals on the terrace under the sombrero patio heaters. It seemed strange to want the best vantage point. After all, he knew he was being tailed and watched.

Since he'd come to this small corner of western Belgium, he'd learnt much – not enough in connection with the case, certainly, but more about the First World War and more about the continent. One other thing confronted him in the shape of a menu. Belgian food and cooking lacked imagination. The menu in one place was almost exactly the same as in another. Omelettes, spag bol, croques, mussels and chips, dames blanches – you knew what was in store. He sighed as he looked down at the options. An omelette would do this time, and it was time too to try a Hommelbier as it appeared to be the local brew. He felt the customary pang for English beer and the pub.

He was busy admiring the work of the tall, straight-backed young waiter as he plied back and forth from the terrace with trays of food and beer. His apron flapped as he glided and swayed up and down, now putting a tray on a table and distributing its contents, now acknowledging with a curt nod requests for the bill or to take another order. He would get the tally-slip, present it, take the cash offered and deftly pull out change from the money pouch tied around his apron, finally tearing the slip to indicate that the bill had been paid.

In Sterling's admiration for this easy professionalism, he had been neglecting his surveillance of the square. As he took the first bite of his omelette, a shadow passed over his eyes and a lanky figure sidled into the chair opposite. Lennon seemed taller close up, but very much like the former Beatle in his early 30s. His eyes behind the round-framed glasses were a cold blue. If Lennon was opposite, the others couldn't be far away.

Sterling felt butterflies. The omelette and the beer didn't seem so appetising now. But with his unease came resentment. He looked up from his plate and fixed Lennon with a cold stare of his own.

'Firstly, you're blocking my view. Secondly, I don't know you. So thirdly, piss off.'

Lennon slouched further into his seat, his long body curved behind the table. 'That's not the kind of attitude you expect from someone just eking out a living. You'd expect a bit of politeness, a bit of willingness to have a listen.'

'I'm having my dinner. I'm not interested in anything you might have to say to me. In fact, I'm sick of your presence around every corner. Sod off, before I complain to the management.'

'You need to be careful, Sterling. It's a wicked world out there, and I really don't think you know what you're getting into.'

Sterling put down his knife and fork and took a pull of his drink. It wasn't bad, but it wasn't as good as his usual pint. He steepled his hands under his chin. 'Alright, now you've got my attention. I'm all ears. Why don't you tell me who you are, how the world is wicked and what it is that I'm getting myself into?'

'You don't need to know who I am. Just that for the moment, I'm your fairy godmother.' He produced a thin smile. He seemed pleased with his little *bon mots*. 'I know that you're on a little mission for our mutual friend, but you're not the only one who's, shall we say, active in the field. In fact, unless I've got it wrong, you've already had one or two unpleasant indications of other people's interest.'

Sterling thought back to the two assaults. 'So it wasn't you who punched me in my own hallway, or tried to throw me off the ferry.'

'Sterling, if I wanted to dispose of you, I wouldn't mess it up.'

'OK, fairy godmother. I'm getting deep into something that could cause me some harm. Any more pearls of wisdom before my omelette goes completely cold? Because if not....'

Sterling was sure Lennon would have stayed longer if he had been more receptive. Something was troubling the thin young man. Instead, he slid from the other side of the table. Upright, he loomed over Sterling. His cold stare fixed him again for a long moment. 'You're a cocky bastard,' he said finally.

Sterling turned pointedly back to his plate. When he looked up a minute later, there was no trace of Lennon in any part of the square in front of the window. He was left wondering about such a pointless conversation. Now he had some nagging doubts of his own. If Lennon had stayed, perhaps Sterling would have learned something useful. It was too late now.

As he patted his pockets for the roll of euros he needed to pay his bill, Captain Casey's leaflet about battlefield tours fell onto the table. He glanced through it casually as he tried to catch the waiter's eye. When he spotted the word, he knew he had to telephone Angela again. Tonight. Now. Why did the waiter choose this of all times to disappear, to avoid casting his eyes over the tables for the next order to take, or for the next request for the bill? Sterling added up what he'd had and what it cost. The tip was generous. Finally the young man came with the slip. He smiled. But Sterling had already put on his jacket and stumbled off into the night.

At the hotel, Christina, but 25 years or so older, was at reception. Her mother's face looked careworn, and her red hair was faded and had little flecks of grey. Christina had made a secret offer of the laptop under the desk, but although her mother had a kindly look, Sterling did not think that she would be so accommodating. He needed patience and contact with Angela. He cursed when her phone went straight to voicemail. She would be in the pub with Jack and the others.

'Angela, it's Frank. When you get to that bit of research for me, I think 'Pop' refers to a town to the west of Ypres – Poperinghe. That might help you with the rest of it.' He turned to the wonderful Captain's leaflet and continued. 'I've got some kind of tourist guide here, and here's what it says: "*Part of the tour will include a visit to Poperinghe, which would have been well known to very many Allied soldiers who fought in the Ypres Salient during World War One – Ypres was just 12 kilometres away. Poperinghe, known as 'Pop' to the soldiers who rested there, was a forward base for the Ypres Salient from autumn 1914 onwards.... "'*

He hung up. All the gang would be in the pub, and he felt lonely again – another emotion to add to the unease and all the other things he was experiencing.

He looked out over the Grote Markt. Under his breath, suddenly angry, he muttered, 'Right, all you bastards. No invitation to you for the next part of the journey.' He went to bed hoping that his hunch was right, and hoping that Angela's magical skills would give him the result he needed.

In his dreams later on, he was at a party. He was naked and embarrassed, but no one there seemed to notice. Angela was there, busy with her laptop, and Christina. Lennon was on the fringes, where he always seemed to be. Then Sterling was at a railway crossing in Canterbury, in the Peugeot. When the barriers went up, he didn't go over the tracks to the other side, but found the car's wheels on the tracks and himself unable to get the car off them.

In the morning, a pale, tired face stared back at him in the mirror. His hair stuck out in different directions – evidence of all the tossing and turning. He could present a cool face to Lennon, but the real story was different. The case was exciting, but he was scared.

Over breakfast, with Christina still absent and her mother standing in, he looked in detail at the map of Ypres Martin De Groot had given him and worked things out. He knew he needed to phone Gloria Etchingham to give her an update (he had promised her Thursday), but right now, Angela was the priority. He knew she got in to the library early. It was twenty to ten in Ypres. He dialled her library number. Straight away, he knew she'd found something. This time, it was she who did not bother with chat. There was an excited, urgent catch to her voice.

'I think I've found something, Frank. Your idea about Poperinghe is looking good. I'll run through it, and you can see if it's plausible. There's a lot about the town, but I thought I'd look at in the context of the First World War. That was the breakthrough. I found a site, and on that was Talbot House – a kind of rest club for Commonwealth soldiers away from the front. TH. Except, as it turns out, not the TH in your puzzle.'

Sterling listened hard. Angie was a librarian, and she loved a search. But he was keener on the answer, not the journey. Still, he was getting a big favour, so this was not the time to ask her to cut to the chase. As he listened, he occasionally threw in 'OK' and 'uh huh' to speed things along.

When she had finished, they were quiet, because there was a grim story behind the answers she had found. Now he knew his next destination, and although he felt the exhilaration of the earlier part of the journey, this part would be more sombre. On the reverse of the Ypres map was a smaller scale inset of the town in relation to the rest of the West Flanders region. It looked as though Pop was the end of the railway line that linked Ypres to the rest of Belgium. This time, Sterling wanted some peace from all those poking into his case. He picked up what he needed. Christina had been right. He had no trouble remembering the code to the garage where his hire-bike was propped up against the wall.

He wheeled the bike out through the yard to the front of the hotel. His posse of followers was all assembled – Lennon and the others he had spotted. He imagined that cars were parked in the square ready to follow the Peugeot. He sniffed the Ypres air as the watery low sun gave off a faintly warming heat. He hadn't cycled since he was a teenager, but he wouldn't be going far. To orientate himself, and to whet the interest of his pursuers, he wobbled his way through a couple of circuits of the Grote Markt.

At the bus stop outside the Lakenhal, a gaggle of onlookers watched curiously. He noted the cars stationed to follow – Lennon's silver Ford and a new one, a dark blue Saab. It was time to make his move. On the next circuit, he turned right into Sint Jacobstraat, and increased the pace a bit, rattling over the cobbles. The map was fixed in his brain. He passed a Novotel on his left hand side, and a bar, The Old Bill, on his right. In the bicycle's mirror, a nice touch from De Groot, he could see if he was being followed. He swung right down Paddepoelestraat. Timing was everything. He touched the brakes – and then turned left into Bukkersstraat. It was perfect.

As he hurried down the narrow street, a VW Golf edged in the opposite direction. Lennon's car was met with an angry blast of the horn and a shaking fist from the startled driver. Sterling could even see the beginnings of an argument as the drivers left their seats for an angry confrontation. The Golf driver, another fairy godmother, pointed vigorously at the 'No entry' sign above his car. The blue Saab eased discreetly past the snarl-up in the only direction it was legal to go and disappeared.

'Uitgezonderd!' Sterling shouted into the wind. No entry – except for bikes.

Still chuckling, he made his way up a ramp onto the cycle path around the Ypres ramparts. There was nothing like schadenfreude as a little motivator. According to De Groot, one way led back to the Menin Gate. The other finished near the railway station. Sterling felt sure he had a day free of all pursuit. He slowed down. He might as well enjoy the ride. From Vauban's star-shaped ramparts, he looked from under the trees across the water-moat to the fields and suburbs beyond the town. A small suspension bridge that looked newly built glinted as an elderly woman wheeled her bicycle to the other side from a gap in the fortified wall of the town. Abutting the ramparts in the other direction, he could see over a high brick wall topped with barbed wire into a car park. The blue and white marked cars in it, and the telltale cluster of radio and telephone aerials on the squat building behind them, told him it was the police station.

He crossed the main road over the archway at the Lille Gate, ducking as he went so that no searching eyes would spot him from below. In a menagerie further on, a tiny goat chewed passively away, its companion on a tree trunk looking placidly back at the doves and rabbits in the rest of the compound. When the path ended, he hurried over to the station. He had wasted his time worrying about where to lock the bike so that it could not be spotted. In the huge cycle park, there were three hundred bikes, and at least half were black, sit-up-and-beg ones like his own.

He waited ten minutes for a train to Poperinghe, climbing up the steep, grilled steps into the carriage. The plastic seat was a bare and functional brown within a beige and brown colour scheme throughout. He calculated that the journey was no more than ten or fifteen minutes. From the window, fields of sweetcorn swayed languidly in the breeze. They would be ready to harvest soon. A pair of ducks swooped low and splash-landed, webbed feet splayed and wings flapping, into a pond a hundred metres from the track, surely quacking loudly, though Sterling could hear nothing through the thick glass plate of the carriage. Before the train moved on, they were composing themselves and ruffling their feathers. The girl opposite looked on with unseeing eyes as her telephone conversation droned on.

Only the Dutch signs at Poperinghe station indicated west Belgium. The tracks, the short low platform and the tiny station hall could have been anywhere from Plymouth to Philadelphia. A sign indicated 'Centrum', and Sterling began his trudge. The modern streets merged nondescriptly one into another. He had to fix on landmarks – a 'Brood 'n Banket' bakery, a bright red pair of shutters and street signs – to be sure that he would find his way back. He imagined that 'Pop' had been knocked about much like Ypres in the Great War and afterwards, but it was clear that it had not been rebuilt on any historical pattern.

Ten minutes later, he emerged in the town centre near a large church, and cast around for Angela's interpretation of the first letters. He felt a quickening of excitement as he saw the building in front of him – Poperinghe Town

Hall – the *Stadhuis*. This was the Pop TH. So far, so good. He checked behind and all around, as he had done since he'd stood on the steps of the train at Ypres station. He was certain he had not been followed. He had a sudden realisation that he was no longer working just for the fee or because he wanted to curry favour with Gloria Etchingham. Somewhere in the journey, his drive to solve the mystery had developed its own momentum.

The paved courtyard of the Stadhuis and its modern frontage were like Poperinghe station. It would not have been out of place anywhere in Europe and beyond. A white car, perhaps a bureaucrat's, was parked in one corner. A bicycle rack with ten bikes was in the opposite corner. Some skilfully placed shrubs gave an impression of colour and greenery. Sterling ducked into the cool, dank air of the cellblock to the side. On the whitewashed walls were photos of soldiers, and here he found Angela's interpretation of 'SaD'. These were the 'cowards' and 'deserters' who were shot at dawn. A plaque in Dutch and English told the story in scant detail. On a wooden banquette in one cell wreaths, small bouquets and wooden crosses with poppies pinned at the heart were strewn around. On the wall racks of another were more, and, bafflingly, even a large tribute – 'We will remember you' – from the Mid and West Wales Fire and Ambulance Service.

Outside in the courtyard, the air was fresh and felt clean. At first, Sterling could not see Angela's final suggestion, the Exec P, the execution post, expecting it to be in the middle, but wreaths, poppies and tributes drew his eyes to the wall next to the entrance of the Stadhuis, which he had overlooked when he had first gone in. It looked very ordinary, but behind it on a slab of dark grey granite was a Kipling epitaph, 'The Coward'.

He breathed in deeply, straightened, and flexed his shoulders. This was very different from listening to the Last Post at the Menin Gate or visiting the cemeteries on the plains around Ypres, leaving poppies and noble words. It took a particular kind of imagination and compassion to do that here. He fretted about whether in extraordinary times, he would find the courage to do the right thing, or be disgraced as a coward or deserter. He and Angela had marvelled at the scope and focus of the website of the Commonwealth War Graves Commission. But it said nothing about soldiers shot at dawn. No sign outside proclaimed the 'death cells' and execution post. This felt like a dirty secret.

Complex emotions were beginning to get in the way of his work, so Sterling tried to refocus. Everything fitted with what was on the scrap of paper he had found at Chester Farm, but he did not know what he was looking for now. There was nothing obvious on the execution post. He scanned the epitaph, but that didn't seem promising either. He crouched down and sifted through the wreaths and tributes. Rain and sunshine had drained the colour from the older poppies and the ink from some of the texts.

As he began to doubt, he saw something – a small photo fixed with clear tape on the right hand side of the execution post within a clear small plastic folder. Freeing the folder, he popped the fastener and slipped the photo out. It was a picture of a memorial draped in a flag with a white cross on a dark blue background. On the back was printed just one word – Etchingham – and Sterling was back on track. Perhaps an ancestor was a traitor or deserter, and perhaps he himself was getting to the heart of the mystery Gloria Etchingham wanted him to solve. He thanked Angela for her brilliant research.

Still crouching before the execution post, he glanced around the courtyard. He planned it so that it would seem to any onlooker as though he was examining the tributes, and he was. But he would not have been expected to take something away. He slipped the folder and the photo into his pocket, stood up and wandered out into the street. He would have a closer look later on.

He checked his watch. There was no train back to Ypres for an hour so either he could go for a beer, or he could see the Toc H house that Angela had found for him. He decided that some more background might help with the case.

His wanderings around the Flanders countryside, and all its associations, were making him morbid – all the poppies and graves and memorials and noble words, and the sentimentality associated with them. Talbot House, a hundred metres or so from the Stadhuis, made him feel different. He soon learned that the large house, donated by its owner early in the war, was taken over by the army, and a chaplain, Philip (Tubby) Clayton, set up a kind of club for soldiers resting away from the front. The house became Toc H in the phonetic alphabet of the time.

He wandered through the museum and house. Tubby Clayton's humour appealed. 'The boss may not always be right, but his decision is final. He is, after all, the boss'. It reminded Sterling of a police inspector he'd worked for, one of the only ones he'd actually liked. Toc H seemed to be as true a taste of the Great War as all his other encounters, but less grim. By the time he returned to Blighty, (his historical immersion continuing) he'd be an expert in the subject.

As he signed the visitors' book in the main house at the end of his wanderings through the house, a Welsh voice lilted behind him.

'Did you enjoy your visit, boyo?' Sterling turned and saw a short, wide man with a full head of white hair and blueness in his watery eyes that reminded him of David Lloyd George, his father's Liberal hero.

'It was very good', he replied. 'Something a bit more accessible, and even cheerful after a diet of cemeteries, memorials, and of course, death cells and execution post.'

'Ah, so you have been to the Town Hall then.' The Welshman shook his head. 'Very sad. Very sad.'

After that, it didn't take long to find out what James Williams was doing in Talbot House. His interest in Sterling's visit was momentary. Far more important was his work as a Toc H volunteer on his wonderful gold-plated pension (accumulated not by luck, but by youthful foresight). He was 'doing a bit of good post-retirement, putting something back' after a glittering career as a teacher and then head teacher in a wide array of South Wales schools, all of which had inevitably been pulled up by the bootstraps during their exposure to his leadership genius. The cause and fortunes of South Wales education had never before or since improved so rapidly. Sterling glanced at the two Belgian women in the admission booth behind him, just in time to catch their smirks as they cast their eyes busily down to their paperwork, doing everything to avoid engagement.

The sensible thing would have been to turn around and march firmly back to Poperinghe station, to avoid being the new victim of boredom beyond endurance, and, as things turned out, other, far worse consequences. But Sterling was the only visitor to Talbot House that afternoon and he had time to spare, so when Williams the Bombast offered him a cup of tea in the part of the house he was staying in, he was too slow-witted to refuse. Sometimes, people who deliver monologues think they are in a conversation. In this case, Sterling could not be sure, but after twenty minutes, he knew he had to staunch the flow, otherwise he would not have been able to resist breaking the teapot over the bombast's head. Sterling was never noted for his spontaneity, but showing the photo might provide a diversion. In a brief lull, he took it from his pocket and pushed it across the glass coffee table.

'Just before you get on to the next stage, I'm going to have to run for my train. Before I do, I wonder if you know where that is.'

Williams reached inside his shirt pocket for his reading glasses. The tortoiseshell frames stood out on his ruddy face below the white hair. Unused to interruptions, he had a piqued, resentful air. He looked closely.

'Well, that's certainly the Scottish Saltire', he said, referring to the flag on the memorial, 'and it's just below a Celtic cross. It's the new Scottish memorial they put up in 2007. And I know exactly where it is – on a cycle path just off the main road between Ypres and Zonnebeeke. I went there with a Scottish pal a little while back. You English got us Celts mixed up in your wars even as you oppressed us,' he said in a sly aside. 'What was the ridge called? Frieburg, Freeburg, no – Frezenburg. It's only a couple of miles west of Ypres.' He looked at Sterling, a shrewd, sharp, suspicious glance, over the top of the glasses. 'What's your interest, boyo?'

They always asked him that. Jack wanted to know his business, De Groot wanted to know it and Lennon certainly wanted to know it. The bombast's interest was more tiresome than anyone's. Sterling had another flash of irritation, but balanced against that was gratitude about making more progress, and much more quickly than he had imagined. He prevaricated. He was following in an ancestor's footsteps and following up his cousin's research. It didn't sound convincing, even to him. Williams held his gaze for a moment. Sterling looked down at his teacup and then at his watch. There were twenty minutes till the next train. He stood up.

'I've got to get going, Mr Williams. Thank you very much for the cup of tea.'

Relieved to have escaped, he found the various landmarks on the dusty streets back to the station without much difficulty – the bakery, the shutters and the street signs. All in all, it had been a fruitful afternoon. But if he'd known what angst showing that photo to James Williams was going to cause, what pain and difficulty, he'd have kept it firmly in his pocket and found the answer in a different way.

8

The shadows were lengthening over Ypres as Sterling pedalled back from the station through the quiet streets, by the direct route down Stationstraat and Boterstraat now that he did not have to throw off pursuers. Shopkeepers and commercial folk were putting out their rubbish and sweeping out their doorways. Flattened cardboard boxes leaned against walls. Two schoolboys, straining over the handlebars of bicycles like his own, their dark hair plastered to their skulls by the slipstream, raced neck and neck over the cobbles. A woman ducked into a delicatessen for a final purchase – perhaps a loaf for dinner. Sterling stowed his bike away in the hotel shed. As he entered the lobby, he was pleased to see that Christina was back.

'How are you, Frank?' she smiled.

'Much the better for seeing you, Christina,' he said. 'But I haven't been away. It's you who went missing.'

'Even hotel staff have to have rest, Frank.' He could tell from her small smile that the compliment he'd slipped in had pleased her. Then a cloud flitted across her face, and frown lines appeared over her eyes.

'You've had some visitors.'

'Visitors?' he said neutrally.

'Two men, asking if you were in or if you could be contacted. They said you'd know what it's about.'

'In chinos and jackets? Smart. Big-looking blokes.' He stated it, rather than asking a question.

'That's right, Frank. They said that it wasn't worth leaving a message. You obviously know them.'

'In a way, Christina.' He was thoughtful. 'Thanks for telling me. I expect we'll catch up with each other in due course.'

He'd check the Scottish memorial in the morning. It was too late now, with night stealing the last of the pale daylight. Tonight, he thought Gloria Etchingham could do with an update.

In his room, he reflected that he was growing accustomed to Ypres; accustomed to Flanders. All the buildings in the centre of the town had been rebuilt in the same image after the end of the Great War. The frontages, in brick crenellations pointing upwards in gradations making half diamonds, reminded him of Sandley. He remembered why from one or two history classes in which he'd paid some attention – how Flemish refugees in the 16th and 17th centuries had fled from religious persecution in what was then the Spanish Netherlands. Their farming, drainage and weaving expertise had been a real boon to Sandley, though like all migrants, they were resented. So many houses in Sandley had the same frontages. Sterling was a hopeless traveller, and often homesick, but when he gazed out over the square, he was reminded of home. The trouble was that there was menace in Ypres, for him, at least.

It was six o'clock in Belgium. Five o'clock in England seemed a very reasonable time to telephone Gloria Etchingham.

She picked up the phone after five rings and said, 'Hello' – a husky hello full of nuanced promise and mystery, or so it seemed to Sterling's naïve and foolish part.

'Mrs. Etchingham?' he started formally, as if it might not really be her.

'Frank', she breathed. 'I've been wondering how you're getting on. Tell me you're getting somewhere.'

'Well, I've made a good start, I think, Gloria. Your husband had an ancestor from the Great War, and he seems to have left a trail for someone to follow. It's a history lesson for me – and for you when I get to the end of it. I've been to various memorials and other places. By the end of it, I'll have the answer. At the moment, I'm thinking that there may be some dishonour in the family that he may have wanted to get to the bottom of. Sometimes, descendants want to right the wrongs of the past. I don't know what your husband was like in that respect. Do you think it's possible?'

There was a pause. 'Keith was an interesting man, Frank. I think that's the kind of thing that would have got him going. I'm very keen for you to continue your work on my behalf,' she said, with an odd formality. 'What else have you found out? It would be nice to have a bit more detail for this outlay.'

That was the thing, in Sterling's limited experience of his client. She could cause ripples and a quickening of the pulse, and not just his. But she was never very far from the money.

'Well, I found one of his ancestors at a cemetery to the southeast of Ypres, towards Lille. That took me to Poperinghe, a little town to the west. The next indication is something at a Scottish memorial just short of Passchendaele – the scene of some massive, costly battles around 1916, so the guidebook says.'

'But what have you found out, Frank? This gallivanting about sounds all very fine, but I can't see where it's leading to.'

'I don't know myself yet. As soon as I do, of course you'll be the first to know. But considering that it's about something in your husband's family history, there's an awful lot of interest from third parties.'

'What do you mean?' Some note had crept into Gloria's voice, perhaps suspicion, but Sterling couldn't quite identify it. 'What third parties?'

'There's a bloke, about my age, maybe a bit younger. He looks a bit like John Lennon when Lennon was into leathers. He's been following me. He's threatened me a bit, too. Does he ring a bell?'

'Not at all.'

'What about four other blokes? Big. Jackets and slacks. They've been hanging around, as well. In fact, it's felt a little bit crowded at times, with so many people interested in my business. Or rather yours, Gloria.'

Now there was a pause. 'No one else knows about my business – not from me, anyway. Keith was doing some family history. Then he disappeared. I think he's dead. Now I just want a bit of closure.'

Sterling sensed that his client was about to cry, but what he couldn't tell was whether or not the tears were genuine. 'Listen,' he said, 'don't get upset. As I said, I'm making progress, and when I have something more definite to report, you'll be the first to know.'

After he'd hung up, he stared for a while at the wall. There was a tiny crack jagging down from above the bedspread, as if someone with a fountain pen had left an ink trail. He was missing something, but he couldn't tell what it was. Maybe the Scottish memorial would give him some answers, though his instinct was that it was just one more staging-post in the journey.

Much later, after re-sampling Au Miroir's spaghetti bolognese, he went to find Christina's company in the lobby. He got them drinks from the bar. Christina sipped her Pinot Grigio. His Keizer Karel blond slipped smoothly down his throat. The night was warm, and so was their conversation. There was plenty of comfort in that.

—⁓—

Overnight, the dreaming continued. Angela would tell him that it was probably to do with the case. If he remembered to report his dreams to her, they could analyse them for hours. This time, he was in cricket practice. His catching was poor. The coach said, 'Don't snatch; step back – let the ball come.' The ball kept coming from dark to light, making it harder to catch. Then an Australian test cricketer was hitting his bowling for six, and after that, Sterling was wading with someone through a field of long, dead stalks of cane, thinking that chopping them down would be a big job. He wondered if he actually needed Angela for interpretation this time.

He was sure that an Indian summer had come to West Flanders and Saturday was warm and sunny like previous days. In the Grote Markt, it was market day. Stalls covered the square, probably established since daybreak while he was sleeping. There were different types of townspeople milling around – the weekend set. An old woman in a black shawl felt an orange at a nearby fruit stall. A young boy howled and resisted as his mother pulled him brusquely by the hand into the main temporary alleyway of the market.

At the entrance of the hotel, Sterling checked his map. Old Lloyd George Williams, the cocky Welshman at TocH, was right. The bicycle was ideal for this stage, and Sterling ducked back into the hotel yard and wheeled it out of the shed. There was no hurry – not for him, anyway. The posse would have to take its chances. It was 10 o'clock when he did his customary wobbly parade around the square. Even if Lennon and the others intended to follow him and were ready for his 'Uitgezonderd' tricks, it would be impossible. He could get to his destination entirely by cycle path. Strangely, and unsettlingly, there was no sign of them. Sterling had become so used to some kind of cat-and-mouse prelude that as he set off through the Menin Gate, down Zonnebeekeweg and onto the cycle path he felt stirrings of loss and neglect. If his enemies were not close, where were they and what were they doing?

The Saturday market crowd left quickly behind, he pedalled east along the leafy cycle path, strewn with twigs, pebbles and assorted litter. He soon realised that he was out of condition when a gentle incline had him panting and sweating. He wondered whether it might have been better to bring the Peugeot. He hardly had the concentration to look around at the Flemish homes on this prosperous side of town – bourgeois, chalet-style houses, raised up above the surrounding land, with driveways leading down into inbuilt basement garages, in grassy islands within fences of concrete posts and green wire. They looked like Roman villas or medieval fortified manor houses with a modern twist.

It wasn't long before suburb gave way to farmland. Next to one of the last bungalows, he could see just the disembodied heads of two children bobbing through a field of mature rapeseed. When he came level with the beginning of the path, he pulled up to rest for a moment. The vista far down the tunnel-path of dry cracked mud was like the parting of the Red Sea – but instead of water, there were huge clusters of starry rapeseed pods interspersed with a mass of poppies in a threadbare red carpet, long into the distance. The children were not children, but teenagers, walking abreast, hand-in-hand, and already a hundred metres away.

He pushed on. It couldn't be far to the memorial now, as he seemed to be cresting a ridge. And there it was, a hundred metres in front – a monument with three building blocks of stone and a Celtic cross on the top, and the countryside of immaculately cultivated fields stretching flat right into the distance towards the north. He took the photograph from his pocket and looked across from the pathway. He was in the right place, even though the Saltire draping the cross had long gone. He began a gentle cruise down just below the ridge. While he had Gloria's retainer, he did not mind his wanderings around Ypres and its environs, but he wanted to be able to report real progress.

As at Chester Farm and Poperinghe, he did not know what to expect, but he felt that he was getting to know how Keith Etchingham had operated. Although the memorial could have been no more than three miles from the centre of Ypres, it might as well have been in the middle of the Gobi desert. Beside it, a farm track led off to nowhere. A narrow tarmac road probably led to the larger road the Welsh bombast had mentioned, a few metres to the south, but out of sight. The cycle path led on to Zonnebeeke and Passchendaele. Sterling could smell the agricultural smells of late summer – mown hay and dry manure – and listened to the faint rustling of the trees beside the cycle path. A blackbird foraged in front of him, pecking vigorously into the grassy verge, pausing, looking around, pecking again – a small, dynamic automaton.

As he approached the monument, a cloud passed in front of the sun, and the temperature dropped a noticeable notch or two, as it had done before during this spell of weather. But it wasn't just the sudden coolness that made Sterling uneasy. All police officers develop an intuition when something isn't quite right, and the intuition doesn't go when you leave the service. Something was wrong. Behind the monument he found out exactly what. The man Sterling knew as Lennon was lying on his back. For a moment, it looked as though he was asleep. It was peaceful, after all, in that open landscape, and not at all cold. But a pool of blood had oozed and dried in a widening puddle from the side of his head, and his eyes stared sightlessly into the wide blue Flanders sky. He wasn't asleep. He was dead.

9

Sterling might have panicked if he had not once been a policeman. The first thing to do was to make sure Lennon was really dead. It had never happened to Sterling, but he'd heard plenty of stories in the force, or from neighbouring forces, about corpses that had 'woken up' – at the scene of an incident, in the ambulance, on the mortuary slab; occasionally even in the coffin. He knelt beside the body and felt Lennon's neck for a pulse, remembering to use a tissue to avoid leaving fingerprints. There was nothing. In one way, that made things easier. Lennon was dead. There was nothing Sterling could do for him. There was no point in pedalling to the nearest farm and gesticulating to be allowed to use the telephone.

He allowed his sense of self-interest and preservation to kick in. He took care not to search the body, or disturb it in any other way. He expected he would find out who he was when the powers-that-be reached him. Sterling did not want his fingerprints found on the wallet, if he still had it, or endless interrogations. He did not want to explain his business. If he was arrested, he knew he would be the only suspect.

He envisaged what might happen. He would be charged and swallowed up by the Belgian justice system. There would be the insinuations of his interrogators, and the plea to confess: 'You argued, so you lashed out. You didn't mean to kill him. Unburden yourself. You'll feel better.' This is how things worked, and a lazy investigating team would not want to listen to anything that might get in the way of a quick result.

He stopped this worthless train of thought. It was more important now to try and establish when Lennon had been despatched. Now Sterling was thinking *alibi*. He looked at his watch. It was quarter past eleven. The blood around Lennon's head was brown and dry in the sunlight, so he had been there for a while. Fastidiously, out of fear of leaving evidence rather than distaste for the corpse (Sterling had seen plenty of those), he felt an arm with the back of his hand. Lennon was cold, as well as lifeless.

Sterling calculated that rigor mortis had been and gone. That was twelve hours. From the dew, the leaves and twigs and other bits of vegetation on him, the temperature and the blood, he calculated another few hours, and that he'd been in the open overnight. Sterling had last seen him himself when he had thrown him off track yesterday morning. If his thinking was right, someone had bashed Lennon's head in sometime yesterday afternoon. Sterling had been on the train to Poperinghe and at Toc H. He still had his train and Toc H tickets, and that made him feel better.

To the west, the memorial, the body and Sterling were sheltered by the ridge he'd just crested. To the north and east, there was nothing but fields and hedgerows, and a series of pylons behind the memorial. He was most anxious about the south, but luckily (at least for his own self-preservation purposes), Lennon was sprawled behind the memorial and out of sight of the tar macadam lane that led to it. With a forensic eye, he looked for evidence of his own presence and for the person or people who had bashed Lennon's head in and left him to die. It looked as though there had been no rain for a fortnight. His bicycle had left no tracks in the dusty pathway or in the concreted area around the memorial. An ambitious forensics investigator might have found evidence of a scuffle around the corpse, but Sterling didn't believe there was anything substantial. More importantly, he was sure nothing led back to him.

Now he was torn. He didn't want to be found at the scene of the crime, but he desperately needed the Scottish memorial to yield its little secret before it was taped off and a couple of guarding gendarmes made it inaccessible for the next week. In the end, rashness conquered caution.

Leaving the body and the scuffle marks, he went around to the front of the memorial. He copied down the inscription – the English version and what he thought was probably Gaelic. The monument was relatively new. It had been put up this century, so it was, up to now, plain and unadorned. He was agitated, but told himself to concentrate. Gingerly, he made a slow circuit. There was nothing obvious, but he knew he had to be patient.

His eyes flitted from the Celtic cross to the terrain around it. At any moment, perhaps a detachment of Scottish descendants of a First World War Highland regiment would swing into view and have unanswerable questions about the body and the blood staining the white concrete. Sterling began to think he would have to wait until after the official investigation. Then he saw something that chimed with what he was learning about

Keith Etchingham's little ways. He could ignore the inscription. Much more promising were the marks on one of the grey bricks above Lennon's stoved-in skull. They went into his notebook. He tried to capture every little nuance, even as his copying hand shook. He did not want to have to return.

He picked up his bicycle and gave the scene one last careful survey. In places, he scuffed the dust to cover an imaginary shoe-print or cycle track. He tiptoed over the springy grass verge back to the cycle path, carrying the bike by the frame in front of him. On the path, hundreds of tracks mingled together. He was lucky that this was a region of cyclists. He felt more confident as he made the gentle climb back to the top of the ridge. The adrenaline that had coursed through him a few minutes earlier was wearing off. As he went back to the town, he began to tremble with relief. He would work out how to report the death when he got there.

In Ypres, he stole into the side entrance of the hotel. At this moment, even seeing Christina would be unwelcome. He opened the shed and slipped the bicycle in. He might not need it again, but he was not ready to return it to De Groot and face another interrogation. He decided to avoid Au Miroir. Now anonymity was what he wanted most of all. Just off the Grote Markt, he had noticed a small brasserie, t'Ganzeke, and he decided to gather his thoughts there. Inside, he found out what 't'Ganzeke' meant. China geese, brass geese, wooden geese and geese of other unidentified material flew, threatened, squawked and walked on almost every surface. Grey geese, Canada geese, white geese and seemingly every other type of goose was represented. Sterling made his way to the back, and sat down in a booth beyond the sight of anyone who might be prying from the door.

Geese aside, t'Ganzeke was like most other cafes he'd been in Flanders, with wood panelling and dark furnishings. It was full of people taking a break from market day, and in some cases, settling down for a bite of lunch. He was already beginning to feel at home. The menu could have been from any café in the square. A young waiter brought a cappuccino – in Flanders, a strong black coffee with a large sweet blob of whipped cream on the top.

Sterling settled into the booth, got out his notebook, and took stock. He owed it to Lennon to tell the local police where he was. He had to do that first. Then he could think about the rest of it. He caught the waiter's eye and asked if he had a telephone book, and moments later it appeared on the table. What was 'police' in Dutch? Sterling tried 'police' and 'polizei' first of all. Nothing was straightforward on this job, but he found 'politie' and that looked right. He banked on the operator speaking English, and established that there was a payphone around the corner from the café.

He indicated that he'd be back to finish his coffee. His palms were clammy and sweat prickled on his forehead as he dialled the emergency number. He placed a discreet handkerchief over the receiver. If it was as it was in England, all calls would be recorded. A voice in Dutch replied straight away, and even though Sterling did not know the language, he did know the spiel. When it was over, he ignored what was probably the bit about name, address and where are you calling from and launched straight in. He pitched his voice high for extra disguise and added what he thought was an Irish lilt, feeling ridiculous. He wasn't, after all, in a spy film, or giving a coded IRA warning.

'Go to the Scottish memorial, the Scottish memorial, between Ypres and Zonnebeeke at Frezenburg. Behind the Celtic cross, you'll find a man's body, already dead. Got that? Scottish memorial just off the road between Ypres and Zonnebeeke.'

The emergency call voice switched expertly into English. 'Sir, sir, one moment. Your name and where you are calling from.'

So, Sterling's disguise had not obscured his gender, and obviously not his first and only language. He repeated the key words and hung up. They'd have got the message. He didn't think he could be clearer. Back in the café, he needed another cappuccino for the caffeine and the sugar, glad to have done the most difficult thing, and a croque monsieur to blunt his sudden hunger. It was approaching one o'clock. The shock of the morning had slowed time down.

He took out his notebook. He would do a review after his croque. First, he needed to look at his note of the etchings at the Scottish memorial. As he ate, he examined what was in front of him: the letters **StGMCY** and a shield that looked like a coat of arms. He squinted at his sketch. Across the top of the shield was a rectangle, and within the rectangle, a horizontal bar. From the base of the shield, it looked as if an ear of wheat was growing. And that was all.

He would need Angela again, and wondered how thrilled she would be with another research task – or whether she would be thrilled at all. So far, the trail had been local. He assumed that the next destination would also keep him in Ypres. He set aside the latest code for a while, sat back in the booth and put his hands to his face, squeezing and rubbing it. He felt so tired suddenly. He ran his hands through his hair, as if the follicles, disturbed and stimulated, would unplug all the blockages in his brain.

The attacks, at home and on the ferry, must be connected with Gloria Etchingham's case. He had nothing else on, so there was no other explanation. But where was the trail going that he was following? If one of Keith Etchingham's ancestors was a deserter (Sterling could not bring himself to think of him as a coward), he could not make the connections between Chester Farm, the execution post at Poperinghe and the Scottish memorial. Etchingham was more likely to be Welsh, or perhaps his ancestor was from the distaff side. Perhaps the trail was about more than one ancestor – the Frederick Etchingham at Chester Farm, a deserter at Poperinghe, and someone else from the latest stage.

That did not explain Lennon, lying in his lonely spot in the Flanders countryside, or the other men who seemed to have faded from view, even though Sterling knew they could not be far away. Perhaps Etchingham had a secret from the First World War that would embarrass and discredit certain interests, and their representatives were making sure that it did not surface. It was as if there was a key to a locked, dirty window, and once he had it, he felt sure that he would be able to open the window to see everything. The key must be with the latest code.

Two middle-aged Flemish couples at the next table were finishing their jolly and boisterous lunch. Their table was a mess of discarded napkins, empty beer glasses and baskets of uneaten French fries. They just made Sterling feel alone. He mimed writing the bill with his hands, and settled it when it came. He was reluctant to leave the haven of the booth in t'Ganzeke, but knew he had to keep the momentum going. He walked back to the Hotel Sultan with a thought. Maybe his own dedicated tourist guide would have some ideas about the code. He would probably have no further need for the bicycle, anyway.

At the entrance to the hotel, he watched as two police cars, one unmarked led by one with blue light flashing and siren, sped around the Grote Markt and up Meensestraat towards the Menin Gate and beyond. His message had got through. He slipped through the side entrance to the shed and pressed the combination of buttons. He wheeled the bicycle the few metres through the Grote Markt and around to Diksmuidsestraat. He did not run. He did not dawdle. He aimed to be entirely ordinary – if not a local, then just a tourist going about his holiday business.

At the cycle shop, De Groot had customers. A young family was buying a birthday bicycle for their five-year-old daughter. Their son, who looked a few years older, hovered nearby, looking at the more exotic of the mountain bikes. De Groot nodded to Sterling and he faded into the background to wait, down by the counter at the far end of the shop with his bicycle. He could hear De Groot exhorting the parents to have mudguards fitted to the bike they had selected, while everything in the little girl's manner and attitude indicated how hopelessly passé that was. It didn't matter that he was speaking Dutch. If he had been speaking Urdu, Sterling would have understood. Even from the back of the shop, his voice took on a plaintive note, almost a whine. It sounded like, 'When it rains, she'll get a dirty, wet stripe up her back'. He was a crusader for mudguards, with his eccentric passion. He made the sale, but with or without the mudguards, Sterling could not tell.

He came down to the back of the shop. He and Sterling looked at the hire bicycle. The tyres had white dusty stripes from the cycle paths.

'Any problems?' he asked.

Sterling shook his head, choosing to think that the question was just about the bike. He had very big problems, including the biggest problem you could imagine having, but he did not share that. Although he was already full of milk and caffeine, he accepted the offer of some more from De Groot's cafetiere. It felt safe in his office-cum-workshop refuge, with a friendly acquaintance in a hostile landscape. The two men sipped their coffee in a comfortable silence for a few moments.

'There's been something on the radio in the past hour. In fact, I think it's going to be on the radio for the rest of the afternoon. The police have found a body.' De Groot spoke casually and looked down at his coffee. A wisp of steam rose sinuously upwards following the contours of his face before it disappeared in the air. Then their eyes met. Sterling shifted slightly in his chair.

'Yeah?' he said neutrally. 'Whereabouts?'

'A couple of miles from here, out towards Zonnebeeke. A man. Mid-thirties. Not many further details at the moment. The radio's just spouting hot air.'

'Where's Zonnebeeke?'

'Just before Passchendaele. East from here. There's a bicycle path.'

Sterling turned his mouth down and pushed out his lower lip, thoughtful. 'And you're thinking ... what?'

'Not thinking anything, my friend. Just making conversation. Just letting you know there's crime here in beautiful Ypres just like everywhere else.'

Sterling stared down at his cup and shook his head again, this time in wondering disbelief. 'It's a wicked, wicked world.'

'Amen to that.'

It was time to change the subject. 'Martin, your English is astonishing. It's like being in the pub back at home. Just a little bit of attention to that accent and…'

'… you could pass for an Englishman.' Martin finished the sentence and they both chuckled in their chairs.

Then Sterling leaned forward – all business again. 'So, Mr Tourist Guide and polymath, I've got a more pressing issue to explore with you. If I was looking for coats of arms – you know – shields of ancestral families and things – where in Ypres would I go?'

'Coats of arms, coats of arms, shields. Something like the black lion of Flanders?'

Sterling knew what he meant. The black lion on yellow was everywhere in the region. 'Yes, exactly like that.'

'Well, you might try the museum in the Grote Markt, called 'In Flanders Field', about the First World War. Like my fellow citizens, I never go in any of the tourist places in the town, but you might find something there. Or there's the town museum, but from memory, a lot of that is about religious feuds in our wonderful education system. I'll think some more, but maybe those places have what you want. Which is what exactly, Frank?'

If it had been Lennon, or maybe Jack from the café, or the irritating little Welsh bombast at Pop, Sterling might have tapped his nose with his finger, but De Groot deserved much better.

'Martin, I just can't tell you at the moment. I'm on a job for someone and I'm at a difficult stage. There's nothing illegal in it and I haven't done anything wrong. When I can tell you something, I will.' It wasn't quite the truth. There would be some Belgian law about failing to identify yourself when reporting an incident, just as in England. If it wasn't breaking the law, it wouldn't exactly be approved of either. Sterling was theoretically withholding other information, too. However he looked at it, his position was shaky.

De Groot took the empty coffee cups and saucers and the cafetiere and washed them up. A crisp tea towel appeared from somewhere and everything was dried and put away. The bell in the shop rang, and from the artfully placed mirror by the door Sterling could see customers, two young men, enter the shop.

'As you said, Frank, it's a wicked world out there. You seem a decent bloke. Our coffee sessions have been good. I wouldn't want there to be no happy returns. You should be careful.' De Groot went to greet his customers.

Back in the Grote Markt, Sterling looked up at the great Lakenhal and the pennants fluttering in the afternoon breeze. The In Flanders Field museum was open, and he would be able to go in again. He could not remember any shields or coats of arms from last time, because he had not been looking. Around the entrance, a gaggle of old men and women with what sounded like Canadian accents debated loudly about whether there was time to go in. For Sterling, there was. He had a particular aim in mind – and if he didn't find what he wanted here, perhaps there was time to take in the town museum in Boterstraat.

10

Two hours later, Sterling was back in the hotel. There were one or two coats of arms in the In Flanders Field museum, but nothing like the one he'd sketched in his notepad. De Groot had been right about the town museum. It was determinedly parochial, as if to emphasise that there was far more to Ypres than the small matter of total devastation early in the 20th century, including religious struggles in the school system. There was plenty of evidence of the black lion of Flanders and its yellow background, but no coat of arms anything close to the one Sterling had found at the Frezenburg ridge.

He had tried from the other end of the riddle, too – juggling a bit with the initials, feeling that he was getting to know Keith Etchingham and his cryptic ways. But there was nothing even closely resembling StGMCY in either place. IFFMY would have been In Flanders Field Museum, Ypres, and SMY Stadhuis Museum, Ypres. They didn't work, but on the other hand, maybe they showed Sterling the way to go. He felt his shoulders slump, but that was because he and Angela had been so successful up to now. He adopted his serendipity attitude. Something would turn up. It was like a crossword clue. Sometimes you couldn't solve it, no matter how hard you worried at it, and then when you returned to it after a break, your subconscious had done it for you.

The lobby was empty and no one was staffing reception. Although there was still plenty of daylight, someone had switched on the little table lamp by the lobby sofa. The day had been tiring. Sterling sprawled on the sofa and closed his eyes.

It was the perfume that he was aware of first, finding its way into his consciousness. He sat up from his half-slump and rubbed his eyes. For a moment, he was disoriented, like a lost tourist with a useless map. Then he felt Christina's presence beside him. He rubbed his eyes and massaged his cheeks, feeling that vulnerability of the sleeper who wakes and knows he's been observed.

'Poor Frank. You looked so worn out, I couldn't think of waking you.' Her eyes were full of concern. The quizzical, raised eyebrow approach seemed to have been abandoned.

'Hello, Christina. It's been a long, long day. Very tiring. I've taken the bicycle back to the shop, so the shed's empty again. I'm going to go and wash my face.' Something in her face gave him a little bravado. He quickly gabbled on before he lost his nerve. 'I wonder if you have got any time off this evening. We could go out and get something to eat. You could show me your Ypres, not the tourist one.' He could not decide whether he was more surprised at asking for a date or still having the energy for a diversion with all the difficulties unrolling before him.

Sterling could sense her making calculations. 'That could be possible. Could you wait till about half past eight? I think I could get someone to take over then.'

It was tempting to be over-gallant and swear to wait through all eternity, but that was stupid. She'd already said 'Yes'. 'That would be fine, Christina, if you could manage it,' he murmured. 'Shall we meet here?'

'It would be better to meet at the side entrance, just by the shed.'

He nodded with a small smile and went over to the stairs. 'See you then.'

He was hungry two hours later when he slipped out of the side door. Christina's mother was at the reception desk, and she didn't look very pleased. He wondered if she knew about her daughter's date, and who she was going with.

Christina herself had changed. The blue jeans and green halter top had been replaced by a short black dress and a little denim jacket. Sterling noticed from a discreet sideways look that she might strain to do the top buttons of the jacket up, not feeling proud of his slyness. Her hair was tied back into a ponytail. He noted new mascara around her eyes. He felt shabby in his jacket and trousers. He had not packed for anything but the job.

'Ready?' He offered his arm as they stepped into the Grote Markt. She grasped at it with both hands and giggled. He felt the momentary, gentle press of her firm slight figure. 'Where to?'

She wheeled them both around and they lurched off across the square and past the museum in the Lakenhal, not used enough to each other to be in step. Gradually they got into a comfortable walking rhythm. In the square, the Saturday night crowd was out. Groups of youngsters moved about the square with loud excited voices and behind them at the chip shop was a big crowd. Sterling realised that it was a meeting point and not just a chippy. Older, more sedate couples wandered about, enjoying the lively, carefree weekend atmosphere. Lennon was dead, but there were no other men, either – that he could see. A bicycle lay temporarily abandoned by a lamppost, its back wheel spinning and its rider nowhere visible.

There was an archway at the far end of the Grote Markt that Sterling had not noticed. They ducked through there and past the large church behind it. They worked their way through small streets in the opposite direction to the Menin Gate. Sterling was soon lost. They came out in at a large hotel in front of a canal. He thought for a moment that that was where they were going, but they ducked into a small café opposite, the Casa Nova. In the dark interior, with scenes of Polynesia or perhaps Hawaii painted on the walls, some kind of European pop music was playing. Sterling thought it was pap, but was careful not to share that with Christina. She might love it.

They found a little table and settled down with drinks. She seemed familiar with the place, nodding to the barman and to one or two of the young set on bar stools or engaged in cheerful banter in large groups at tables pushed together. She persuaded Sterling to have another Belgian beer – this time a Trappistenbier Trippel. He could taste the alcohol and knew it was strong. Good. It would loosen his tongue and give him the confidence that always flowed through him with a drink or two. Monks – they did good work.

Christina didn't look at the menu because there wasn't one. She had acquired the air of a guide taking tourists off the beaten track. 'We'll have the Flemish stoemp,' she said assertively.

It was Sterling's turn to raise his eyebrow. ''Shtoomp?'

'It's a kind of beef stew with potatoes and other vegetables – I don't know the English words. It's really good in here.'

'It will make a change from the croques and crepes around the rest of Ypres,' he said, 'and the salads that go with them. Forgive me for saying it about your hometown, but I've never been in a place with such dull and samey menus. Maybe you can confirm this for me. There's a grated carrot train, isn't there, that goes around the back of Ypres town centre.'

'A grated carrot train?' Christina frowned and looked blank.

'Yes. A steam engine. All around the back of the square, underground, on a single-track railway driven by an ex-Belgian railways train driver with a big moustache and a peaked cap. He circulates with a great big specially designed crate of grated carrot at a little depot supplied with carrots from local farms. A vast carrot grater moves up and down on pistons as naughty Ypres boys and girls who bunk off school are punished by having to hold carrots against the grater.'

'Frank, what are you talking about?'

'The train stops at the back of every café, bar or restaurant, where chefs with tongs lean down over the crate and nimbly scoop up portions of grated carrot for the salad garnishes that go with the croques and crepes.' Sterling mimed the chefs' actions with tongs – transferring grated carrot from train to plates. 'The customers don't get their orders till the train has done its rounds.'

'Oh, the grated carrot train. I didn't recognise the English words. Yes, you're right, but we call it the

Geraspte Wortel Trein – the GWT. And of course, those naughty schoolboys and girls have other duties, as well.'

'Other duties?'

'Well, that piece of mayonnaise you get with your croque monsieur.'

'The blob of mayonnaise. The dollop of mayonnaise. With ridges.'

'Yes, OK, the blob, the dollop.' Christina repeated the new words. 'Those same boys and girls have to work the mayonnaise machine and the blobs are transferred by the same train. Another machine does the French fries. It's the big secret in Ypres. You don't go back to staying away from school after you've been made to help with the GWT. How did you know about it, Frank?'

He said nothing, but tapped his forefinger against the side of his nose. They smiled and sipped their beer. The girl was wasted running a hotel.

In cafes or restaurants, Sterling normally could not help his eyes flicking from table to table in a restless, jerky sweep, even while conducting a conversation. Tonight, his attention did not waver from Christina. He concentrated on her delicate neck, her animated green eyes, and her little habit of tossing her head and laughing. He listened to her talk with a steady gaze and an easy laugh. This Belgian girl in the small provincial bar had him forgetting danger, law-breaking and murder for a few welcome hours.

The 'stoemp' was everything Christina had promised. Talk of a diploma in hotel management and involvement in the family hotel soothed him. Stories about customers and their quirks amused him. It was good to hear about ordinary things, and when he learnt that she was twenty-five, he did not feel so old himself. He sensed that although she was happy enough, life was dull, or at least routine. He was sure that that was part of the reason she had come out with him.

'And what about my quirks, Christina? Will you be dining out on them sometime?'

'Well, if I could understand what 'quirks' are, and 'dining out', I would be able to answer. You haven't done anything very bad, if quirks are bad, but you are....' she looked for a word, '....mysterious.'

Sterling leaned back and smiled. 'International man of mystery, me.'

Later on, as the bar emptied and it looked as though the barman was beginning to close up for the evening, it was time to go. They walked arm in arm through Ypres's cool evening streets back home to the hotel. This time, they walked in perfect harmony, perhaps helped by a certain tipsiness. Now it was Christina Sterling asked about shields and coats of arms, like the black lion of Flanders.

As the church behind the Lakenhal loomed, she murmured 'Maybe you could try there – the church. St Saviours that one is. There's St Jacobs in Sint Jacobstraat and one I can't remember in Rijselsestraat. All of them have associations with local families and of course some military ones, also.'

They stole like thieves into the side entrance of the hotel. Christina detached herself from Sterling's arm. His throat was dry, as if no glasses of strong local lager had ever gone down it, and he was suddenly sober, too. There was a kettle, tea bags, milk and coffee in his room.

'Perhaps some tea or coffee to finish the evening,' he said, but the alcohol that had fuelled his confidence now deserted him.

Christina looked up into his eyes. 'I don't think my mother or Guy would think that a very good idea.'

Sterling knew her mother, and he had a good idea who Guy was. But he needed to check. 'Boyfriend?'

She nodded, a sad little nod.

He nodded back. 'Never mind. It's been a lovely evening, Christina. Thank you very much.'

He was careful not to show his disappointment. There was no point. It would seem churlish and sour the end of the evening. Courtesy and generosity make the best impression, and of course, there was the matter of pride. In this frame of mind, he began the walk up the stairs to his room. He didn't skip, but he didn't trudge either. He felt Christina's eyes on his back. In his room, he leaned against the door and blew out his cheeks. He was tired. He didn't have time for a date, if that's what the evening was. For God's sake, he was working on a case. He was being hunted, threatened and attacked. And he didn't suppose Christina entirely welcomed disruption either, given the stability and contentment of her life.

He would try and crack the latest code in the morning. He was too tired and unsettled now. He would visit the churches Christina mentioned, as well. He didn't think that they had any answers, but there might be something. Given Keith Etchingham's previous form, a church would be somewhere he'd at least have considered. As for the code, it was possible that Sterling's subconscious would do some of the work, as it sometimes did. He washed his face and brushed his teeth. It was funny – when he had been with Christina in the bar, he had felt alive. His eyes were clear and his face ached from smiling. In the mirror, he looked ill at ease and tetchy. Worry lines appeared on his face.

As he was slipping off his shoes, there was a soft knock on the door. He tensed, immediately alert, a knot in his stomach. He had been attacked twice and followed almost constantly. This could not be a friendly evening visit. He looked around for some kind of weapon and found an iron – unwieldy and the wrong shape, but better than nothing. He stretched himself flat with his back to the wall next to the door. His pulse throbbed in his neck. He seemed automatically to have put on the latch chain, though if someone was going to crash in, the flimsy door and chain was not going to stop them.

'Yes?' he called out.

'It's me,' said a small soft voice. It was not very helpful. You – and who else? Sterling thought.

'Me,' he responded neutrally.

'Me, Christina.'

He opened the door as far as the chain would allow. She looked up at him through the crack in the door. 'Christina, I thought we had said our goodnights.'

That made her smile. 'Yes, I thought so, too, but I have remembered something that might be helpful.' She cast her eyes down for a second and then looked back up at me. 'May I come in? It's a little public here in the corridor.'

Sterling put down the iron. What would she think if she saw that in his fist? Then he closed the door and fumbled the chain from the catch with clumsy fingers. When he opened the door wider, she glanced quickly up and down the corridor and slipped inside. The adrenaline that had made Sterling wake up so sharply switched to other bodily duties. It was no longer about fight or flight. He wasn't very optimistic about what Christina might or might not have remembered. Surely she had other motives. But he thought he should play along.

'What about that tea or coffee?'

She nodded eagerly for coffee and he waved vaguely to indicate the chair for her to sit on. She perched on one of the beds while Sterling busied himself with the kettle and the sachets of coffee and milk. She spread her hands around the coffee cup as if they were cold. Sterling sat down beside her, leaving a respectable gap. He found himself imitating her hand-spreading gesture around his own coffee cup. He looked at her profile and struggled to concentrate. His voice sounded thick as he asked her what she'd remembered.

She ducked to take a sip of her coffee. Speaking to the floor in front of her, she said, 'There's another church here in Ypres you could try, as well as those others. I only thought of it after you'd gone. It's really got lots of coats of arms and shields in it, far more than the others. I've only been in it once, when I was a Girl Guide, and that's why I didn't remember it. It's the English Church here in Ypres.'

Amongst all the different and conflicting emotions Sterling had felt this evening, another one arrived. 'Can you remember what it's called?'

'I think it's St. George's.'

Sterling put down his coffee cup and fumbled for his notebook. StGMCY. That could be the start of it. It was certainly worth a try in the morning. He wondered what 'MC' might stand for if he was right about the first part. The 'Y' might be Ypres. Christina could tell he was pleased as he enveloped her in a grateful, spontaneous hug. It was awkward sitting side by side with a little gap in between, and Christina still with her hands fanned around her own cup, but she laughed and was in the spirit of it.

When she put down her cup, she turned back to face him. He could not quite read the look. Then they kissed. Sterling could taste coffee on her breath, and her perfume mingled in the cool bedroom air. He ran his hand down her back. She shifted a little to make it easier. He could feel her hand move to his neck. They broke apart a moment later, almost startled at what they'd just done. She fiddled her jacket straight and pulled at her dress, while Sterling hitched up the back of his shirt collar. A moment later, the same respectable gap had reappeared between them.

'I'm very confused,' she said softly.

'I know. So am I.'

'I think I should go.'

'Yes, I think you should,' he said.

They moved to the door together and Sterling opened it gently, peering back and forth along the corridor, nodding the all clear. The difference between her slipping out and her having slipped in half an hour before was that this time, eyes brimming, she reached up and kissed his cheek softly before she was gone. By nature, he was a jealous man, but he had learned how to curb it. He still hated Guy, whoever he was, and Christina's mother.

11

The dream Sterling remembered that Sunday morning was unusually optimistic. He had been in some kind of art class, though he had never had much talent, as far as he knew, for painting or drawing or any creative activity of that kind. The class had to put on some kind of exhibition. He was open with the teacher, a young woman he had never met in any conscious state. He couldn't draw or paint, so he was going to do some photos and make a montage with connecting text. She was very pleased. It was going to be a perfect solution, and Sterling was pleased in turn about her unconditionally positive reaction. He was no dream interpreter – he generally left that to Angela – but he associated it with progress in the case. He was anxious about the night before, but as things had been cut short, of course any subsequent awkwardness would be avoided as well, and probably regret.

In the breakfast room, the clink of cutlery and the rising sound of conversation seemed to show that a new intake of customers had come in late last night. It was much busier than yesterday. An American woman in a floral blouse asked loudly where the ketchup was. Christina, on breakfast duty with the kitchen staff, looked flustered, and perhaps a little tired. She was back in jeans and green top, and her hair had lost a little of its lustre. Sterling wanted to see how things were between them. When he caught her eye with a small grin and an even more discreet, waist-high thumbs up, she smiled and returned the thumbs up.

As he was eating his bacon butty, he felt her presence by his table.

'Tea or coffee, sir?'

'Coffee, please. Busy this morning.'

'New people in last night.' Then she whispered. 'I don't think my mother was very pleased with me for going out.'

'I had a good time.'

Then, the status of the friendship confirmed as healthy, she was gone, emerging a few moments at the other end of the room with a high chair for a baby and her hard-pressed parents. Sterling finished his breakfast and coffee, and slipped away.

The Grote Markt had been vibrant the night before. In the gritty, breezy morning, it looked like the aftermath of a wedding reception. Chip papers eddied and plastic bottles clattered around the cobbles. There was the occasional stain of what looked very much like vomit. There was a general air of bedragglement. The older local crowd picked their way to worship. Sterling could see the noses of a grey-haired couple in their Sunday-best black suits near him wrinkle in prim disgust as their steps grew daintier to avoid the rubbish.

He had forgotten his map, and Christina had forgotten to tell him where St George's was located. He couldn't be bothered to go back to his room, and was unwilling to upset the delicate equilibrium they had established this morning. He strolled over to the In Flanders Fields museum to look at the town map there. He was sure it would be in the centre, and he was right. Elverdingsestraat was just down the road from t'Ganzeke, about five minutes' walk away. He gave the square a quick sweep. He had not been followed since Lennon's murder. He did not think that made him safe, but it looked as though he had Sunday off, as well.

At St George's he knew straight away that he was back on the trail, and felt the familiar surge. The gold lettering on the red-painted noticeboard had the title *St George's Memorial Church, Ypres*. StGMCY. He muttered his thanks to Christina.

It was time for the early morning service, and a meagre crowd of churchgoers was trickling inside – excellent cover for a man away from home and needing to worship. Some kind of lay officer, lanky and grey, welcomed Sterling as he went through the heavy doors. Given Ypres' associations with Britain and the Commonwealth, he was sure the congregation was used to strangers. As he entered, he looked all around and felt for his notebook. There were seats and not pews, in the continental style. He chose one halfway up from the altar at the far end, needing a panoramic view.

He tried to remember when he had last been to a church service, and failed. Was it as far back as school? Maybe a funeral. It didn't really matter. What mattered just then was that all over the brightly lit, richly carpeted church, with its generously whitewashed walls and vaulted arches, were coats of arms and pennants, hanging everywhere, arranged around the sanctuary and embroidered on the hassocks themselves. There were hundreds of them. He knew he was in the right place. On the other hand, Keith Etchingham had chosen his hiding place well. No one was going to waltz in here and find what they were looking for straight away. His coat of arms was almost as well disguised as Sterling's bicycle at Ypres station.

Sterling was the youngest person in the congregation. He was the youngest person in the whole church, including the choir. It was a disadvantage, because he was attracting attention. Attracting attention meant that he had to concentrate on participating in the service and not looking on walls or hassocks for the coat of arms or pennant whose description he had in his notebook. He needed to be patient through hymns and psalms and liturgy and sermon, and when everyone was invited for coffee and cakes in the hall next door, he began to think he'd never be able to get on in peace.

But the home-baked cakes were light and sweet, with a still lingering warmth from the oven, and the coffee was freshly ground and just brewed. This was not Anglicanism as Sterling had known it. The lay officer who had seen him in and the vicar who led the service were both happy to chat, but not intrusive. Sterling got the impression that odd visitors were received courteously, but there was no investment. They'd be going back to their own congregations, or in his case, his local. He asked if the church would be open for the rest of the day – he would like to explore it for a little longer. Even on Sunday, they told him, closing time was not till at least 6 o'clock, according to who was on the rota.

So back in the church, under the lights that were still on, Sterling looked again at his sketch. He needed to be methodical in his search, from walls to hassocks and altar area in manageable lines. He began at the wall on the left of the church. The shield he had was so distinctive he did not really need to keep referring to his picture. Nothing on the left wall matched it, and nothing on the chairs on the left of the aisle. He moved to the right of the aisle and from there to the right wall, his eyes getting used to the gloom. Moving around the cool church kept him relatively warm. He finished scanning the hassocks and the shields and pennants on the right of the church. He had found nothing, but was not discouraged. Etchingham's previous riddles had yielded up their answers. Sterling knew that he was in the right place, and was being careful enough not to gloss over any of the heraldic evidence in front of him.

He started to move up towards the altar. Perhaps it was a breath of air from the door opening at the back of the church that caused a momentary stir in the still atmosphere under the whitewashed vaults. Perhaps a slight new smell provided a contrast to the mustiness shared by all churches. It wasn't the Holy Ghost, but Sterling felt a presence that prickled the hairs in his neck. He turned around, hunching slightly in the movement. Just by the inner door, a man slouched on the wooden partition, hands behind his back, looking like a football coach supervising training from beneath a baseball cap. The baseball cap with jacket and slacks, and the gloomy interior, meant that Sterling could not clearly see his face, but what he could see lacked all expression. He assumed that it was one of the pursuing posse. The man stared for a good few seconds. Sterling felt the force of malevolence. Then the man slipped away.

If he had aimed to intimidate, he'd succeeded. Sterling sat down on one of the chairs, jittery. It was one thing to be in a group of police officers in a ruck outside a pub on a Saturday night and breaking up a fight, or sorting out a Fascist march that has been infiltrated by the Anarchists and Socialist Workers. You got stuck in without thinking. You were with your colleagues, who were also your mates, and you felt that no one could get you, even while the missiles were flying. It was quite another thing to be doing all this creeping around Ypres, alone, with people in the shadows, the odd sneak attack, and then murder. It wasn't just the fear, but how Sterling was dealing with it. He was learning things about himself that he did not like, in addition to things he already knew. Resting his arms on his thighs and clasping his hands, he looked down at the hassock in front of him. There are elements in you that indicate a tendency to cowardice, he thought. No, be honest – you are a coward. You should scuttle back to England and get a safer life.

It was a minute or two before he could get started again. Some trainer in the police had said that confronting your demons was halfway to getting over them. Sterling had come this far, so he should keep going. He moved up towards the quire and the aisle. This was the only part left.

'Bingo,' he whispered. His sketch was in black and white, but there they unmistakably were in full colour: the ear of wheat, yellow on a rich blue background, the white rectangle and the horizontal red bar, embroidered on a cushion amongst a line below the altar rail. Good old Keith. Sterling felt warmly disposed to him, whatever the circumstances. He'd played fair up to now, like a decent crossword setter. But surely there wouldn't be too much more of this. Sterling did a quick check to make sure that he was still alone, and then knelt by the cushion. Along with the others, and next to another set to the right of the entrance to the altar, it was set in a long, rectangular tray. He simply eased it from its place. There was nothing in the tray, but a slip of paper was taped on the reverse of the cushion. He eased off the black tape and looked at the business card he'd just found.

Marc Mehrtens, Chocolatier, 7 Grote Markt, Ypres.

There was a phone number and even a website.

In a biro on the back had been printed 'Pay the bearer on demand'. Sterling shook his head, ruefully. He had traipsed about the whole Ypres district day after day, from cemeteries to museums to execution posts to churches. He had been followed and menaced and threatened. And now he would be ending up at a chocolate shop a few doors down from the hotel, having come full circle. If Etchingham had just disappeared, and wasn't decaying in the cold ground or scattered as ashes somewhere in the wind, he'd surely be chuckling at the circularity he had engineered. It was now that Sterling began to believe that this was not about any of Keith Etchingham's ancestors, not about a death in the trenches or in front of a firing squad, and not about putting right a family wrong. There was no issue of honour or disgrace here. The coat of arms had no significance, except as a hiding place for the latest clue. Etchingham had probably picked it because its design was so plain and easy to scratch onto stone. Something else was behind Sterling's treasure hunt.

He left the church with excitement and fear grappling in his head. It was Sunday, about midday. He wondered if Marc Mehrtens's chocolate shop would be open. Surely, if there were tourists, it was likely. He set off back to Grote Markt, scanning the street in a way that had become automatic. As he passed the hotel, with the cluster of chocolate shops a few metres on, he decided to duck in to reception. Maybe Christina would be free for a moment, and he could congratulate her for that midnight moment of insight. He wanted her to carry on thinking well of him, too. He pushed through the doors and entered the lobby. Straight away, he wished that he hadn't.

12

Christina had made the transition from breakfast bunfight manager to receptionist, and as Sterling approached the desk, she was dealing with a loud and protracted query from floral blouse woman, but this time not about ketchup. Around her, members of a small family were hopping from one foot to the other. They wanted to check out, but Floral Blouse was too busy to notice them. Sterling went to join the little knot of agitation. He was in no hurry.

As he got closer, Christina looked past the little crowd and saw him. He caught her urgent little gaze straight away. Her eyes flicked behind him to where he knew the sofa was. He should have given the tiniest nod and peeled off to the stairs and out of sight up to his room. He should have waited for Christina to catch up with him later, either by phone or by coming to his door. He should have done a whole series of calm, non-instinctive, subtle, sensible things – in fact, anything except turn around and look directly at the sofa. Instead, he turned around and looked at directly at the sofa. If a paparazzo had been looking for the perfect shot, with perfect lighting and setting, there it was, and there Sterling was in the centre of the viewing frame.

On the sofa were two men. One was lanky and dark, with a sour, cynical look on his sallow face and small, glittering, suspicious eyes. The sofa was not large enough to accommodate his long legs, and his thighs emerged from his trunk at a steep upwards angle. The other's feet barely touched the floor, and combined with his billowing white hair, gave him the ridiculous look of a garden gnome. It was the Welsh bombast 'Lloyd George' Williams.

Sterling had no time to react.

'That's him.' The bombast practically squeaked, struggling to get out of the sofa that was enveloping him. 'He's the one who showed me the photo.'

Sterling hadn't liked the Welshman from the moment he had first met him. Now dislike turned to loathing. On the outside, though, he tried to feign bewilderment. He was just an innocent tourist. 'What's going on? What's this all about?'

The tall man stretched up off the sofa. Sterling heard one of his knees creak. Two other men emerged from corners of the lobby. Even if he'd thought of running, there really was nowhere to go, and no point. The tall man spoke for a few moments in Dutch to one of his associates, who turned to Sterling.

'This is Inspector Broussart of the West Flanders police. He does not speak much English, so he's asked me to translate.' He gestured to the other man and himself. 'We are part of his team. We are investigating a suspicious death just outside Ypres. That man,' he pointed to the bombast, 'saw a report on the television news with a picture that you also possess and which you showed him. He thought you might be of interest in our enquiries.' He waited until Broussart, who seemed to be following the little speech, spoke a few more words. Then he turned back to Sterling and continued in his clipped, precise, accented English. 'Inspector Broussart wants you to come with us to the police station. If you are not willing to come as a volunteer, we will arrest you. It's your choice.'

Sterling looked at Williams, who was red with excitement. He wanted to punch the self-importance from that gloating face. He put his hands in his pockets and clenched them into fists.

'Well, I'll come,' he said with a shrug. 'Why not? But I really don't understand what it's all about.' He turned to the bombast and spoke softly, using one of the only Welsh words he knew, once winkled light-heartedly out of a God-fearing colleague called Jones from Caernarfon who had fetched up in Folkestone nick.

'Just doing my duty as a citizen,' he replied indignantly in his ridiculous Welsh lilt. He seemed shocked at being called a bastard, in Welsh to boot, and then affronted, as if his high-mindedness far outweighed any inconvenience to Sterling.

Andy Nolan and Sterling had often talked about grasses, another topic that helped them while away the small hours. They could bear grasses who grassed for the next few pints or packets of cigarettes. Those ones lived on the margins and got money where they could. They could bear the ones with scores to settle. It wasn't pretty but you could understand it. The worst grasses were the ones who did it from allegedly noble motives. The bombast was the easiest classification ever. Sterling turned away, dismissing him, and handed his passport to Broussart for inspection. He flicked through it and slipped it in his pocket. Sterling wondered if he was allowed to do that. It was hard to resist presenting his wrists for handcuff. The three policemen coalesced around him and they shuffled awkwardly to the door, Broussart leading the gloomy way and his detectives at each shoulder.

Sterling glanced back at reception. Christina's face, already pale, had become ashen. He hoped it was because she knew him well enough to believe some mistake was being made, rather than that she'd had a lucky escape from getting mixed up with a criminal. He tried a small smile of reassurance, but it was probably a rictus. The mouth of the woman in the floral blouse formed a little 'O'. When Broussart's detective had begun his little speech, the lobby had gone quiet. No one wanted to miss any of the drama. Sterling ducked into the unmarked police car. He needed to use the journey to the police station to sort out what he was going to say.

There wasn't much time. It was a short drive – just to Rijselsestraat, as expected. They went past the pedestrian entrance, turned left through an archway attached to the station and swept into the car park at the back. It seemed a long time since Friday, when Sterling had looked down here from the ramparts now behind him. The gates and wall seemed higher too, and the rolls of razor wire more menacing.

Sterling felt alone. Following the surly Broussart's example, no one spoke. The little group went into the station by the back door. It might have been in the heart of Flanders, but it was no different from police stations everywhere – the nondescript green walls, the clutter, the general air of shabbiness that no one who worked there noticed anymore. At the end of the corridor leading to what Sterling thought was the custody desk, someone had not quite hit the target of a wastepaper basket with a banana skin. Half of it was in and half out, and it balanced precariously. As the little convoy passed by, there was a faint banana smell.

Broussart turned his head back slightly as he walked on, giving his two detectives instructions. At the custody desk, he turned right and the translator and his colleague steered Sterling to the left. There had been no frog-marching or brusque handling, but he had no doubt at any stage about what was required of him. He was left in a small interview room and invited to sit on the chair opposite two other chairs, with a rickety table in between. He knew how things worked. The mirror at the back was two-way. He wondered whether he was in for questioning or full-on interrogation.

'Coffee? A cup of tea?' asked the translator.

'Tea would be good,' Sterling replied. 'Milk, one sugar, not too strong.'

The detective's expression, previously completely neutral, changed fractionally. It might have been a tiny smile. If he'd said anything, Sterling thought it would probably have been, 'You English, you must have your tea.' They'd get Sterling's fingerprints and DNA, of course, but he didn't mind. He was convinced they would find nothing to link him with the crime scene. If they asked formally, he wouldn't object, either. He calculated that a stance of openness and bewilderment was the best strategy.

When the detectives left, he tested his chair for wobbles. One leg at the front was shorter than the other three, and that would get irritating after an hour or two. He seemed to be pitching forward, too, so the legs at the back were longer than those at the front. He'd be wriggling and shifting and constantly trying not to slip forward. He tried the other two chairs facing him. He swapped one for the one allocated to him. He didn't care that someone was watching him through the glass. When they found out that he was a former policeman, they'd realise that he knew the tricks the police use everywhere.

He leaned forward in his new chair, put his elbows on the table and his hands under his chin. He would have to give Broussart some account of what he was doing in Ypres and where he had been. He could say that he was researching an ancestor during the First World War. After all, he had looked for Sterlings on the panels at Menin Gate. He had been out to Chester Farm and over to Poperinghe. It wasn't an absolute lie. It just fell well short of the truth. A lot depended on the questions he was asked. He was tired, and he needed to concentrate. If he played open and bewildered, and his story fell to bits, he would look all the more suspicious. He had to keep in mind that he knew much that would help the West Flanders police, but he was not the one who'd bashed Lennon's skull in. He was fundamentally and indisputably innocent. In fact, he didn't even know Lennon's real name. He had just found his body.

He needed to concentrate on what he wanted, his *aims and objectives*, as a particularly boring trainer had tediously but unforgettably put it at police college. He wanted to emerge from the interrogation and get out of the police station. He wanted to get to the next stage of his own investigation, which meant going to the chocolatier, and then he wanted to solve the case altogether and report back to Gloria Etchingham. He knew that if the police found out who had killed Lennon then that would help him. The ifs and buts swirled around in Sterling's head like a chess problem. He was facing checkmate in three moves against any defence. The next few hours would be tough. He couldn't think clearly any more, so he closed his eyes. Maybe a brief nap would help before the show started.

It might have been ten minutes later or it might have been longer when the interview room door opened and Broussart and his translator entered, the offsider carrying a Styrofoam cup of tea, which he put in front of Sterling, who assumed that others were behind the screen. The offsider took the chair rejected by Sterling and put it against the side wall. He left the room for a moment and came back with another chair, presumably with legs all the same length. While he was doing this, Broussart stared at Sterling impassively, the sour expression permanently fixed on his face.

Sterling put his hands flat in front of him, palms down, the acme of openness and relaxation – as adrenaline made his ears roar. Broussart and the offsider got out their notebooks and pens. The first part was pre-planned.

'Mr Sterling, my name is Detective Pieters, and I have introduced Inspector Broussart at the hotel. We have invited you here as a volunteer to ask you some questions about a man who was found dead yesterday at a location between Ypres and Zonnebeeke.'

Pieters's English was excellent, but Sterling longed to tell him that in English it was 'voluntarily', rather than 'as a volunteer'. He had a fleeting picture of himself stuffing envelopes with Save the Children fund-raising appeals here in the station. He kept quiet and took a sip of tea, giving Pieters a little toast of thanks as he lifted the cup. There wasn't enough milk, and there was too much sugar, but it was welcome, anyway. They always messed up the drinks. It was part of the same strategy of discomfort as the wobbly chair.

'What will happen is that Inspector Broussart will ask questions and I will translate. When you answer, I will translate your answer for the inspector. We should,' he considered for a moment or two, looking for a suitable phrase in English, 'get the handle of things quickly.'

'Get into the swing of things', 'Get the hang of it', Sterling thought, but just nodded. Pieters did not look as though he was yet thirty. His blond hair was cut short, almost in a crew cut, and he had an earnest way about him. They would be just sticking to business, and not exchanging banter about the intricacies of colloquial English.

Broussart knew that the introductions were over, and his harsh, impatient voice made Sterling realise that he needed to improve his concentration. Broussart spoke directly to him and fixed him with a sharp, knowing gaze, and then Pieters translated. Pieters was right. A rhythm developed – a question from Broussart, translation by Pieters, response by Sterling, translation by Pieters for Broussart.

'You are Frank Sterling.'

'Yes.'

'You are a policeman.'

Sterling's little performance with the interview chair had told them that.

'Ex-policeman. Currently, I'm a tourist.'

'Ah, so you are here in Ypres to….?'

'Well, be a tourist. I'm sorry, Inspector Broussart.' Sterling looked directly at the man running the interview. 'But I'm not sure how this is relevant to what you're investigating – this "suspicious death".'

'We're just establishing background, Mr. Sterling,' translated Pieters. 'Surely British procedures are similar.'

Sterling leaned back and yawned, taking care to cover his mouth with his hand to avoid any impression of insolence. 'Excuse me – a tiring week.'

The questions and answers flowed back and forth, like a particularly long baseline tennis rally. Sterling realised he was becoming more confident. He wasn't telling the truth, the whole truth and nothing but the truth, but he wasn't exactly lying either. He was glad he was a 'volunteer'. He had not received the Flemish equivalent of a caution – all that 'you are not obliged to say anything....' stuff – so that made for less pressure. Broussart and Pieters had no evidence pointing to him except his possession of the photo of the Scottish monument – highly circumstantial. All Sterling's pre-interview preparation had not been entirely necessary.

'To summarise, Mr. Sterling, you are here in Ypres as a tourist, but in England you are a private investigator and at one time, you were a policeman,' stated Pieters.

'Yes, that's about the size of it,' Sterling replied, but he could tell from Pieters's face, and Broussart's when the translation was done, that they knew there was more to it. It seemed thin even to Sterling.

From underneath his notepad, Broussart drew out an envelope, saying a few words in Dutch as he did.

'Moving on then,' said Pieters. 'On Saturday 5th September we received a telephone call, in English, from someone who reported finding a body at the Scottish memorial at Frezenburg ridge. According to papers we found on his body, it was Thomas Jackson, a 29-year-old Englishman.'

Broussart pushed some photos from the envelope over to Sterling's side of the table. Poor Lennon, or Jackson as he supposed he would have to think of him now. He looked more forlorn in death in the photos than even in the flat Flanders landscape, the head wound more gory and pronounced.

'Did you do this to this man?' he asked in blunt, heavily accented English.

Sterling was caught by surprise. He sensed that Broussart could understand English. He had known when to speak and when to wait for Pieters to translate. But this was a new development.

'Of course not,' Sterling replied, but there was unintended bluster in his voice.

'Do you know him? Did you follow him? Is anyone here with you in Ypres who could be involved?'

The pace of the questioning quickened as they came to the heart of it. Sterling made himself remember that he was entirely innocent. He did not even need to have reported anything. It was time to try and shift the balance – not go on the attack but move from openness and bewilderment to indignation. He really felt it, too.

'I may have seen him around the town. It's hard to tell. His head's been bashed in. But yes, I could have seen him around the Grote Markt. I don't really know anything else. If you're accusing me of something, shouldn't you tell me what?'

Being 'a volunteer' worked both ways. Sterling did not have to tell them everything, but they could also keep things from him.

On his own initiative, Pieters said, 'We're not accusing you of anything, Mr. Sterling. You're just a volunteer helping us by answering our questions. If the situation changes, of course we will tell you.'

'Well, speaking as an ex-policeman, I would say that this man Jackson has been murdered. You've told me that the body was found yesterday, and I would imagine that your forensics people would know by now when the assault took place and how long he's been dead for. I reckon that I can pretty much account for my time while I've been here. Why don't we take things from that angle?'

Pieters turned to translate, but Broussart waved him angrily away. He knew what Sterling was saying. He knew Sterling wanted them to show their hand. Sterling was becoming aware that Broussart could understand English perfectly adequately, and even speak it when he wanted to, though not particularly well. The translation performance gave him time to observe and evaluate. It was an effective technique. Sterling wondered if Broussart ever thought he was a suspect, or whether he believed that, although Sterling was not directly involved, he knew more than he was saying. Broussart reminded him of a detective sergeant at the Folkestone nick – also cynical, always looking on the dark side of people, always looking for lies – but always exactly right in his appraisal of a situation. The legs of Sterling's chair were four square on the floor, but he shifted and squirmed.

Broussart and Pieters had a protracted conversation in Dutch, Pieters nodding and deferential, but throwing in the odd point of his own. At the end, it seemed as though Broussart had made a decision.

Pieters spoke in English. 'OK, Mr. Sterling, our forensics people believe that Mr. Jackson was killed sometime during last Friday, almost certainly in the middle of the afternoon. His body stayed there overnight and we were informed the next day. So, speaking to you of course as a volunteer, can you please tell us what you were doing on Friday afternoon?'

The questioning had gone on for some time. Sterling had a headache from the effort of concentrating and not making any slips. There was an ache in the small of his back. The interview room, dingy, over-heated, ill-lit and painted a particularly unappealing olive-drab colour, had also begun to smell of cologne and body odour. He noticed a few scratches on the tabletop for the first time, formed into two faint words – *sauve moi* 'save me'. But he had his second wind as he looked up into Broussart's eyes.

'Friday afternoon....' He pretended to think and not look triumphant before the slam-dunk. 'On Friday afternoon, I went by train to Poperinghe. I've still got my tickets somewhere. You can find my signature in the visitors' book at Talbot House, and I had a cup of tea with that little Welshman. The same silly prat who involved me in this whole ridiculous mix-up.'

Broussart had understood what Sterling had said, but he still waited for Pieters's translation. They conferred again in Dutch. Sterling considered how things would have worked if the processes were anything like those in England. Someone gets murdered. The victim is from out of the area. There are no immediate clues. It goes out on the TV news. There's an early lead, in this case 'Lloyd George' Williams's swift betrayal. Having no other leads, the police follow the one they've got as a priority. They get their man – an early breakthrough. Everything happens too quickly to do timelines and sort out glitches. Then it all unravels in the first round of interrogation.

For the moment, Sterling thought he might have gained a bit of time.

Abruptly, both men got up and left the room. Pieters had, up to now, been reasonably polite, but this time he said nothing. Sterling supposed that the team would be conferring behind the glass or in the squad room, and checking his story by sending someone to Talbot House to look in the visitor's book and talk to the Welsh bombast. Broussart wasn't the kind of man who needed to save face. He just did what he had to do. But maybe his superiors would be sensitive to criticism about detaining and questioning a tourist with a solid alibi. Sterling rested his forehead on his hands.

An hour later, he looked at his watch. It was five o'clock. He had been in Ypres police station for four hours. Twenty minutes later, Pieters appeared at the door. There was no sign of Broussart.

'Thank you for coming to the station to answer our questions, Mr. Sterling. You are free to go now,' Pieters said with his now customary courtesy. Sterling's alibi had held up.

'That's it? Good,' he replied. 'Inspector Broussart took my passport. Can I have it back?'

'We're going to keep your passport for the moment, Mr. Sterling. Please don't leave Hotel Sultan, and don't leave the town. We will have more questions for you when we've got further into our investigation.'

'Can you do that? Keep my passport? Tell me where I can or can't go? Surely I've got rights.'

Pieters looked at him. 'I wouldn't,' he searched for the right words again, 'boot up too much of a fuss if I am in your place. We think you have more to tell us. You've been a policeman. You will not be too surprised at what we can do.'

'Don't lose my passport. Where's the way out?'

This time they went to the front entrance, approaching the security door that divided the back office from visitors. The glass would be bulletproof. Things were the same everywhere. Just before Pieters punched in the code, Sterling noticed the photographers and reporters in the street outside the front doors. He put his hand on Pieters's arm and he looked back.

'Do I have to go through that lot?' asked Sterling. 'I'm just a tourist. I really don't want to get into all that.'

Pieters knew he was not just a tourist, but he seemed a decent bloke. Sterling could almost see the calculations he was making, too. It would probably be to the advantage of the West Flanders police for the first person 'helping them with their enquiries' not to have to run the press gauntlet. The two men backed out of sight down the corridor.

Pieters spoke a few words to a uniformed policeman in one of the offices, and they all went back through the car park. Sterling blinked in the outside light. It was like coming out of the cinema after watching a matinée all afternoon. In the corner of the wall abutting the bottom of the rampart slope was a heavily bolted and reinforced door. The uniform got out a heavy set of keys and set about the locks.

'Go up the steps and turn left to go to the Menin Gate. From there, you can find your way to the Grote Markt and your hotel,' said Pieters. Sterling knew that already, but kept it to himself.

'Thanks, Detective Pieters,' he said.

He nodded curtly. 'We'll see you again soon, Mr. Sterling.' Sterling did not doubt that, the way he said it.

The door clanged shut as he scrambled up the uneven steps to the track on top of the ramparts. The cool early evening air smelt woody and fresh. He took in a deep breath of freedom. The feeling in his gut told him that it wasn't going to last long, and his gut was rarely wrong.

13

Sterling was confident that only the police would know that he was walking on the ramparts pathway towards the Menin Gate. He wanted some time to himself, to take stock again and address his depleted state. If Christina was worried about him after he was taken from the hotel by the police, he'd reassure her later. He needed to update Angela, and perhaps Gloria Etchingham herself. He wondered who Thomas Jackson was, and how he was connected to the case.

Sterling had not eaten since the cakes at the church, and the tea in the police station had only made him thirstier. He wanted a quiet café where he could just fade into the background, away from the tourist haunts and his band of stalkers. He suspected that Broussart and Pieters would be replacing Jackson. As he walked, he looked over the moat-water to the flat, cultivated countryside stretching into the distance, and then in the foreground at the solid well-to-do Flemish villas on the roadway running parallel to the moat. The calm evening and the Sunday teatime normality soothed him. It felt as if he was the only person out of doors.

'That's enough excitement for one day' was a catchphrase in Sterling's family as he was growing up. He remembered it as he was deciding what to do after reaching the Menin Gate. The chocolate shop was close by in the Grote Markt, but Keith Etchingham had been gone a good few months, so cracking his secret wouldn't be affected by one more day of waiting. Sterling decided to do a discreet check about when it was open and then find that something to eat. At half past six, it was too early for the Commonwealth Last Post crowd. Some chocolatiers and gift shops were open as he cut down Meensestraat. A few locals were out for a pre-prandial stroll. In one of the spots on the square, someone had parked a pick-up truck. Strapped in the back was a forlorn little mobility scooter, looking as if it had broken down and been retrieved.

He ducked down one of the side streets opposite Hotel Sultan and near Au Miroir. Not far from De Groot's cycle shop, he found the only food place open, a little Turkish pizzeria. Thinking that this was surely a contradiction in terms, he found a small table for two overlooking the street. The dark-set young man who served him seemed to be something between a waiter, pizza oven operator and family shop manager. As he went back towards the kitchen, he twirled the tray on two fingers. Sterling doubted whether he noticed that he was doing it.

After the pizza and beer arrived, the café was quiet. It was Sunday evening, and most people were indoors. Sterling realised why he was by himself when he saw the young man join a table of fellow Turkish people a few doors down on the other side of the street. They had chairs out, and were smoking, drinking tiny cups of strong black coffee, whose aroma Sterling caught even from up the street, and laughing in the fading evening. It seemed jollier there than where he was, and it would have been good to join them. He remembered his need for some quiet obscurity, and concentrated on the rubbery cheese and tired fragments of onion and tomato. It was just the stodge he needed to stave off the hunger that had made him tremble on his walk along the ramparts.

It was a struggle to pay the bill. There was too much entertainment for his server to drag himself from the little party down the street. In the end, Sterling went to him with his euros and carried on back to the hotel. The little Turkish crowd waved a cheerful goodbye, and Sterling thought of the pub. He slipped quietly into the hotel through the side door. There was no one at reception. He climbed the stairs softly and slipped into his room. Taking care not to flick the curtain, he took a sidelong glance out into the square. The light was fading quickly now, but the streetlights had come on.

He tried to remember when it was that he had last seen the burly, smartly dressed men watching him. It was one of them, surely, whose malevolence Sterling had felt in the church this morning, but before that, they had faded from view. They had switched their attention to Thomas Jackson. It must be that. Sterling scanned the square from his vantage point at the side of the window. Now that the dead hour between late afternoon and evening was over, there was more activity, even though it was Sunday. The zombies were beginning their swarm to the Menin gate. Odd couples and knots of people milled around. There might even have been one or two police officers. But the people whom Sterling feared – really feared – were not in the square that night, and for some reason, that made him feel worse.

He had to speak to Gloria Etchingham again. She knew more than she had said so far, and what she wasn't saying was putting him in danger. He dialled for the outside line and pressed her number. The dialling tone started.

'This is Gloria Etchingham's telephone. I can't take your call right now. Please leave your name, a message and your contact details, and I'll get back to you.'

'Damn,' said Sterling softly. He wanted to get information, not give it. More loudly, he spoke to the voicemail. 'Gloria, it's Frank. Things are getting... intense. There's been an... incident. Do you know anyone called Thomas Jackson? He's involved somehow. And I've got another lead that I'm following up tomorrow. I'll telephone then – about this time. I think that's it for now.'

He was almost glad he had lost his mobile telephone. Now he was controlling the flow of communication. In Sterling's view, people talked to each other far too often and far too inconsequentially. On reflection, he was not too sorry that Gloria was unavailable. He had the latest lead to occupy him, and he would have more to say tomorrow evening.

He was more successful with his second call, to Angela. She picked up after a few rings. He knew she'd be in. Sunday evening, for her, was ironing, domestic chores and getting ready for the next week's work. No pub, no crossword.

'Angela, it's Frank.'

'How are you, Frank? How's it going over there?'

The sound of her voice warmed and reassured him. He gave her a brief summary of what had happened since she had solved the Poperinghe stage of the puzzle. There was little point in leaving anything out. She was quiet as Sterling told her about Poperinghe, finding Thomas

Jackson's body at the Scottish memorial, the visit to St George's, the silly small treacherous Welshman, and the police questioning. They had last spoken on Friday morning. Now it was Sunday evening, a lifetime further on. Sterling thought he was being coherent, but every now and again, Angela asked a question, and at each point, he added another layer of information and understanding.

When they had finished that part of the conversation, there was a lull. Sterling could hear Angela's light breathing on the end of the telephone. It was quiet in his room except when the occasional car glided by around the square outside. Although there was silence, he felt connected to home.

'You need help,' Angela said eventually. It was a statement and not a question.

'I've got some allies here,' he said, thinking of Christina and Martin De Groot. 'But no one I'm really sure enough of or know well enough to rely on.'

'Hmm,' she replied. There was a knowing tone in her voice. 'I expect you have, Frank. You've got the knack, though you came unstuck a bit with James Williams. I'm thinking that you need a bit more than that now. Strange country. Strange language. Murder. Suspicious police force. Other interested parties.'

It was the other interested parties that worried him most.

'Any ideas welcome, Angela,' he said.

'There is someone. I'll ask,' she said at the end of the call.

Tomorrow, Marc Mehrtens the chocolatier would be open, a few doors down, and Sterling could carry on with his investigation. There was little he could do before that. Maybe he could have telephoned and asked for a meeting, but he could not think of how to avoid suspicion. He rehearsed a conversation in his mind, assuming that the chocolatier would speak English. 'Hello, Mr. Mehrtens, my name is Frank Sterling. I'm a private investigator from England. Can you interrupt the rest of your day to solve a piece of the puzzle that I'm investigating? Perhaps meet me at your shop?' The whole thing lacked any plausibility. It was much better to wait till tomorrow.

His watch said 8:30. It was only fair to tell Christina or her mother that he was back in the hotel, that he hoped to stay a few more days, and that despite his visit to Ypres police station, his continuing presence was nothing to worry about. Only the last assertion was doubtful. He was relying on Christina to protect him from her family, who might fear the hotel's reputation being besmirched by scandal. He washed his face, not daring to look in the mirror, and smoothed down his hair. He gulped down some water. The tea and beer had just made him thirstier. Then he went downstairs to reception. There was reassurance to be doled out.

But no one was behind the counter and the restaurant was empty. The hotel had the air of the *Mary Celeste*. It was tempting to postpone the reassurance conversation, but the bell on the counter would summon someone, and long experience instructed Sterling that postponement was always the worse option. He hoped for Christina rather than her mother as the tinny sound echoed through the lobby. From the back office, her mother emerged. She stopped for a moment as she passed through the door from the office to the counter. Sterling could see questions and doubts in the worry lines of her face more than the good looks she had passed on to her daughter.

'Mr. Sterling. What can I do for you?'

'Mrs... ?' He realised that he did not know Christina's surname.

'Mrs. Van de Velde.' She was not going to be very forthcoming.

'Mrs. Van de Velde,' he repeated, and took a breath. 'Mrs. Van de Velde, you may have found out that the local police came to the hotel this morning and invited me to go to the police station for questioning. Perhaps your daughter said something.'

'She did mention something, yes.' Just like her daughter's, one of her eyebrows went up, and there may have been a small smile just in evidence around her lips.

'Well, I did accept the invitation and I did answer a few of the questions the police officers asked me. I spent quite a lot of the afternoon at the station.'

'I know. Ypres is a small town, Mr. Sterling.'

'Oh.' He was nonplussed, but in a way not surprised, either. Sandley could be twinned with Ypres, and the situation there would be just the same. 'Anyway, Mrs. Van de Velde, I just wanted to tell you that I answered the police questions, and they appeared to be happy with my answers, so they've let me go.'

'As I see, Mr. Sterling.'

She was definitely laughing at him now. He was certain of it. She was very much like her daughter, or her daughter was very much like her. Sterling remembered how his friend Nicky Moran had not met his natural father, who ran a shoe shop in the Isle of Wight, till he was 25, but when they walked along together, their mannerisms were identical. He came back from his musing, feeling himself blushing. A place like Hotel Sultan in the middle of the square must have some little drama or other every third day – a guest not paying a bill, a fight outside the door, plenty of police visits. Sometimes, Sterling had delusions of grandeur. His trivial little escapade probably caused little stir after the initial police visit.

'So I'll be staying on for a few more days if that's OK.' He started to turn away, back up to the stairs.

'Fine, Mr. Sterling.' Something steely in Christina's mother's voice made him pause for a moment. 'There is another matter, Mr. Sterling. Christina is a very happy girl. She has a very kind boyfriend. He's an optician in Kortrijk. We're all very fond of him in this family. We would not like Christina to become sad for any reason.' The English was stilted, but the message was not.

He felt another surge of blood to his cheeks and stumbled quickly back up the stairs. 'Guy the optician,' he thought mischievously at the top, his embarrassment receding. 'How dull.' But he would take care not to share his amusement with Christina. She might not find it funny. And anyway, why should opticians automatically be dull?

That night, Sterling did not sleep well. His pursuers were relentless. He fretted about Thomas Jackson's murder and how he might be being linked to it. William's betrayal had disconcerted him. Now that he was known to the Ypres police, he felt certain that they'd wish to interview him again. He wondered about Christina and the beginnings of that 'friendship'. Solving Keith Etchingham's puzzle absorbed him more than anything.

He dreamed that he had just attended a conference with a Scandinavian man who wanted Sterling to take home some papers left behind at the meeting. He was reproachful when Sterling was reluctant to do that (arguing that he'd just have to bring them back the next week). When he woke in the morning, the sheets and covers were crumpled all over the bed and his hair was a shock of disorder. He was counting on the visit to the chocolatier to dispel his feelings of negativity and unease.

14

Sterling stepped out of the hotel into the Grote Markt at 10 o'clock. Breakfast, supervised efficiently and discreetly by Mrs. Van de Velde, was uneventful. He wondered where Christina was. Perhaps her mother, alarmed at how things were turning out, had locked her away. No more consorting with English strangers for you, my girl. More plausibly, she might have gone off to the optician in Kortrijk, which, Sterling had noticed when he was at Ypres station, was a few stops down the railway line towards Brussels and the east. He was disappointed. It didn't seem like the Christina that he'd been with in Casa Nova on Saturday night just to fade out of sight. He hoped she knew that he was out of the police station. Away from Sandley, he needed his allies.

He lingered for a moment on the step of the hotel's front entrance. The weather had changed. It was cooler and overcast, with a hint of drizzle. Whilst the sunshine had lit up everything – people's faces, the crenellated façades of the buildings, the brewers' signs for Stella Artois, Jupiler and Maes Pils over the hotels and cafes – the overcast sky and the dampness made everything grey. Few local people sat outside at the cafes, whose waiters and managers had clearly not banked on the sunshine ending, since tables, chairs and awnings were set out as for summer. On the other side of the square, at Au Miroir, a solitary old man wrapped in a scruffy raincoat sipped at his coffee under one of the awnings, puffing occasionally at a brown cigarillo and reading the local paper spread on the table. A bit of cooler weather was not going to disturb his routine.

No one seemed to be watching for Sterling, but that meant little except that the watchers had probably become much more circumspect. He turned up the collar of his jacket and buttoned it at the middle, hunching his shoulders forward. It wasn't really necessary because of the coolness, but it made him a smaller target for the drizzle. His umbrella was in the Peugeot. Anyway, it was only a few metres to the chocolatier. He could hardly envisage anything more innocent than going and buying some chocolates.

Marc Mehrtens's shop was in a little cluster of chocolate shops. If Ypres had been larger, and not just a small provincial Belgian town unfortunate enough to be in the middle of the military deadlock between the Great Powers almost a century ago, the area might have been described as the chocolate shop *quartier*. As it was, there were about five or six establishments in the corner of the Grote Markt interspersed with restaurants and clothes shops. Some were part of a chain. Sterling recognised the blue and gold branding of Leonidas from somewhere in England, maybe the West End.

Mehrtens was an independent. He had set up his business in an old tearoom. The door and the panes of glass above the main plate glass shop front windows reminded Sterling of the leaded windows of churches back home, or, as he thought about it a little more, the leaded door and window panes of 1930s semis along ribbon roads from towns throughout England, urban fingers creeping out into the countryside. He thought of the pub windows too, the 'Cobb and Sons, makers of fine ales and beers' and the ketches and barges in rich translucent red and green in a miniature Victorian seascape. They were just beside the spot where he and Angela did the crossword. Above all, he thought of the windows in Angela's library.

He peered in, hands against the glass over his eyes to shield them from the window's reflection. There was an 'Open' sign in the window, but no one seemed to be in the shop. He tried the door, and a bell over it rang out somewhere out to the back. Did all the hotel and shop bells in Ypres have the same supplier? Everything was old-fashioned in a way he appreciated. He had a moment or two to look around. On the right was a glass counter full of Belgian chocolates – white, light brown and dark, and full of golden boxes of different sizes wrapped with red ribbon. A till and some weighing scales sat on an adjacent lower counter.

On the other side were all the tools of the chocolate trade in a kind of display. If they were intended to inspire confidence in the customer, indicating that this was the shop of a craftsman-chocolatier, they succeeded. A pair of white gloves for handling the chocolates was draped over the weighing pan lip of another more delicate set of scales. In the coolness, there was a sweet rich complex confectionery aroma (it was too subtle and elegant to be a mere smell) that reminded Sterling momentarily of Nestlé's white chocolate and the Milky Bar kid.

From a secret side door, or that's how it appeared, a short, slim, compact, gentle-looking man emerged. Although his shoes were an elegant brown, with subtle patterning over the uppers, the Flemish equivalent, Sterling imagined, of Russell and Bromley, the rest of him was grey – from the corduroy trousers to the sleeveless cardigan and cotton grey and white checked shirt. They matched his rich, thick head of straight grey hair and his Marshal Pétain moustache, both beautifully cut in what Sterling was learning was the continental manner. This was a man from whom men, women, boys and girls would be equally happy to buy their chocolates – a man exuding confectionery solicitude, trustworthiness and expertise.

Sterling had chosen his moment well. At just after 10 a.m. on a Monday morning, trade was rarely brisk, and for Ypres chocolatiers, clearly there was no exception.

Mehrtens spoke in English. Sterling had become used to the fact that Flemish people knew from what Jack Cook would call 'the cut of his jib' that he was English. 'Good morning. I expect you're here for chocolates.' The little joke seemed astonishingly fresh, even though he had probably used it a thousand times.

'Actually, maybe I am and maybe I'm not. I don't quite know yet. I suppose that depends a bit on you.'

Mehrtens frowned a little, but not in a hostile way. Sterling wondered if the chocolatier had ever had a similar reply. 'If not chocolates, then....?' He trailed off, not quite so confident that the conversation was going down the customary tracks.

Sterling reached into his pocket for the card he'd found in the church. 'My name is Frank Sterling. I tracked this down. It asks you to pay the bearer on demand. I wonder if you know what it means.'

The chocolatier looked from behind the counter out of the wide window into the street. He knew that seeing in was more difficult than seeing out. He might once have known the scientific explanation, as Sterling did for about two days when he was a teenager – it was to do with the refraction of light and glass as a highly viscous liquid. 'Does anyone else know you're here, Mr. Sterling? Keith was very definite about that point.'

'No, I don't think so. You knew Keith Etchingham?'

'Keith….' Mehrtens looked up to a corner of his shop. Sterling's arrival had triggered a small, unexpected reminiscence. 'I'd never met anyone like him. I am not sure how you say it in English. In Dutch, it would be something like, 'Kracht van de natuur'. He had a very big personality. I didn't know him until I met him in one of the cafes here. He asked me to recommend a beer and we started a conversation. My God, I don't really drink beer, but my mother was looking after the shop that afternoon, and then I was going with Keith around all the cafes in Ypres. I did not think that would happen. He told me afterwards what it was we had done. Pub crawl.'

He laughed at the phrase. 'I didn't get back home till about 11 o'clock that evening. My mother wasn't very pleased with me. I had such a good time. Life can be a little quiet in this town. It wasn't that day with Keith.' He smiled at the memory. 'He said it would be urgent if someone came to me. How long have you had my card? You should have telephoned me if the shop was closed. Explained who you were. Said the magic message.' Sterling thought he meant "magic words". 'I would have come in and opened up.'

Sterling tut-tutted mentally and made a note: do things as soon as possible; progress might be surprising. He filed away the information about Etchingham.

It added to the knowledge he already had. 'And … can you pay the bearer?'

'He was a very nice man to be with,' said Mehrtens, not appearing to have heard the question. 'But he was scared of something or someone. Really scared. He was very secretive, as well. As we were walking from café to café, I began to think that it was not just the start of us being friends. He was … testing me. To see if I could be trusted. That was very important. His words were that he wanted to believe in human beings again. At the end, he did trust me. He gave me something. That's what I have to give to you.' Mehrtens ducked out of sight behind the counter and emerged with a small golden box of chocolates wrapped with a red ribbon and bow. He offered it. 'This is what Keith told me to hand over. We made it up together, but he added something. He told me not to look. I think you should be careful.'

'Thank you – I will be. It's been eventful enough up to now.'

Being in the chocolate shop made Sterling think of Christina and Angela. They deserved presents for what they had put up with. 'While I'm here, could I have two more boxes of chocolates the same size as this?'

'Of course,' said the chocolatier. He slipped on the white gloves and became a magician. 'Are you buying for yourself or are the chocolates presents?'

'Presents,' Sterling said.

'OK, presents. Would you like me to make an appropriate selection?' Now Mehrtens was in his element – cool, measured and assured. The two golden flat pre-shaped pieces of cardboard were swiftly transformed into two boxes, and when two layers of assorted chocolates were added, his deft fingers unwound the red ribbon from the dispenser, wrapped it neatly around each box and completed the bows with a flourish. He marked Etchingham's box with a little 'x' on the bottom.

Sterling could not hold back from asking. 'Weren't you tempted to find out what was in the box?'

'Yes, but Keith was made it clear that it was dangerous. You must understand, Mr. Sterling. To go out with Keith that day was a very unusual thing for me.' He searched for the appropriate English words. 'I am a person who does the same thing every day. To do a different thing – that is very odd for me. And I just make and sell chocolates. It is safer not to know than to know.'

Sterling nodded. 'Thank you again, Mr. Mehrtens. I expect it will all come out eventually.'

'What has happened to Keith?' asked Mehrtens abruptly, just as Sterling was turning to go. 'He said that someone would pick up the box – he didn't know who. But where is he?'

'I'm not sure. He's disappeared, presumed dead in the circumstances. If I knew more, I'd say. I'm sorry. Sorry about Keith. Sorry to be the one to tell you.'

Sterling made his way out of the shop. As he opened the door, a boy and a girl waited for him to pass. They looked like twins – twins at the onset of adolescence, and just a little awkward and gawky. Their soft Scottish accents contrasted with the usual loud squawking of the battlefield tourists. From the outside, he could just make out Marc Merhtens greeting them with his chocolatier smile, a little forced this time. Perhaps he was asking them if they were there for chocolates. As Sterling turned away, back to the hotel, Mehrtens caught his eye and nodded. Sterling could not see clearly through the glass, but he was sure the gentle face had also acquired some sadness.

The room at the hotel was the obvious place to open Etchingham's box of chocolates. Sterling wondered now what he thought about the whole affair. He wanted this to be the last part. He wanted to get back to England, report to Gloria Etchingham and get back to his sheltered life. Surely the chocolates had all the answers he needed. As he entered the hotel, Christina was at reception, her eyes fixed on some papers in front of her. So she had not gone to Kortrijk after all. It was his chance to give her the little gift of chocolates. He began the little journey from the glass doors, extracting one box of chocolates and concealing the bag with the other two boxes as he went. She looked up just as he arrived at the desk.

'Hello, Christina. I see you're back on duty.' There would be no prize for originality, but he tried a light smile.

'Hello, Frank. My mother told me you were back.' She smiled back, and he felt encouraged. He offered her the box of chocolates. 'I know you're probably familiar with these, but I thought you might like them anyway. It's a thank you for your company on Saturday night. It was a nice evening.'

'I enjoyed it very much, but my mother isn't very happy for me to be with a foreigner who the police want to speak to and who makes things so difficult. You've caused many arguments, and not just between me and my mother.'

He did not think that was very fair. He did not frogmarch her down to Casa Nova, or choose her optician boyfriend. People have free will. He'd always believed that. But he could be canny. Dealing with abusive drunks with painstaking politeness on Folkestone High Street on Saturday nights had honed that skill. He looked at the floor and shuffled his feet.

'I'm sorry I have been unsettling.' He looked back up into her face and felt a bit of mischief. 'I'm not used to such an intriguing receptionist.'

'Thank you for the chocolates, Frank.' Christina was dismissing him, and she looked back down to the paperwork on the counter, but he saw a small return smile.

Sterling went up the stairs to his room, reassured that things were still good between them. Knowing that helped in the nightmare that followed.

15

It's little things that tell you something isn't right. In this case, it was the faint smell of a man's cologne or the scent that comes with shaving foam. That hadn't been in the corridor to Sterling's room, and he knew that it had nothing to do with him. He looked around for other signs – and found them. The bars of the fire escape door, with the sign of a little green man in a pose of flight down some cartoon stairs against a white background, were not quite aligned. He could see the faintest sliver of light, like a long stiletto, in the bottom gap between the door and the wall of the cleaning cupboard. He went for his room key, and even went so far as scratching it in the lock. Then he thought: the room will be the trap. There was no obvious way out except through the door. He had been too complacent to examine the possibility of an exit from the window.

He had more manoeuvrability outside. The person waiting for him must have echoed his thinking. As Sterling put the key back in the pocket, the cleaning cupboard door opened and one of the gang of men following him stepped into the corridor. He didn't just step into it. He filled it. It was time to go. When teachers on occasional school outings used to shout out, 'Don't run, walk', the walks – to be first in the ice-cream van queue, to be first to jump in the sand on the beach – were always on the verge of erupting into runs. That's what Sterling remembered as he scuttled back along the corridor and clattered down the stairs. When he burst into the reception area, he stopped and pretended that he had forgotten something.

'Christina,' he hissed softly. When she looked up, like a boules player he tossed the bag with the remaining chocolates across the room to the counter. She was quick, catching the bag one-handed. She was quick to clock the situation, too. The bag was slipped under the counter just as his pursuer jumped from the last stair into the lobby and Sterling dashed out through the side door.

He wanted to get away. Find somewhere quiet to regroup. Think about how he could extricate himself from this dangerous, deepening mess. Beyond escape, his thoughts were vague. There was no plan. As things turned out, he did not need one. He'd been concentrating on who was behind him and how close he was. He did not notice the large, smartly dressed man he cannoned into on the pavement. The man noticed him, though. He was expecting him. As Sterling stumbled, he put an arm around his shoulders. To the world, it was a friendly and good-natured gesture of support, the smiling face indicating, 'Accidents happen. Here, let me make sure you don't fall over.' To Sterling, it was very different. The other arm ended in something that was being poked into his ribs, something small, hard and round – very possibly the barrel of a gun.

The other man fell out of the side door of the hotel. A car pulled up on the other side of the road. It was the dark blue Saab. While the original pursuer pirouetted over to open the back door, Sterling and the bear shuffled over like two beginners making a hash of their first dance, steps out of kilter, one determined and one confused in their firm embrace. Sterling was shoved into the middle of the back seat and boxed in by his captors. The journey from outside his room and into the car had taken under two minutes. He felt bile in his throat. And panic. There was a word for all this. Abduction.

You expect clichés at these times. But the car did not make a clichéd getaway, engine howling, tyres screeching. It accelerated gently away from the kerb and turned right smoothly and quietly into D'Hondstraat. Clichéd questions came into Sterling's head. 'Who are you? Where are we going? What do you want with me?' And clichéd statements: 'There must be some mistake. You won't get away with this. I've got friends who know exactly where I am and will come after me.' But he thought that things would become clearer soon enough. He concentrated silently on trying to control his fear.

The car moved down D'Hondstraat. It followed the one-way system in the same leisurely manner into Rijselsestraat. In a moment or two it passed under the ramparts bridge at the Lille Gate and into the countryside. Sterling looked wistfully up, his ruse with the bicycle and *uitgezonderd* a quickly fading memory.

He thought he had better go through the motions. 'I didn't want to make a fuss before,' he said. 'I thought it would be dangerous. But I'm sure there is some mistake. Why have you picked me up off the street? Where are we going? Are you the police?'

His abductors stared ahead. Doubtless there would be time for talking later. These were definitely the men who had been following him since he left England a week ago, or perhaps following Thomas Jackson. The two men boxing him in were bruisers. Sterling was big enough, but he felt small squeezed between their combined bulk, and for that matter, scruffy. The driver was different. Although smartly turned out, like the others in blazer and slacks, he was smaller. His driving was nervous, with little flicks and glances into the rear view mirror and the cautious air of someone who didn't quite know where he was going and wasn't always getting it right. Sterling kept an eye on the signs. He hoped that there would be an opportunity for it to be useful.

After the Lille Gate, they had turned left at one roundabout and again at the next, on what seemed to be some kind of outer ringroad. In the middle of the one that followed was a huge blue tap sculpture with a red handle hanging from the sky, water gushing in a torrent from the spout to a pool below. In the back of the car, their heads swivelled in unison to look at it as the car snaked around the roundabout. No one spoke, but the unanswered question floated around their heads: 'How did they do that?' In any situation other than a kidnap, they might have chuckled.

Eventually, they were going out in a south-easterly direction towards Menen on the N8. Sterling knew his passivity was disadvantaging him. It indicated acceptance. But there seemed no point in anger, indignation, bewilderment or any other kind of behaviour after his half-hearted little speech. He knew these men, and they knew him. There was no point in pretending. And he was sure that, unfortunately for him, they would shortly get to know each other much better.

They did not drive for long. After a few kilometres, with the driver slowing down and peering with nervous concentration for a right hand turning, they pulled off down a small farm track. There was no signpost, not even a junction sign. The track was a bridleway of concreted blocks joined with strips of tar. Sterling's uncle's bungalow on the edge of Herne Bay was serviced by just such a type of road. His road, and the others on the estate, were named after an older generation of long-disappeared cars – Alvis Avenue, Daytona Close, Wolseley Way. As usual, at times of stress, Sterling was thinking irrelevant thoughts. This road was nameless, and so harder to find. But who would be looking for him? His spirits sank a little more.

Four hundred metres down from the main road, they pulled into a courtyard on the left. Sterling could hear the faint irregular thrum of the traffic from the main road they had just left. In front of the courtyard was a country cottage with a red roof in the West Flanders tradition, but new, with the window frames painted a dark brown and a matching front door. The brickwork had recently been repointed, and the mortar made a fresh white contrast with the older brick. It was just the place for a gentle family holiday, or a lovers' hideaway. Or to keep someone captive and out of sight.

His companions quickly got out of the car, and the larger one hauled Sterling from his place. There was no display of kindness this time, feigned or otherwise. His arms were gripped and he was marched roughly towards the front door. He did not give serious thought to making a break for it. In the wide farming landscape, there was nowhere to go. But he worked quickly to try at least to get familiar with the surroundings. As he faced the cottage, the track was to the right of the courtyard, and the main road was behind it. He could see that the cottage's garden surrounded it on the remaining three sides and was laid, relatively recently it looked like, to a simple lawn with the odd shrub. A short wooden palisade marked off the cottage and its small estate (the garden and courtyard) from the track and the dilapidated barn, sheds and sundry other farm buildings he could see at the back. The fence could be hurdled by anyone even slightly competent, but Sterling couldn't see how he would get the chance.

The group went through the front door, no longer three abreast, but with Sterling in the middle and shoved in. The door gave straight into the living room area, which was tiled in a dark rust colour. A black flat screen television took up a corner away from the front door, next to a hearth and fireplace, and two substantial sofas were arranged at right angles in twin homage in front of them. To the far left, the living area gave way to a dining area with a solid table and six chairs. Sterling assumed that the area walled off to the far right was where the kitchen was. At the wall between the living and dining rooms were some spiral stairs in cast iron, artfully done to blend in. The men had made themselves very comfortable, and renting a place like this gave them an admirable anonymity that did not bode happily for Sterling.

He only had a few seconds to look around. From the dining room window the outbuildings seemed closer, but they were not where he was being taken. The spiral staircase curled down as well as up, and down was where he felt himself being propelled. At the bottom of the staircase was a solid wooden door. The lock was old, but the brass bolts near the top and bottom looked bright and new. One of the thugs opened the door and the other pushed Sterling in. With the door slammed shut, he heard the lock click and the bolts slide across. He was going nowhere.

The cellar smelled musty and fruity. In one corner were some bags of coal, some firewood and some kindling. In the other, apples and pears were laid out on newspaper, picked from trees he had not seen outside. He thought the landlords were being optimistic if they were offering a nice homely touch and a cooking opportunity. He could not imagine any holiday tenants, and certainly not the thugs upstairs, taking the trouble to peel, spice, sweeten and boil these for pear and apple pie. High in the wall adjacent to the track was a small window of frosted glass. At a pinch, he thought he might be able to get through it. There was only the small hindrance of climbing the smooth wall with his bare hands and removing the iron bars embedded in the concrete frame.

He found an empty space under the window and sank down with his back to the wall. One of the pears had a ripe, rosy tinge. He reached over and picked it up. The flesh was dense and sharp, but had a sweet, natural aftertaste. He bit into it methodically. Only three of the gang had whisked him away. He waited for his interview with the fourth, the one he tagged as the head honcho.

They hadn't taken his watch, or his shoelaces, for that matter. They had checked that he had no mobile telephone. But he hadn't been tied up. They were confident that he could not get out. It had been about twenty past eleven when he was put into the cellar. Time was passing, and he was getting scared. They would bank on that, but boredom was also a problem. Sterling had always found it difficult to sit still and do nothing. He tried to work out his story, which needed to be very different from the one he had told to Broussart and Pieters. It depended on what the kidnappers knew.

What was bothering Sterling more and more was how open everything had been. He had been taken in broad daylight and there was no attempt to conceal their destination. It all added up to something very ominous. They couldn't let him go. As the implications, worried over for hours, began to sink in, he began to swallow nervously. The cellar was cool, but that did not stop the sweating and trembling. He needed to compose himself for the first interrogation. The less they knew, and the longer he could spin out his story, the safer he was. When they had collected Keith Etchingham's chocolates from Christina's desk in the hotel, when they knew his secret, when he was surplus to requirements, he was finished.

16

Three hours later, his ears attuned to every possible noise, Sterling heard footsteps and then the bolts being drawn back. 'Here it comes,' he muttered as his trepidation returned. The door eased open. Perhaps his captors believed he would be hiding behind the door and would spring out with deadly chops and kicks, but he was a sad shadow of an action man. When the two men saw him at the opposite wall, the larger one jerked his head and Sterling got to his feet. He thought he would let them come and get him, so that they did not have all the psychological advantage. They went up the spiral staircase in single file, Sterling again in the middle.

A kitchen chair had been positioned between the television and the sofas, and he was pushed roughly into it. Lounging on one of the sofas was the fourth man. Sterling could see that he was stocky and far from tall. His grey hair was cut short – between a crew cut and completely shaven – and was full on his head. His fingers were stumpy, extensions of his squat body, and his head was large and out of proportion. He had the pasty, clammy skin of a butcher working all day in low temperatures. He could imagine those stubby fingers around the handle of a meat cleaver.

'Before we go any further...' Sterling squeaked, despising himself, and then as he recovered a bit and found a lower timbre, 'I really need to take a leak.'

A shadow passed over the boss's face. He motioned with irritation to the others and they began the single-file procession up the spiral staircase to the top floor. As the bathroom was pointed out, Sterling caught a glimpse through the doors into the other rooms, clothes and shoes and other junk associated with partnerless men abroad strewn untidily around. If they had been ex-Services, he felt sure the rooms would have been neater. Again, he filed away the information, though it was as much use as a match in a gale.

'The window is locked, and there is a bloke beneath it,' said the larger man, 'so don't try anything.' His voice was light for such a big man.

Sterling realised with a slight shock that this was the first thing he or the other two had said. The door was ajar and when he was finished, it was back to the chair in the living room. The larger man, whom Sterling believed was number two, tied his hands to the back of the chair. His stomach lurched as the boss stared at him from his sofa. He recognised those malevolent eyes from St. George's Church.

'So,' said the boss. 'The tinpot detective. The cycling detective.' He rolled the words around his mouth, pleased with his efforts. 'The slippery detective. The loner. The *amateur*. You've caused us a bit of trouble and confusion.'

'Purely unintentional,' responded Sterling. This was not a man to alienate, though as the encounter went on, he was certain that he would not be able to avoid it. 'I don't even know who you are.'

'How rude of me,' said the boss. His manner was cheery, but there was no twinkle in those cold dark eyes. 'Well, I am Smithy. My colleague to your left is Fred and the one by the wall is Jason. The one patrolling outside' (and here there was a warning in his voice) 'is Simon. Not our real names, of course, but convenient enough for our purposes. And of course, you are Frank Sterling.'

Sterling said nothing. He could not imagine any name for Smithy more incongruous than the one he had chosen. And he also thought, if he knows what he seems to know, he must know much more, too. He reflected on Smithy's description, sadly noting that there was a sound basis for his contempt. He might almost have added 'dilettante'.

'Well,' said Smithy, 'let's not beat about the bush. You need to get me up to speed. Your connection with Gloria Etchingham and everything to do with it.'

'Or....?' Sterling replied. It might have indicated bravado, but he did not feel it.

'Or we won't bother with 'comfort breaks' and any notion of a civilised approach. We'll get what we need … in another way.'

Sterling swallowed. It was good that he had relieved himself. Otherwise there might have been a trickle down his trouser leg. 'Mrs. Etchingham engaged me to do some research for her after her husband was murdered or disappeared or whatever. That's what brought me over here. There were various things amongst Keith Etchingham's papers, and I had to track them down.'

'Good start, Frank. OK if I call you Frank? We don't want to get too formal around here. But I think I can say that we know that already. It's detail and *results* that we need. In short, what have you found out?'

Sterling was finding the cheery approach mingled with the utter menace of Smithy's manner unnerving. In one way, it was a good thing that he had not reached the end of his search. If he did not know the results, he could not convey them.

'I came from England last Monday. I've been here over a week. I'm sure you know that. In fact, didn't you come over on the same ferry? Someone attacked me on the deck. My mobile fell into the sea....' Sterling let the words hang for a moment. He might as well try and get some information back whilst he was being interrogated. Perhaps Smithy would admit responsibility, but he stared stonily ahead and Sterling carried on. 'The first part of the trail led me to Chester Farm Cemetery on the Lille road – not far from here, I should imagine – and the grave of one of Etchingham's Great War relatives. Mrs. Etchingham wanted some closure from her tragedy, and she thinks all this is connected with her husband's family honour.'

As Sterling began to talk with more fluency, though not more confidence, he began to see a strategy that might keep him safe for a little while – a mixture of the convincingly open, but occasionally selective.

'At Chester Farm, I found another reference, and that took me to the Town Hall at Poperinghe, and the execution post where British Army deserters were shot during that war. I was thinking that maybe one of Etchingham's relatives was one of those soldiers.'

Smithy stared on, and Sterling took that as a good sign. If he'd been impatient or had interrupted, he would have known he wasn't satisfied. So far, everything fitted with what he already knew. Sterling was making sense. That afternoon at Poperinghe was when he had given Jackson and Smithy's gang the slip with his bicycle heroics.

The story was emerging with glibness and conviction, but in Sterling's mind was turmoil. He had to get the pitch right. 'At Poperinghe, I found a photo of a war memorial, and as I had no idea where it was, I showed it on spec to a Welsh bloke who was staying at the museum there. He recognised it as the Scottish memorial between Ypres and Passchendaele, so I got lucky there.' He looked up at Smithy as if to say, 'With me so far?' and he nodded.

'The next day – I can't remember which now – I went over to the memorial. This is when things really did go bad. While I was there, I found a body. I didn't know who it was until later, when I was questioned by the local police. Someone called Thomas Jackson. English.' Sterling waited. As he was speaking, he wasn't fixed on Smithy's probing, uncompromising eyes, but on a small picture in the Impressionist style, all fuzzy and vague, entitled *Windmill at Pitgam* on the wall to the left of his head – to indicate that he was in full and honest story-telling mode. Now he looked back at a face that was still completely inscrutable.

'I got out of there quickly. It was nothing to do with me. I knew his name was Jackson because the police picked me up not long afterwards and told me. The Welsh bloke had shopped me.' He almost gave a little rueful look, but thought that would overdo it. Sympathy was not a characteristic he was associating with his interrogator. 'I told the police I was a tourist, and I had the Poperinghe alibi for when the police had worked out that the murder had been committed. In the end, they had to let me go.' He paused again, trying for reasons he did not understand to make shifts in the situation so that it was not all one-way traffic. 'I'm getting a bit croaky with all the talking. Could I have a glass of water?'

The man Smithy motioned to Jason, who eased himself off the wall behind and around to the kitchen. He put a small tumbler of water in Sterling's hand and he took a sip.

'Before I left the Scottish memorial, I found something carved on one of the stone blocks.'

At this, Smithy's body tensed in its lolling position and he became even more watchful. Sterling was beginning to get the impression that other people had been following Keith Etchingham's trail with less success than him.

'It was a kind of picture or diagram with a bit of lettering. I was stumped.' In Sterling's head he was doing plenty of editing. 'In the end, and after a lot of traipsing around Ypres, I found the place the letters on the memorial stood for – St George's Church in Ypres. That's as far as I've got. I reckon it's all about some relative of Etchingham's and that all the places are connected.'

'That's as far as you've got?' said Smithy incredulously, ignoring the red herring about Etchingham's mystery relative and the connected places. 'That's as far as you've got,' he repeated as a statement. 'This is very disappointing. Actually, for you it could be painfully disappointing.'

'I would have got further. I think the diagram was a coat of arms, perhaps from Etchingham's relative's regiment. But someone was following me and it put the wind up me.' Even though Sterling was quavering, he did not miss the sly opportunity. The more he thought about it, the more certain he was that the presence in the church that Sunday was Smithy's. If it sank in that he was the one who had stopped Sterling from making any more progress, he was the stumbling block and Sterling was the innocently interrupted investigator. No blame could be attached to him for that.

'Where's the diagram now?'

'In my room at the hotel.'

Smithy tut-tutted and swore very softly. It was the first time he had shown anything other than cold neutrality. Sterling was scared, but he felt a small bloody-minded thrill of satisfaction.

'Why did you go to the chocolate shop this morning?'

The sudden switch of direction was startling, but Sterling was helped from revealing the truth by his smart-Alec side. 'To buy chocolates,' he replied. Without intending to be facetious, he had been exactly that.

Smithy's eyes flicked to Fred. Sterling didn't understand the gesture straight away. He understood it very clearly when he received the cuff on the side of his head, the force of which tipped him and the chair sideways for a moment, with two legs slightly off the floor, and then back to its original position. His ear roared and his head stung as blood flooded to where the blow had been. In a way, the sudden physical violence was better than the threat of it. He realised how tense he had become. Now he had more of an inkling about what he might expect.

'Don't get cocky, Frank. We can easily get out the plastic sheeting and spread it out under the chair,' said Smithy in a tired voice.

Sterling was tempted to whine, 'There was no call for that', but it might have made things worse. 'Honestly,' he said again, 'chocolates for my friends back home and for the hotel receptionist.'

'Ah yessss,' Smithy replied in a Gollum voice, 'that pretty little red-haired thing. The one you went out with the other night. Where does she fit into all this, I wonder?'

Sterling said nothing while he tried to keep thinking things through. It made sense that Smithy knew so much. The thugs had been much better at keeping out of sight when Thomas Jackson had been removed from the scene.

'Where are the chocolates, anyway, the package he was carrying?' Smithy said sharply – to the men slouching against the wall rather than to Sterling. 'He should have been carrying the bag when you put him in the car.'

'He had it in the corridor, a white bag,' said Jason, 'and he didn't open the door to his room. But it wasn't in his hand in the street.'

'It was just chocolates,' Sterling protested.

'If you're messing about with us….' said Smithy.

Woe betide me, Sterling thought.

'Find the bag and bring it back here. You two go', Smithy said to Fred and Jason. 'Simon can stay here with me. Untie him and take him downstairs.'

Back in the cellar, Sterling flexed his hands. He loved the pins and needles feeling of the blood rushing back into circulation. That first round could have been much worse. He rubbed his head and it felt sore, but he'd held up well enough. Bought himself some time. Been appropriately selective. Not been the coward he suspected he might be. Smithy had been sharp, though. Sterling thought about the cross at the bottom of Etchingham's chocolates, and what the consequences might be if Fred and Jason got hold of those chocolates and brought them back to base.

He fretted about the gaps in his story that he might have to supply in the second round, and what could be worse than cuffs around the head. The frosted glass in the cellar window high in the wall was becoming a dirty grey as the day drew on. Hell could freeze over, he thought gloomily, and the window would still be too high to reach, the bars would still be just as strong, and their ends would still be just as deeply embedded in the wall. He sank back down to wait in what had quickly become his usual place.

17

In the hours that followed, Sterling spent much of the time continuing to think of ways to protect himself. Part of that was making everything he knew about the case fit together coherently. Even in his confused and fearful state there were ways to work out the blend. Smithy and his gang knew much more than him in some aspects, but he had the key information, even if he had said that he hadn't. They couldn't dispense with him until they were sure he had told them everything he knew, or until they had access to what he knew and could get the rest themselves. With Angela's help, he had developed a good success record on his trail around Ypres – better than Thomas Jackson and better than these thugs. He began to see how he might give himself a chance of getting out of his prison. He could be the Sherpa guiding them to where they needed to go. Then he would be safe until they reached the end. It was better than this, he thought, as he looked around the cellar.

He asked himself what would happen when he became redundant. The best prospect was being locked in the cellar while the gang disappeared off somewhere. He had little doubt that they had murdered Jackson. Maybe they didn't want the danger of another killing. After a while, perhaps the landlords would get a telephone call, or a farm labourer would hear Sterling banging and shouting. But if he knew too much, and he was straying into that territory, a body in the cellar of a rented-out cottage might not be discovered for weeks. Smithy was a hard and ruthless man, and so were Fred and Jason.

The gang's interest in him had been quite recent. Supposing it was Jackson they were following originally, and not Sterling. That would explain why Jackson approached him at Au Miroir. He wasn't just warning him. In his awkward way, maybe he was looking for help. After killing Jackson, the gang had switched focus to Sterling. The attack on the ferry: if it hadn't been Jackson, maybe it was Smithy or one of the others. At that time, Sterling could have been a threat.

Why did they kill Jackson? It wasn't a clinical assassination, a single bullet through his forehead. It was more opportunistic, even accidental. Smithy looked capable of rage. They had killed Jackson because somehow Sterling had become the better bet. Jackson had provoked them, or defied them, or had become worthless to them. Sterling wanted to avoid the same end. There was no element of client confidentiality in this, no notion of protecting Gloria Etchingham's interests and the integrity of the case. All the hot air about the Etchingham family honour was exactly that. Sterling's priority now was to save his skin. He waited on. He fretted on.

At five o'clock, the man called Simon brought a lump of cheese, some bread and some water, and left them by the door. He wouldn't talk, but he was different from the others – not just smaller, but nervous, as he had been earlier, driving the car, and ill at ease. Before he withdrew, Sterling called over softly. 'This isn't legal.

This is kidnapping, whichever way you look at it.' He wouldn't look at Sterling, either, and when the door closed again, Sterling could hear the bolts shot back with depressing finality.

Later on, he found himself comparing the two interrogations. The police one, by Broussart and Pieters, was civilised enough, though Broussart was surly and ill-tempered. Sterling did not have any qualms about his physical health or even, in the end, his liberty. It was what the questioning was about that was disconcerting – murder, and his perceived role in it.

In the countryside, Smithy was no longer concerned with Thomas Jackson, who had clearly served some sort of purpose. Smithy was interested in what Gloria Etchingham was interested in, and Jackson's murder and Sterling's abduction indicated how high the stakes were. There was no handbook containing the 'do's and don'ts' of police interrogation procedures to hold him back, either. Sterling could face another beating or worse, and of course he was a prisoner. He would likely be another victim, too. He felt almost nostalgic for Ypres police station and the reinforced door backing on to the ramparts.

Fear, brooding and boredom: the three staples of the abduction victim. There seemed to be so much hanging about, though those upstairs might also be feeling some pressure from everything they set themselves to do. The brooding stopped when Sterling heard a commotion. It was almost seven o'clock. Something was happening, and he was going to be part of it. He expected the footsteps down and the drawing back of the bolts. He decided that he preferred the boredom to the dread that rose up in him. He wasn't ready for the second round, and never would be. Fred and Jason knew he was reluctant. They came over to the wall opposite the door and grasped him by the arms. There was an ugly, deep scratch on Jason's hand. The cologne Sterling had smelt on him earlier had faded. Now it was mingled with sweat. The tension in them translated into rough treatment as they frogmarched Sterling to the door. He was about to protest, but instead he relaxed and tried to harmonise his movements with them. It was important not to be provocative.

On the spiral staircase up from the cellar, his eyes came parallel with the ground floor parquet. From there, he could just see a slight figure deposited on the opposite sofa from Smithy's, mouth taped over, hands tied and legs drawn up underneath the body. His heart gave such a start that it seemed to be trying to make an exit from his chest. It was Christina. And as Sterling stepped off the staircase and into the room, there was another shock. His interrogation chair was stationed on a square of thick plastic sheeting.

On the other sofa, Smithy was leaning forward, his elbows on his fat knees and his hands clasped under his large square chin.

'Ah, Frank, thank you for rejoining us.' He made everything seem as if Sterling was doing them all a favour.

'Christina has absolutely nothing to do with this,' Sterling said in a low, intense voice. His anger in the circumstances surprised him. 'What the f....'

Smithy put up the palm of his hand, like a police officer stopping traffic. 'We've gone a long way beyond that, Frank. Everything is too important, and we are in a hurry. You must take your share of responsibility for these unfortunate circumstances. Plan A was just to get the package you keep telling us is so insignificant – so we could check for ourselves. It wasn't so difficult to work out what might have happened when you didn't bring it with you. But the girl on reception' (he nodded towards Christina) 'refused to co-operate with us. Sadly, we had to invoke Plan B. Easier said than done, I have to say.'

As he said this, Jason gingerly touched the scratch on his hand.

Sterling looked over at Christina. She was a small-town girl, twenty-five years old. She helped her mother (and for all Sterling knew, her father) run a family hotel. She had an optician boyfriend in Kortrijk, a few railway stops away. She had a diploma in hospitality and hotel management from a college in Roeselare. She said she hadn't been anywhere much or done anything much. She had been snatched from the street by two large (and in Sterling's view, extremely threatening) Englishmen and taken to a cottage in the countryside for no apparent reason. She should have been terrified. Certainly, she was dishevelled. There were streaks of dried tears down her cheeks. There was the beginning of a dark bruise over her left temple. But when Sterling looked at her, really looked at her, and caught her gaze boring into him, he saw anger and defiance. She had not submitted meekly to a one-track fate. She saw forks in the road. Choices. His own defeatism shamed him. He needed to find some backbone. Now he knew where he'd get it from.

No one else seemed to notice the exchange. When he looked back to Smithy, he had sat back on the sofa, legs splayed, hands behind his head, the essence of relaxation and control.

'Really,' he said to the ceiling, 'we need to know two key things. The full story. None of this, 'That's as far as I've got' crap. And linked to that, where that package is. It's going to mean some hurt for one of you.' He thought for a moment. 'Now, who's going in the Mastermind chair? I think it had better be you, Frank.'

Fred and Jason dragged Sterling over to the chair and the plastic sheeting. He resisted more this time, in a kind of reflex action. He really did not want to be subjected to what Smithy had in mind, and now that he had seen Christina's attitude, more steel had come into him. It made no difference. They were large and strong, and he was seated in the chair and tied up with little delay.

'So, Frank, let's consider the first thing. You haven't told us the full story. It's time to tell it now.'

'This is really outrageous. You can't just kidnap two innocent people and keep them prisoner. You can't threaten us like this. Let us go before it really gets out of hand.'

Smithy didn't even bother with the 'spare me this', traffic policeman hand. His eyes flicked to Fred hovering behind Sterling with the look that now he recognised instantly, and he received another hard cuff.

'That's assault,' he said. 'It's getting worse for you.'

Out of the corner of his eye, he noticed Simon slouched against the wall behind and to the left of Smithy. He shuffled and took a deep breath. His face was white. Sterling was resisting out of a foolish stubbornness and to show Christina there was some-thing to him. But another motive had emerged. Simon wasn't like the others. He could see the consequences of being caught. He might be a weak link, and Sterling was speaking to him.

It made no difference to Fred. Sterling received a cuff on the other side of his head, which was spinning and buzzing. Protesting that he knew nothing became Sterling's own name, rank and serial number mantra. Fred undid the top button of his shirt and loosened his tie. Doing the hitting was warm work. Sterling avoided looking at Christina. He was responding to the rhythm of blows around his head, on his shoulders and on his forearms, grunting with each one. He still had time to think, but he was thinking things that did not help – about whether pain lessened the more you had of it, and whether torture was effective in getting the truth. On the torture front, the gang were amateurs, but they were learning quickly. After some minutes, Smithy ordered a halt.

'Why are you doing this, Frank? It's going to get worse. This is just the start. The sooner you tell us everything you know, everything, the sooner all this can stop.'

Sterling shook his head. People would surely notice that he and Christina were missing. There must be some alternative to this.

Smithy changed tack, all cheery again except for the soulless eyes. 'We're not really allowed to smoke in here – it's part of the letting agreement – but desperate times call for desperate measures.'

He took a cigarette from a packet on the arm of the sofa and lit it up, handing it fastidiously to the man Fred. Sterling felt a wide-eyed dread. Reality was even worse than anticipation. In one smooth movement, Fred swooped in and squeezed his balls hard with one chubby hand, and with the other stubbed the cigarette on his neck. Sterling screamed long and hard like an animal in a trap and writhed helplessly in the chair, trying to stand up, trying to breathe, trying to do anything to assuage the hurt. Through the waves of pain and his watering eyes, he saw Fred smile down on his handiwork, pleased with the results. Jason watched impassively from the sidelines. Smithy nodded as if to say, 'I expected that'. The squeamish Simon had turned away. Christina's eyes were filled with tears as well, but Sterling could still see no fear. His body was in shock and he throbbed in his groin, in his neck and from the cuffs to his head and body.

'You look the worse for wear, Frankie-boy', said Smithy. 'I think it's time for a break. We need a bit of supper, and you and the girl could do with some confabulation. We can lay on another session like that, or you could do it an easier way. Tell us what we need to know and it all stops.'

Jason untied Sterling from the chair. Only some misplaced sense of pride stopped him collapsing into his arms. He shambled down the staircase as Simon opened the door. As Sterling shuffled into the cellar, he murmured, 'I wonder how many years inside you'll do. It'll be just as bad in Belgium as England.'

Christina followed him into the cellar. The tape had been taken from her face and her hands untied. Someone had given her a small bottle of surgical spirit and a wad of cotton wool. They could reach the window now, one on the other's shoulders. All they needed was a hacksaw or bolt cutter (of industrial strength) for the bars and glasscutters for the windows, fitted with silencers (if they existed), and for their captors to be struck deaf and blind.

Sterling sank to his usual spot. Christina crouched down with the surgical spirit and the cotton wool.

He winced as she dabbed the sore on his neck, but managed a kind of pained smile, getting one in return.

'Christina, I'm really sorry I've got you into this mess.'

'Well, it's not going to help to just get upset about it,' she replied matter-of-factly.

He could tell she was grasping for the English words she needed. He thought about saying, 'It's no use crying over spilt milk', but this was no time for an English lesson. His neck was stinging fiercely, but it seemed to be enhancing his alertness and clarity.

'The man is right, Christina. We need to sort out what we're going to tell him. It's not that I mind the torture,' he lied. 'It's how we can use what we know to get out of here. What did you do with the bag I threw over to you?'

'It's under the desk at the hotel, right where I was when you threw it to me.'

'OK, well, I think I'm going to tell them about one of the boxes of chocolates in that bag. It's a special one I got from the Mehrtens chocolate shop. It'll get us a bit of time when they go and retrieve it. And if they get what they want, they'll let us go.'

He was lying again, trying to convince himself as well as keep Christina's spirits up. She was sharp, as well as brave. The quizzical eyebrow went up. If she'd been a teenaged girl in Sandley, she would have said 'Yeah, right'. To try and establish some basis for hope, he asked her when she would be missed.

'They came for me just as I'd finished my duty for the day. I'm not back on till Wednesday. Tuesday is my day off. My mother will think that I have gone over to Kortrijk.' She searched for the appropriate words again. 'I am twenty-five now. I don't have rules that I must follow.'

Sterling mused and nodded. Things were not looking good. Smithy and his gang were amateurish in some ways. He and Christina hadn't been tied up. Questioning him had been brutal and unpleasant, but not systematic or entirely effective. He had told them some things but not everything. But the stakes were high and the prize would be large. That's what was making Smithy ruthless.

'One of those men, the one called Simon, the smallest one, is not comfortable with what's going on. When I was being driven here, he was nervous. The others don't think anything's going to happen to them. They think they can get away with all this. He's much more sensitive to the fact that what they're doing is seriously illegal. I've been reminding him. Maybe we can use him somehow.'

They talked quietly on. Sterling told Christina, in broad outline, what he had been doing in Ypres and why he was there. It seemed only fair, given what he had drawn her into. They explored what they might do and what they might say when they were next taken upstairs. They thought of ways they might escape, which became more and more outlandish: Sterling would pretend to be in pain in the corner and the men would come to examine him, giving Christina the chance to sprint up the stairs, burst through the front door and dash to freedom; as Christina slipped off her clothes to divert the thugs, Sterling would spring on them, overcome them with his fabled police crowd control skills and make for the kitchen knives.

'There's a problem with that last one,' he said. 'If you slipped off your clothes, I'd be diverted as well, so we wouldn't get anywhere.' They both smiled at that.

'Perhaps we could escape on the grated carrot train,' he said finally. 'Drop down in a soft damp landing right into the middle of all that orange.'

'I don't think it comes all the way out here,' she replied sadly, and they fell silent for a time.

When the gang had first abducted Sterling, and Jason and Fred lurked out of eyeshot behind him as Smithy began the first interrogation, expecting the pain and the blows was worse than actually receiving them. Now the sore on his neck and his painfully squeezed balls told him the real pain he could expect. Waiting for the next instalment in that cool, silent cellar would have been agonising but for Christina's resolute presence.

It was nine o'clock when Fred and Jason returned to fetch them back upstairs. The dining chair in front of the sofa was still there and so was the sheet of plastic around it. Sterling could hear a bit of clattering in the kitchen area. Maybe Simon's importance to the group was partly to do with his catering abilities. Sterling gulped and started trembling, hating himself all over again. The bolstering of morale in the cellar had evaporated. There was no tough-guy detective. There never had been.

'I don't think you'll need to tie me to the chair,' he said to Smithy. 'I've thought about everything and there may be one or two things you need to know that I didn't think were too important at the time.' His self-justification seemed pathetically flimsy and weak.

Smithy looked pleased. He lolled back on the sofa. He could add psychological analysis to his list of criminal talents.

'Go on then,' he said, 'sit down and tell me. I'm all ears.'

'Well, the sketch I found at the Scottish memorial – I found the real thing at the church. It was on a pew cushion. Underneath that was the card for the chocolatier, Marc Mehrtens. The card kind of instructed me to go to that chocolate shop and, as it turned out, pick up the package. When your bloke came for me, I threw it to the girl on the way through the door.'

'You could have saved us a lot of time, and yourself a lot of pain, if you hadn't been so stupid,' said Smithy.

There was that look again. Because Sterling was telling the truth and the whole truth at that point, he didn't recognise it quickly enough. Fred did, though, responding from behind with another cuff, knocking Sterling and the chair over. He was almost too startled to feel the stinging on the side of his head. If he had been Smithy, he, too, would have been furious about having lost a few hours.

Smithy turned to Christina. 'So, girl, we know now that the package is important, and we know that he threw it to you. Think very carefully before you answer. Only the truth will do. If we don't get it, Frank here will suffer. Maybe you will, as well. It's all the same to Fred. In fact, he might like a bit of a change.'

Sterling thought he saw Christina's jaw jut out a little. It might have been nerves. More likely, it was defiance.

'It's under the counter in reception. Where we keep all the things that our guests lose or leave in their rooms or in the restaurant. You can just ask the person at reception for it. There's someone around until half past eleven.'

'Thank you. That wasn't so very difficult,' Smithy said to them both. His dead eyes shone. 'I fancy a bit of an excursion into Ypres myself. It's been a long day, one way or the other, and I've got a bit of cabin fever. There's plenty of time for further … exploration if things don't go entirely to plan. I will be very agitated if they don't.'

He gestured to Fred and Jason, who pulled Sterling to his feet. The man Simon took Christina's arm. She didn't resist, but on the way back down the stairs and through the cellar door, Sterling caught a glimpse of her mouthing soft words with a fierce gaze that Simon stolidly avoided, his own head and eyes cast down. She caught on quickly. Sterling had learnt that on their evening out.

'That buys us a bit of time, Christina,' he said when they were alone again, the cellar now gloomy and getting darker as night closed in.

He didn't sink down this time. He was standing, flexing his arms, legs, neck – anywhere on his body where he had received blows. The sore on his neck throbbed, and so did his balls, but he felt too prissy to examine them. He thought Christina would have been amused, but he wasn't prepared to risk it.

She had a thoughtful look about her. 'Yes, we'll get a bit of time.'

'What?' he said. 'What is it?'

'Well, everything you told them is true. But what I said was true once, but not anymore. I did put the package under the counter along with the chocolates you gave me, but they're not there now.'

'Christ, Christina. You've seen what that man's like. You've seen what his mate can do. When he gets to the Sultan and finds no package, he's going to go barmy. And when that happens, he'll be back here to bash me about, squeeze my balls and stub cigarettes out on me worse than ever. I reckon he'll get that monster to start on you.'

Sterling was pacing up and down, shaking his head. It was hard to believe what he had heard. A heavier beating, more stubs, more squeezing. He could feel his agitation enveloping him. Christina stood in front of him, and he had to stop pacing for a second. She took both his arms in her hands and looked up into his eyes. He remembered their carefree Saturday evening out – that moment when she had taken one his arms in both of hers and twirled them around into the Grote Markt.

'Frank. *Frank*,' she said more urgently, forcing him to concentrate. You keep saying we can't just let them do what they like. We can't let them drag us upstairs and downstairs and hit you (and maybe me) and then do even worse when they don't need us anymore. When that man comes back without the bag, I'll say that someone moved it. My mother is always tidying up. She tidies the desk almost every day. She will have put it in the safe with all the other lost things. I'll say that I have to go with them. They'll never get in the safe without me. Yes, it gives us time. You're always saying we need time. But it gives us other things, for sure. Chances. I was an actor at school. I can make them believe me.'

He looked down at her. Her eyes searched his face. He had thought her lively and good company on their night out. He hadn't reckoned on plucky and enterprising. He stooped a little, wrapped his arms tightly around her slight frame and buried his face in her neck, her soft hair brushing his cheek. He began to laugh softly, and felt her body shake a little as she joined in, her back arching into him and her arms clasping him tightly in return. They had a chance of escaping from this. But, as things turned out, not in the way they planned.

18

Sterling and Christina calculated that with all the delays and inconveniences that abductions generate (now that they were experts), Smithy would be back from his excursion to Ypres at eleven o'clock, and, if he didn't have what he went in for, he would be in a raging fury. Christina would have to be agitated and insistent to convince him what might have happened. Sterling fingered his neck, reminding her that it was likely to be him who would face the consequences if her performance flopped. Neither of them paid much attention to a scratching, rasping noise as their conversation, sometimes animated, sometimes desultory, flowed on.

A minute passed. Christina put her hand up and cocked her head.

'Listen, Frank. Can you hear that?'

He fell quiet and listened himself. 'A mouse. Mice. Maybe rats,' he said dismissively.

'I hope not. I don't like them very much.'

He smiled in the dark. It was hard to imagine her conforming to stereotype. 'Scared of spiders, too?' he asked.

He felt a little slap on his leg. Then he looked up. The gloom was creating some trick of the light up at the window. There were shadows flickering where once there had been just a dull grey screen. As they watched, mesmerised, they could hear, very softly, the splintering of wood between long intervals of silence. Sterling caught a glimpse of the tip of a jemmy inserted at the top of the window between window and frame. A rhythm began to develop: purchase for the jemmy, soft splintering, withdrawal, insertion a little further along, soft splintering, withdrawal – all happening almost soundlessly. A tiny gap began to appear between the window and frame as the window eased outward from the cellar wall. Sterling felt Christina's damp hand in his. Cool air seeped into the cellar and the temperature dropped a notch. He realised that he was holding his breath.

The jemmy reached a tipping point. Now strong fingers in black surgical gloves appeared where the jemmy had once been, manipulating the glass loose. The gap between window and frame widened. Then the glass was gone. Very good, thought Sterling, but what about the bars? The mystery man behind the window removal must have been thinking the same thing. The silence lengthened for a minute or two but for the sigh of air through the empty window and into the cellar. Then the blades of the largest pair of bolt cutters Sterling had ever seen were wrapped around the bottom of the first bar. He thought removing the bars would be a noisy business, but the blades whispered through the metal. The sheared-off stump shone dully in the gloom. The bolt cutter did not cut completely through the bar at the top, but did enough to bend it into the cellar parallel to the ceiling. There were three more bars and the whispering continued. When all the bars were pointing in, there was more silence. What now? Surely this was not some cruel trick – a ploy by the psychopathic Smithy.

A blacked-up face appeared through the window enclosed by a dark balaclava. A dry, flat voice Sterling could hardly hear mouthed, 'Frank Sterling, I presume?' It was the voice, more than the camouflaged face, that he recognised. The relief made his legs wobble. He leant against the wall and closed his eyes.

'Mike', he whispered, 'Mike bleeding Strange. What the fuck are you doing here?'

'I'll tell you later. Let's get you out of there first. Hang on a moment.' Mike's face disappeared again.

Sterling turned to Christina and said as nonchalantly as he could, 'Friend from home.'

She shook her head. She said something. Dutch oaths sound the same as English ones. There was wonder in her face, disbelief and even wry humour. 'Man of mystery,' she murmured.

After the jemmy and the bolt cutters, Sterling was not surprised to see a small, lightweight, retractable ladder slide down into the cellar. Mike's face again appeared in the window frame. He gestured to Sterling to start the climb. It was going to be a tight squeeze through that empty window. Mike waited for him to get up to it. Then he put a hand on his arm. Their faces were obscured from Christina by Sterling's bulk on the ladder.

'Frank, we should leave the girl,' Mike whispered.

'Leave her? In this rat's nest? Are you insane?'

'She'll be safe enough. I've arranged for the local police to be along soon. The point is, if you stay here, the police are going to find you, take you away and lock you up. They'll get you for something. You're already on their radar. But if they find her and she tells her story, they are going to arrest these blokes.'

It made good sense. Sterling had sprung up the ladder like a gazelle. He went back down like a man stuck in a quagmire. Christina looked at him.

'It's better that I stay here, isn't it?' she said. 'When you have got away, you can send the police here. I won't tell them about you. I don't think that the men upstairs will want to say that you have been here. Why did they kidnap me? Maybe for sex. I could say something like that.' She had taken Mike's cue without even hearing him and embellished it formidably. Sterling added 'very tactically astute' to her long list of attributes.

'Mike thinks that's best.' It was hard to look at her, but he made himself. 'He says that the police will be here soon. I swear I'll make sure everything is alright.'

'OK, Frank. Just don't be long.' She hugged him tightly for a moment and motioned him back to the ladder.

It was certainly a tight squeeze through the open window. One of the bars snagged his shirt and left a small rent in the middle of his back. When he had scrambled through onto the cold grass next to the house, he turned back and put his head through the window.

'Christina, the bag. You said it's not under the counter. Where did you put it?'

'In the bottom of the wardrobe in your room.'

Sterling nodded. The last he saw of her was her pale face looking out of the gloom in the middle of the cellar.

Mike did a crude job bending back the bars and replacing the window frame. Then they crept away across the grass at the side of the cottage to the track. Sterling expected to be led to the right, back up to the main road, but when they'd clambered over the short fence, they turned left down the track and carried on a couple of hundred metres past the farm buildings.

It was a dark, cloudy night and it took Sterling a while to adjust.

A small flatbed truck with a driver's cab loomed vaguely out of the darkness. He lost sight of Mike about thirty metres away. As that seemed to be where they were heading for, he carried on, glancing back at the dark outline of buildings behind. From nowhere, a large figure took form just in front of him, a figure with legs apart holding something two handed straight in front of him. There was no doubt. It was a gun, and he was pointing it at Sterling.

'We haven't finished with you yet, Sterling,' said Jason. 'Let's turn around and walk very carefully back to the house. I'm angry, and that makes me trigger-happy. Smithy, though, is going to go absolutely apeshit.'

Sterling was about to turn, when Jason just crumpled soundlessly to the ground, as if he was a puppet and the puppet-master controlling him had just dropped the strings. A hand shot out to cushion and divert the gun in case of accidental discharge. Sterling rushed up as Mike stood over the body.

'These people are amateurs,' he said. 'He was patrolling outside when I was doing the window. But how did he think you'd got out of that cellar without some outside help? Did he think you were by yourself?' He shook his head.

'Unbelievable,' agreed Sterling, but without conviction. He was not sure how anyone would fare against the unexpected and undeniably professional skills of his publican friend.

'I just stunned him. He'll come round in about half an hour, though he won't be feeling very well. Perfect timing, really.'

Sterling stood next to Mike and looked down at the body. He was angry – angry at the way he'd been treated for the past week, not just about his ill-treatment in the house behind him. Jason was a big man, but lying there knocked out, he looked vulnerable. That didn't stop Sterling. He gave him a couple of swift, hard kicks in the side, and to finish things off, a strong kick in the groin. Mike watched without expression. Sterling thought it would make him feel better, but afterwards, he just felt cowardly.

They slipped noiselessly into the cab, the doors making a faint clunk as they pulled them gently shut.

'You said the police were coming.'

'Yes. And the fire brigade. I told you, I've already put in the call.'

'Why the fire brig….'

There was a huge, loud, but curiously dull 'whump'. Sterling flinched and shaded his eyes against the sudden makeshift daylight. It seemed very close. And it was – the roof of one of the outhouses at the back of the house jerked upwards and detached itself from the walls before collapsing inwards. A fireball rose in the sky and the building began to burn fiercely. The brickwork at each gable pointed up to the sky like jagged teeth.

Sterling looked across at Mike in front of the steering wheel. 'That's why.'

His nod back was deadpan as he slipped from the truck. 'One second,' he muttered as the night swallowed him again.

A few moments later, Sterling heard two cracks, distinct above the crackle of the outhouse's burning brick and timber. Then Mike reappeared.

'Just a smoke grenade into the house, in case any of the law and rescue services get confused about where to go. The girl will be fine in the cellar. I told the police that's where she'll be. The men can't go anywhere. I checked transport. They only have a Saab, and that's in Ypres. Let's go.'

They rumbled carefully up the track to the main road and then turned right towards Menen. Four hundred metres later, Mike did a U-turn, slipped the truck into a small lay-by and turned off the lights. Sterling had the sense that he'd reconnoitred it already. For that matter, the whole thing seemed planned to the last detail. Sterling heard the sirens before he saw the blue lights of police cars and fire engines far down the straight road back to Ypres. The outhouse glowed ahead and to the left in the nightscape. He thought of Sandley's Elizabethan beacons warning of the Spanish Armada, but they were pinpricks in the sky compared to this. As they looked on, the flashing blue procession approached the cottage.

'Good job,' murmured Mike. He looked satisfied.

'Good job, well done,' Sterling replied, turning to face him. 'Thank you. Thank you very much.'

'Well, it's your show, Frank. What now?'

'You're sure Christina will be OK?'

'Yes, I'm sure. The police know about her from my call. I spent a bit of time finding out what was happening and where you were being held. The cellar is the safest place to be. They'll probably take her to hospital to check her over. They might do that with the men, but they'll keep them under guard. I had to wait until one of them took the car. Four of them might have been too many.'

Sterling didn't think he could complain in the circumstances. 'Christina's got a story. I reckon she'll even be canny enough to think up something to explain the bars and splintered window frame in the cellar, which any investigator looking closely would spot. I don't think those blokes are going to be free anytime soon. She'll keep me out of it. The one who took the car was going to my hotel in Ypres to pick up a bag that's hidden there. But it's not where it's meant to be, so he won't be able to find it. I reckon he'll be coming back here, finding it's chaos, and doing a flit. I need to get that bag. Hotel Sultan please, driver. Maybe you can tell me how you got involved in all this on the way.'

He looked down the track as they eased by on the road back to Ypres. Blue lights were still flashing and hoses were trained on the ruined outhouse, but he could see nothing in detail. He and Mike moved on, and he hoped that Christina was alright. He thought of ways of alerting her family to the fact that she might be en route for or actually at the local hospital. Perhaps it was best to let events unfold. Mike had made no mistakes so far. It did not seem likely that he would start now.

'Angela filled me in on the details she had,' said Mike, as he concentrated on the road. 'Not that that was very enlightening. I came over late on Sunday evening. I was around when you came out of the hotel at ten o'clock.'

Sterling did not think it was worth bothering about the whys and wherefores. Mike was eerily experienced in this kind of activity. They approached the giant tap. The water shimmered in the darkness.

'I've been wondering how that works,' Mike said as they snaked around the roundabout towards Ypres.

'The man who took the Saab back into Ypres. Do we need to worry about him?'

Sterling looked at the road in front of him. He remembered the cigarette stubbed out on his neck, the squeeze to his balls, and all the blows to his arms and head. Smithy hadn't delivered them, but he was the force behind them. 'Oh yes,' said Sterling. 'He's the boss - and the most dangerous of all of them. When he sees what's happening at that cottage, he'll slip away. He won't care about the others. But we'll be bumping into him again.'

Mike glanced sideways. 'Noted,' he said. It occurred to Sterling then that this was the longest conversation that he and Mike had had since they had first met a couple of years ago. He had never heard him say so much. Taciturn or talkative, he was glad Mike Strange had come to Ypres, and was thankful for Angela's wisdom.

19

They waited in the pick-up in the Grote Markt, where Mike had parked almost next to the Peugeot. Street lamps bathed the square in an orange hue, while the lights of the cafes and bars had probably been switched off for a good while. A man in a dark windcheater and black jeans walked a white Chihuahua. He was as tall as the dog was tiny, but he was in no hurry, and the dog kept up, occasionally sniffing lampposts and in doorways. It was a practised routine. Someone had a theory that dogs look like their owners. Perhaps the man had a tiny wife.

Sterling looked at his watch. It was close to midnight. His abduction had lasted almost twelve hours. Not bad in the circumstances – short, he imagined, as abductions go, and with a good result. On the drive into Ypres, he worked out that the hotel and his hotel room might be the safest place to be. If Smithy had any sense, he would have gone. His gang would be in custody. The police would be preoccupied with them, and, if Sterling was at the hotel, he'd be exactly where he should be. The more he thought about it, the more sense it made. Mike seemed to think so, too.

'I'll just check everything. Then you can go in.'

Sterling eased back into his seat when he slipped away. His neck and groin throbbed, and he felt an overwhelming tiredness. It had been a long day.

Mike slipped soundlessly into the driver's seat. 'It's all clear. No Saab,' he said.

'Where will you be if something happens?'

'Around,' he said.

'How can I get in touch?'

Mike looked at him. 'Well, since Angela says you've lost your mobile, I think it's going to be the other way round.'

Sterling nodded. That made sense.

He rang the night bell, and an old man in a shabby but well-cut suit and slippers came to the door. The slippers undermined the elegant formality. Show me your room key, he mimed through the glass. Sterling fumbled through his pockets and put it up for inspection. Smithy must have been confident that he would not escape, as he had been allowed to keep his possessions once it had been established that there was no mobile telephone among them. The night duty man checked against a small printed list, and let Sterling in. There was no small talk in the old man – in fact, no talk at all, and as he shuffled back to the desk and the computer screen, Sterling made his way to his room. It seemed incongruous that security at the hotel was sound at night, and almost non-existent during the day.

He checked the corridor, but nothing and no one stirred. His key scratched in the lock, and then he was back in his temporary home. He had not counted on seeing it again so soon. There had been times over the course of the day when he did not think he'd ever see it, or England, or Sandley, again. He slipped over to the wardrobe. When Christina said something was so, it was so, and tucked away in a corner at the bottom was the bag.

He brought it over to the bed, rummaging for the chocolates on which Marc Mehrtens had scrawled the small 'x'. He turned the box over and round. It was just like all the others stacked in the chocolatier's, and indeed in the other chocolatiers' shops around the square, and for all Sterling knew, in the shops in all the small towns from Ypres to Brussels. He pulled the red ribbon gently, and it fell smoothly away from the box. He eased the seal off, and opened the flaps.

There was nothing unusual on the top layer, so he gently tipped all the chocolates in that layer onto a tissue on the counterpane of the bed. He examined the semi-transparent waxed sheet between the two layers, before tipping the bottom layer onto another tissue. At the bottom of the box was a small plastic bag. This was it – the next stage. Sterling flexed his fingers, even though they weren't stiff and didn't need flexing. He just felt that familiar frisson. Sometimes looking forward to something was better than getting it.

In the plastic bag was a sheet of folded A4 vellum, of very good quality and even watermarked. At the top, in full colour, was the black lion of Flanders boxed in its yellow background. He turned the paper to the light, and the lion was also the watermark. On the sheet itself were two numbered items. The item marked 1. was a colour photo about ten centimetres by ten centimetres square. It looked like a shop or commercial frontage, from some distance away, with poorly defined posters or placards behind plate glass. Sterling could just make out some Dutch words *Hier voor u in geld en het leven*.

The item marked 2. started with a small image that looked like a Stetson cowboy hat, the initials **A SL** and a number, **9781847249593**, that had been neatly scored through. Sterling turned the sheet over, but it was blank. Smithy might have killed him for this, or maybe he would have put him to work. Sterling could go to work on his own account now, or rather Gloria's. He memorised the details and slipped the paper into his secret cache with the others. There wasn't any more he could do tonight except get some sleep. He wished he knew that Christina was safe.

He put a chair against the door and wedged the top of it under the handle. It would give him a few moments to collect himself if someone tried to burst in. Then he glanced out through the curtains down into the square. In the misty orange drizzle, everything seemed quiet. That Mike was somewhere close by was comforting. He showered and slipped between the cool sheets. He ached from the beatings, and his body was a patchy, mottled pink, yellow and black, but the throbbing had stopped and there seemed no lasting damage down below. He needed sleep. He needed to be refreshed and alert for tomorrow.

But Sterling's dreams made him restless. He was wrestling for a dagger with someone he did not know. A tall, lanky shepherd with a comb-over, in black Michael Caine glasses was taking him on a cheerful, witty and revealing walk through a flock of sheep. Some of the sheep linked together, horns and behinds, in a stationary protective curve, facing the two men and bleating. 'Why do they do that?' Sterling asked. 'It's to protect themselves and the flock – a kind of sheep wagon train,' said his companion. 'Of course, it's not that effective when the lambs just gambol beyond the line.' Later on, Sterling was edging hand by hand across a crevasse on a length of rope, too far across to turn back and yet not far enough to carry on. When he first awoke, it was only five o'clock, but after that, he dreamed no more and woke from a deeper slumber at half past seven, not exactly alert and refreshed, but recovered to a degree. Excitement and anticipation might do the rest.

Breakfast was the busiest time at the Sultan Hotel, and Tuesday 11 September, one whole week into Sterling's stay, was no exception. Much of the rest of the time, it had a semi-deserted feel to it, but the breakfast room was particularly busy this morning. He suspected a coach party as he looked across the room over a sea of grey heads. He had reached that pitch of hunger that produced a trembling edginess, realising that all he'd eaten that day was the bread and cheese that the abductor Simon had brought at five o'clock yesterday afternoon. Nothing less than a huge breakfast, bolted down quickly, would take away the ravenous feeling.

It was hard to wait patiently in the queue for scrambled eggs and bacon, and put the bread in the toasting machine. Sterling's fellow guests were new arrivals here. They could not find the bread tongs. They wanted to roll back the lids on every chafing dish to see what was available. They enquired loudly where the ketchup was. It seemed a particular problem in this hotel. They jumped queues, left queues and then returned to them in the same place.

When he had finally got his breakfast, and by a strange fluke secured his corner table, the only solitary traveller in the room, Mrs. Van de Velde herself came to ask about tea or coffee.

'How are you this morning, Mrs. Van de Velde?' he said as innocently as he could manage. 'And how is Christina?'

She pursed her lips, her harassed and washed-out face showing a hint of anger. 'I am much better now that Christina is resting at home after her....' she searched for an appropriate word, 'experience, which I am sure that you know something about. And she is OK, I think.'

His face went blank. He had found out what he needed to know. 'I'd like coffee, please, this morning.'

He had grown tired of getting pushed about, and tired of getting all the blame for things that were only partly his fault. He thought he could like Christina's mother. He recognised Christina in her, but if she did not want to get on with him, so be it. He tucked into his breakfast.

'Since you came here....' she continued, returning to her theme from the earlier encounter at the reception desk.

Sterling put down his knife and fork and stared up at her. She looked around at all the people wanting her attention, turned on her heel and walked away. It was almost a flounce. He finished eating, drained his coffee and returned to his room. His first call was to Gloria Etchingham. It was ten o'clock, nine o'clock in England. Late enough.

'Gloria. Frank,' he said after she picked up the receiver. He was terse. He'd been through enough for her and the case to earn that right. And distance had faded the charm that had been dazzling him.

'Frank,' she said. He felt the dazzlement rekindling, despite himself. 'It's wonderful to hear from you. It had all gone quiet. How have you been getting on?'

For some reason, the pushiness of the last conversation hadn't spilled over into this one. Sterling was speaking to a mellower Gloria Etchingham.

'Things have moved on a lot, Gloria. The trek that your husband has been sending me on around the Flanders countryside is, I think, almost over. I don't think I'm going to need to be in Ypres for that much longer. And for the moment, other interested parties have ... fallen by the wayside.'

'Fallen by the wayside.' The phrase seemed to please her. 'So we are ... the only show in town.'

He smiled into the receiver. Gloria Etchingham was many complex things, but he did not have her card marked as a wordsmith. 'That's correct,' he said, allowing amusement into his voice.

'Good,' she said. And then 'good' again, more to herself than to Sterling.

He spent a few more minutes very quickly summarising what had happened, but with many details left out. The deal was about payment by results. Gloria had always been much more interested in ends than means. The conversation drew to a close.

'I'll tell you the whole story when I'm back at the office,' he said.

'I look forward to it, Frank,' she said softly. 'And if there is a successful outcome, we must think about a ... bonus.'

He felt a familiar frisson. But what about Christina, and the danger he'd put her in? Get a grip, for goodness sake, he thought. After Gloria Etchingham, he tried Angela. He needed her research skills again, especially now that Mrs Van de Velde seemed to be 'in dispute', as his former Police Federation rep would have put it. He could hardly ask to borrow the laptop Christina had offered a few days ago.

He rehearsed what he needed from Angela, and reminded himself how much he needed to thank her for enlisting Mike's help. Without both of them, he had faced disaster. But when the library's telephone was engaged for the next ten minutes, he gave up. He took the vellum sheet from its hiding place and slipped it into his pocket. He could try and identify the photograph, even if he couldn't get in touch with Angela for the second item. If Keith Etchingham had been consistent, Sterling expected the photo to be of a shop frontage in Ypres or somewhere close by.

He was careful as he stepped out of the hotel, mindful that last time he'd done it – was it only yesterday? – he had been abducted, pushed into a car and whisked away. He assumed that Mike was close by, but didn't expect to see him. He pondered on the difference between Mike Strange, Thomas Jackson and the gang he'd escaped from. Mike was a professional, even if he was now a publican – and once a professional, always a professional.

Sterling wandered around the Grote Markt with the vellum folded so that the photo would fit snugly into the palm of his left hand. Every few minutes, he glanced down to check it, and then glanced up at the façade that happened to be in front of him. It wasn't a photo of a café or bar. It wasn't a clothes shop or a pharmacy. The more he glanced and compared, the more he realised that he was looking for a bank. But after a whole circuit, he knew that it wasn't a bank in the square. He found himself outside Mehrtens the chocolatier's. He thought he might ask Mehrtens himself, but even then his luck was out. An old woman was running the shop, he guessed Mehrtens's mother. Tuesday must have been the chocolatier's day off.

Sterling once found himself with a then-girlfriend at a falconry on a large estate. In a question and answer session after a display, the falconer had defended the inactivity and shackles on his eagles, hawks, falcons and owls. 'The reality is,' he said, 'that raptors like these birds spend most of the time stationary and waiting around, interspersed with occasional bursts of frantic activity.' His girlfriend and those around her laughed when Sterling had said, 'just like a policeman'.

So he was used to a cycle of waiting and bursts of action, Experience told him that, having got this far, the next bit was going to be like sauce in a bottleneck, coming out in a sudden blob. Or the moon, stars and planets would come back into some kind of favourable alignment. Either way, experience also told him not to force things – today, it was time to go with the flow. He mooched over to the Peugeot, started it up and edged out of Ypres through the Menin Gate. A drive would recharge the dodgy battery, clear his head and make the waiting tolerable. As events unfolded, his experience was proved right.

20

Sterling gravitated to Smithy's cottage on his drive. As he drove past along the main road, he saw part of the blackened ruin of the outbuilding Mike had blown up. There was a police car in front of the cottage. He could see crime scene tape fluttering in the breeze. A smoky, charred smell filled the car. Behind him, Mike's pick-up followed at a casual, discreet distance. He was glad of that, and glad that for once, everything felt calm and ordinary. In this part of West Flanders, pretty much every road leads back to Ypres. Having satisfied his curiosity about the cottage, he turned around and headed for home.

The Hommelbier he had with his croque monsieur at Au Miroir made him think that he deserved a siesta after all the recent excitement. Just beyond the door inside his room was a small envelope. He took it over to the chair and tore it open.

'Dear Frank, as your friend said, I was safe in the end. The police doctor told me I was OK, but said I had to rest. He gave me pills but I don't think it is necessary to take them. My mother also said I must rest. She is cross with you, but she does not know why. I think you already know that. I will be back soon. What happened is not your fault. In fact, when I spend time with you, it is always rather exciting.'

Abduction, Sterling thought. Exciting? No. But he was glad that Christina had confirmed what he had wrung from her mother. She had been generous too. Not his fault? That was debatable. He wondered if she was in Kortrijk with the optician. He settled down to his siesta with other things to think about.

He had two things to do when he woke at four o'clock. With the first, he was lucky straight away. Angela picked up the library's telephone on the second ring. Hearing her voice triggered a melange of emotions. He was homesick, grateful, relieved, hopeful.

'I don't know where Mike is right now, but if you hadn't got him to come over, I'm not sure I'd have survived.' He told Angela about the abduction and the rescue and she listened quietly.

'I said before, Frank. You gather people around you. It's that *je ne sais quoi* quality.'

'Well, if you're going to quote Italian at me ... I've got the next thing for you. There's a photo, which I think was taken somewhere around here, and some letters and numbers. Have you got a pen?'

'Ready,' she replied.

'OK, here we go. Firstly, there's a symbol that looks to me like some kind of cowboy hat – a Stetson or something. Then the capital letter 'A'. Then a gap. Then the initials SL. Then a long number. Here we go: 9781847249593, but crossed out. Got all that? I was going to start off as usual with a Google search, but I haven't got internet access here.'

'Hang on for a few moments, Frank. Customer.'

As he waited, he could hear his own breathing. His mouth felt dry. He had had this feeling before.

Two minutes later, Angela was back. 'Frank, we drink together. We do the crossword together. I've spent time training you up. Filled in all those gaps in your knowledge. You're a good pal. You showed me round when I first came down here. You can be witty. You can be thoughtful. You're even addressing the sexism you picked up in the police. I'm your de facto research assistant.' Why was she saying all this? Sterling waited. 'But have you ever come downstairs from your fancy office and used the library beneath you? Have you ever done anything to keep me in a job when all the county wants to do is close the sub-libraries?' She sounded cross. 'Are you actually a member of Sandley library?'

'My *fancy* office,' he blustered, playing for time. 'My fancy office. I don't think so.'

'Well, are you?' Angela was not going to let it go.

'Not yet. But I've not long been out of the job, Angie. I've been meaning to. So what's this about? Why the sudden hassle about the library?'

'You can be in the library and in "the job", Frank.' She put a heavy ironic emphasis on 'the job'.

'What's this about, Angie?' He was trying to keep calm.

'Really, you don't deserve it. If you used the library, and not just me, you'd recognise the cowboy hat. It classifies a book as a Western. And the number, which I'm just keying into my computer, is probably the ISBN – International Standard Book Number. Yup. And that tells me the title of the book is 'Appaloosa'. 'A' for Appaloosa. It's all here in front of me. I don't know why the number is crossed out.'

'I know I'm pushing my luck here, Angie, but what about SL?'

'What do you think, Frank, taking everything that's happened so far into account?'

'Sandley Library. Do you keep that book in the library? Can you get it for me?'

'I do. But I can't "get" it for you, Frank, because you're not a member of the library.'

'Angela, please.' He noticed that he used her full name as an imploring pitch entered his voice.

'I can't get it, anyway. It's out. It's not due back till Friday. The borrower might renew it online and hang on to it.'

'Let me have the name and address of the borrower. I've got a pen.'

There was a silence on the line, a silence that felt glacial. A librarian's voice Sterling barely recognised, dripping with bureaucratic hostility, crackled over the telephone line. 'I cannot give out confidential, private, data-protected information about library members to anyone. Not even you. Especially, at the moment, not you.'

He recognised his faux pas straight away. If he wanted to retrieve the situation, only a full-scale retreat would give him the slightest chance. He paddled back desperately.

'Angela, that was so thoughtless of me. I didn't mean any of that as a slur on your professionalism. I just got carried away. As a really big favour, which in the circumstances, I recognise that I don't deserve, could you possibly find a way of reserving that book so we can look at it when it comes in on Friday? And of course I'll rejoin the library. I know I should have done that already.'

'What you deserve, Frank? We, Frank? Rejoin, Frank?' With forensic skill, Angela picked out the themes he was using to try and retrieve the situation.

He said nothing. The hole was already too deep.

Her voice softened. 'I'll put a flag on the book.'

'My dad took me to the library every Saturday morning,' he said. 'I loved it. I just got out of the habit. *Meet Lemon Kelly*. When I was a kid, that was my favourite book.' He tried a judicious change of tack. 'What about Keith Etchingham, eh? Alive or dead, he's played me like a professional. I've been dragging myself all around West Flanders and after all of that, we're back bang on where we started from.'

'Yeah, yeah, Frank. I know all you can think about is your case, and God knows, it's got you into a scrape or two. When will you come back to England?'

Perhaps he and Angela were back on track.

'It's too late today. There's the photo I've got to identify, and I've probably got some other things to tie up here. I guess I'll have to tell the local police I'm going home – unless Mike works something out – a motorised rubber dinghy at dead of night from Cap Gris Nez to Sandley Bay, maybe. We won't get the book till Friday at the earliest. I don't know. Maybe tomorrow evening. I'm looking forward to a proper pint and a catch-up.'

There was another silence, but not glacial.

'Look after yourself, Frank', Angela said eventually. 'Keep Mike close.' Then she was gone.

Sterling sat on the bed for a few moments. He stared at the heat ring a careless previous guest had left on the side table next to the bed from a hot mug of tea or coffee. The chocolates were a poor return for Angela, bearing in mind all that she had done for him, and the thoughtless way in which he repaid her. He wondered if he just used people, but took the charitable view.

There was often interesting payback when people got involved in his business.

Having buoyed himself up with the thought of how much entertainment he brought other people, he took himself, glass half full, down to reception. It was time for another encounter with Mrs. Van de Velde. She appeared from the small office when he pinged the bell on the counter. The smile on her face faded when she saw him.

'Mr. Sterling.'

'Mrs. Van de Velde.' They paused, like wrestlers circling in the ring, looking for openings. 'I'm almost finished here in Ypres. I'm just letting you know that I'm probably leaving at around midday tomorrow, maybe a little later.'

'Thank you for letting me know,' she said in a formal voice. 'As you know, rooms have to be free before half past eleven.' She realised that he might interpret this as awkwardness on her part, and continued less primly. 'Of course, you would be welcome to leave your luggage in our locked luggage room if you want to stay a little longer. Have a last walk around the Grote Markt.' She even allowed the little smile to return. Life might return to normal. Her daughter would be back on track. Maybe she could let bygones be bygones. 'I hope you've had a pleasant stay in Ypres.' She didn't mention anything about a return.

'Thank you, Mrs. Van de Velde.' He stressed the 'you' and nodded. He almost straightened up and clicked his heels. 'It's certainly been eventful.' She had no idea how eventful. 'I'll come down tomorrow morning after the breakfast rush to sign out and pay my bill. Do pass on my regards to your daughter.'

They nodded to each other, still wrestling, but in a courtly kind of way, and Sterling made for the door. Even in the drizzle, which had never gone away, the Grote Markt had a grey and orange medieval beauty. The streetlights were on, and the cafés and bars were open for evening business. Across the square, the Lakenhal stood ornate and tall. Its belfry dominated the square and Ypres itself. It dominated the countryside, too, from Chester Farm to the southeast and Vlamertinge to the west, and for all Sterling knew, points north and east.

In front of the Lakenhal, a young couple came to a halt with a baby and pram and turned behind them to look at a toddler lagging a metre or two behind. Something on the stone flags was absorbing her and she squatted down. It was taking too long. Her father, a tall young man in a short overcoat and fashionably small square spectacles, paced back and scooped her up over his shoulder. Her legs kicked out and Sterling could hear her shrill protests from the hotel. Her father good-naturedly patted her bottom. The family strolled on.

Mehrtens's mother was still serving in the chocolate shop. Even at this late hour, she smiled at customers just as her son did. He probably learned it from her, along with his opening gambit. Sterling did not think she would appreciate being asked about a photo by an English stranger, and he had not dared to ask Mrs. Van de Velde. He crossed the square and wandered down Diksmuidsestraat, but on the door of De Groot's cycle shop was a red *Gesloten* sign. He was at home, or maybe in a local around the corner. Sterling would have been in his place. He lingered outside the shop for a few moments. On Sunday evening, things had been different and he had needed to be alone, but usually he did not like to be out of doors in the early evening as darkness enveloped everything, no matter where he was. He called it the lonely time. Tonight, he was immersed in the lonely time. It was when a person should be inside, smelling supper cooking, talking to family about the events of the day, sipping the first pint with mates in the pub. He couldn't do any of those things.

A man in a dark suit emerged from the door opposite, locking it behind him with a large key. The brass plate next to the door said *L. Smid, Advocaat*. His case looked delicate and European – a slim leather affair with no room for lunchtime sandwiches – no room for anything much. He looked across at Sterling loitering as he slipped into a dark Mercedes, suspicious. If he was going home to dinner in one of the outlying villages after some weeknight overtime, Sterling envied him.

There was the Turkish pizzeria just around the corner. Maybe Sterling could sit with the men at the table on the pavement down the street while he ate his pizza. Have a bit of company. In the end, it was better than that. The drizzle had driven the group into the café, where they recognised him from Sunday and made some fuss. Just before he ordered, Mike emerged from somewhere in the shadows down the street and slid into a chair opposite. He said little except that everything was safe and clear.

Sterling spent the evening drinking beer, signing and gesticulating with his Turkish friends, arguing in the international language of football and munching pizza. Ozgur, Yusuf and the others followed Manchester United in the Premier League and the Champions League. Sterling maintained allegiance to non-league Cambridge United in the Blue Square Bet Premier, in deference to his father's passion. Man U were flying high. Cambridge, as far as he knew, were mid-table. The Turks had never even been to Manchester, and he mocked them for it. The only people who liked Man U, he laughed, were Mancunians and foreigners. Even in Manchester, half the population hated them. 'Ah yes, Manchester City,' Yusuf said. But Sterling kept quiet about his last trip to Cambridge, circa 1986, and his own tenuous link to his favoured club. After the backslapping farewells, Mike walked him back to the hotel and saw him in. He didn't say much, but if Sterling had been one to enjoy a flutter, he would have bet that he'd had a good evening. He even saw him smile at the banter.

Sterling's guardian will-o'-the-wisp disappeared into the drizzly night. Sterling stomped into the hotel and up the stairs. He had just missed night-time lock up and suit-and-slipper man. He could smell the damp on his face and jacket. The beer had made his legs heavy. He was alert in a semi-befuddled way, but trusted in Mike to have done the right checks. He slipped into his room, keen to wash his face and brush his teeth before he conked out. Five minutes later, he felt pleased he had managed it.

The soft knock on the door was a surprise, and his tiredness seemed to fall away from him. He thought he recognised it, and when he eased the door ajar, Christina was pressed to the wall of the corridor. He opened the door wide enough for her to slip in.

'Frank,' she whispered. 'Going home tomorrow. My mother said nothing, but I saw a note in the book.' She looked up at him with soft green eyes.

'Yes, home tomorrow, girl. I think I'm getting to the end of this case and that's where the final clue is.'

'We have business that we have not finished. I don't want you to forget me.'

'Business? I don't think so,' he said. 'Christina, you can be sure that I'll never forget you, not after what we've been through together.'

Christina reached up and put her hand around his neck, drawing his mouth down to hers. Her breath tasted minty as they kissed. Still kissing, they did a shuffly *pas de deux* to the bed, where they slipped off their clothes. She did something deft with her hands behind her back, and then she was completely naked. Her pale body looked sinuous and firm in the gloom. They kissed side by side, and then she flipped on top of him. Her hand wandered downwards.

'My God, Frank. You are ready for this,' she giggled. Then she grew serious and determined. 'And so am I.'

Sterling didn't dream at all that night. He'd written it off as a quiet day in Ypres. He'd done one or two things. He'd found out about the book from Sandley library. He'd wandered about, thwarted by the first clue, the photograph. The Turks had been entertaining. But there was no doubt: a quiet day had had an explosive ending.

21

Frank and Christina woke in the early hours with their arms around each other. Before she dressed, he watched her pace around the room gathering her clothes, noting again the curves of her hips, her generous breasts on the slender frame, the flatness around her midriff and her milky skin. There was a small strawberry mark on her left thigh in the shape of Norway. She smiled when she saw him watching. She slipped her clothes on almost as deftly as she had taken them off and came over to sit beside him on the bed. Feeling at a disadvantage, he dressed, too, and made them tea.

'Perhaps it's time we put our cards on the table, Christina,' said Sterling.

'Put our cards on the table?'

'Work out what everything means. Be honest with each other.'

She nodded and took a sip of tea. They were silent as they sat next to each other on the bed, but not strained.

'It was wonderful last night,' he said. 'A lovely surprise. But I think you're happy with your life as it is now, Christina.'

'Yes, that's true. I am happy, and I didn't plan this. But my life is not very interesting. You knew that, and changed it for a little while. But I don't think I want to change it for good'.

'Well, I didn't plan anything, either. You really bowled me over, but I've got to go home today. I lead a strange, uncertain life, but I do as I please, and I'm not sure I want to change that, either.'

'I think we understand each other, Frank.'

'Yes, I think we do. I was never going to forget you before, you know. I'm certainly not going to be able to forget you now,' he said.

'Good. You promise that will tell me how your case works out?'

'Of course. You deserve nothing less.'

'And yes, it was wonderful, Frank.' She leaned over and kissed him softly on his mouth and then his forehead.

A moment later, she opened the door. 'Back to my ordinary life,' she said, and he could not miss the wistful tone. Then she was gone.

Sterling did go and pay his bill and sign out after the breakfast rush, and he did leave his luggage in the small luggage room behind the counter. Christina and her mother were both there to do the processing, for him and a good-natured coach load of tourists whose accents indicated somewhere in Wales. He smiled a secret smile. Mother and daughter both looked happy for different reasons. Christina looked away and smiled a smile of her own. Glad they knew where each other stood, Sterling reckoned he had time to go and see De Groot, and if not him then Mehrtens, about the photo.

But before he stepped out for the last time into the Grote Markt, Pieters stepped into the lobby. He saw Sterling tense and put up a conciliatory palm.

'Have you got time for coffee, Mr. Sterling? I have some information that might interest you.'

They strolled over to Au Miroir. The drizzle had gone overnight, but the sky was grey, and there was a hint of cold that had not been there when Sterling had first come to Ypres. It was a little early for him, as he had just had breakfast, but to keep Pieters company, he ordered a cappuccino, Belgian-style. When they were comfortable sitting next to each other in a window booth overlooking the square, like cinema-goers in front of a big screen, Pieters reached into his jacket pocket, took out Sterling's passport and slid it along the table in front of him.

'Good job you came calling, Detective Pieters,' said Sterling. 'I had completely forgotten about that. I guess that means I am free to travel. And if I am free to go, perhaps you've got some other news for me.'

Pieters sat smugly surveying the square. 'You are right, Mr. Sterling. You are free to go. But of course, we need to know how to get in touch with you in England if we want to speak to you some more. Look over there, at the bus stop. That short man in the baseball cap. Lives in Mesen, to the south of Ypres. Used to come up here to pick the tourists' pockets at the Last Post. We stopped that.'

They were quiet for a few moments, watching, as if they expected the crook to start on those prospective bus passengers waiting in front of him in the queue. Pieters wanted to spin out his news. Sterling knew how to wait.

'Did you hear about the....' Pieters looked for the word, '....explosion out in the countryside, towards Menen?'

'I heard something,' Sterling said cautiously.

'Yes, I am sure you did.'

Sterling waited some more.

'Someone English had telephoned our emergency number about the explosion and about a girl who had been kidnapped – actually, as it happened – the girl from your hotel,' Pieters said. 'What a coincidence!' he exclaimed cheerfully while he fixed Sterling with a sideways stare. 'My colleagues found the girl in the cellar, and also three men. One was lying on a track beside the building that had exploded. It looked as if someone had kicked him, but he said no. The other two were outside a cottage, finding it difficult to breathe from smoke….' He waved his hand around impatiently, unable this time to find the word.

'Inhalation,' said Sterling. 'Smoke inhalation.'

If he had been English, Pieters would have said, 'Whatever'. As it was, he moved calmly on.

'The girl, Christina Van de Velde – you must know her – attractive, red hair – confirmed what the mysterious English caller had said – that the men had kidnapped her. So we weren't dealing with a sort of accident. We were dealing with a serious crime. And that's why Inspector Broussart called our forensic team in. We needed to get evidence. We arrested the men, who were also English, and took them to the station for questioning. They had some silly story about the girl going with them willingly, and being locked in the cellar as a joke, but that girl was a bit scared, angry also, actually, and she comes from a good Ypres family.' He smiled. 'Of course, we are more likely to believe a Flemish person than an English person.'

'Sensible.'

'We got our evidence, for sure, but not quite the evidence we were looking for. In one of the bedrooms of the house where the men were staying, we found a T-shirt with something brown splashed up the back of it, mostly in a straight line. In one of the outhouses at the back, near the burnt out one, we found a bike. That had some dry brown stuff on it also.'

Sterling leaned in towards him. Pieters did not move, so there was just his profile, his short blonde hair shining slightly in the light. It was as if he was reciting an often-told story. His voice had a trance-like quality as he stared forward.

'It was blood. Our forensics people got it to the laboratory people and our laboratory people got the DNA from it. Thomas Jackson. Our murder victim.'

'Good work, Detective Pieters. Efficient. In England we could wait weeks for those tests.'

'I don't think we have so much crime here in Flanders. And for sure we don't often have murders. After that, it got easier. One of the men we concentrated on more than the others. He was weaker, more nervous. Under pressure from our questioning all yesterday, he confessed to us – not what he had done himself, of course, but what the others had done. What do you say in English? He shopped them. All he did, so he tells us, is follow the victim on a bicycle so he would not escape. The others came by car a little later. He must have cycled through the blood pool when he got away from the body. He did not feel the spatter on his back. He panicked, I think.'

Sterling looked out at the square. A young boy was feeding the pigeons. Two British soldiers, padres by the look of the dog collars with their uniforms, walked towards the In Flanders Fields museum in the Lakenhal. He could sense Pieters again looking across at his face. The man Simon, he was thinking. Maybe he and Christina had unnerved him. Maybe Simon was always the one who was going to do the confessing.

'Surely, though, Detective,' said Sterling, knowing that Pieters liked to be called by his title, as he had himself when he was in the police, 'there must be lots of loose ends … The explosion, the smoke. And the motive for the murder. It wasn't random. What was that about?'

'Yes, loose ends, as you say. Our forensics team found a smoke grenade that had been thrown into the house, and the remains of small bomb that blew up the building behind the house. Someone had taken out the window of the cellar and bent the bars back. We thought for a while that the man we found outside had been working against the others and trying to rescue the girl, but that doesn't really fit with the facts. We think the motive for the murder may have been to do with something in English politics. We will know more when we contact the English police about the men we have arrested. And we are looking for a fourth man who was not at the house when all the action happened.'

Then Pieters appeared to change the subject and became more familiar, more chummy almost.

'I have done courses in England, you know, Frank. Bramshill. The National College of Police Leadership. I learned many things there. Like matching resources to priorities – what you have with what you have to do. You were a policeman. You know what happens. We have our murderers. We will look for the fourth man. We will threaten the others if they don't help us with that. But we have our result. We have our evidence. Enough evidence. The loose ends, as you call them, don't matter. In fact, even the kidnapping of Miss Van de Velde does not really matter now. She does not have to go to court. We have larger fish to cook.'

Sterling said nothing. There was nothing to say.

They carried on watching the view from the window, companionable.

'I guess you're going to apologise to me as well, on behalf of Broussart and the Ypres police,' said Sterling after few more moments of quiet observation. 'That scary afternoon of questioning and suspicion.'

'Apologise, Frank?' Pieters seemed genuinely surprised. 'Why apologise if we have done nothing wrong? Anyway, we never apologise except when we absolutely have to, and even then ... It must be the same in England. Broussart does not even know I am here. He would not give a soldier's damn for your feelings. In fact, you should be thanking me for this favour, and feeling lucky that we are not going any further.'

'No harm in raising it,' smiled Sterling. He was not sure if he would see much more of Pieters. He might miss his quirky English.

Pieters got up from the table, clapping Sterling on the arm. 'Goodbye, Frank. Enjoy the rest of your "tourism".'

As he opened the door of the café, he turned back and winked. The last Sterling saw of him was as he ambled off down Rijselsestraat towards the police station. Sterling finished his coffee and caught the waiter's attentive eye. Pieters's largesse had not extended to paying for the refreshments. Gloria would have to foot the bill from expenses.

22

There was that one thing more to do before Sterling left Ypres. He left Au Miroir and strolled across to Diksmuidsestraat. De Groot was in what looked like a complex and animated discussion with a couple of white-haired cyclists with racing bikes. They were wearing the garish gear of club cyclists – Lycra shorts and multi-coloured vests. Their legs were tanned and muscular, but Sterling saw wrinkles and knobbles behind their knees. Instead of cycling helmets, both were sporting little caps with the peaks upturned, like bakers or Norman Wisdom, though not so off-kilter. Neither bike had mudguards.

De Groot nodded and smiled at Sterling, and indicated his back room with a sideways jerk of his head. He crouched down for a closer look at the derailleur gears on one of the bikes. He poked and fiddled with the mechanism with deft hands, getting a delicate screwdriver from his front pocket and beginning to make an adjustment.

In the back office, Sterling sat in his usual place and waited, looking at the photo on the sheet of vellum with the black lion of Flanders. Five minutes later, De Groot came into the office, wiping his oily hands on a rag. When he was satisfied that he had done a good enough job, they shook hands. He went to the windowsill and turned up the volume of the transistor a little. The Kinks were singing in tinny, laconic voices.

'Good to see you again, Frank. Coffee?'

'I'll just keep you company, Martin. I had breakfast and then I had coffee with a policeman. I've reached my limit for the moment.'

'Those old racers. They pretend they're still young, still doing those semi-pro sprints around our towns. They come in more to have a talk than anything else. They know how to fix their own bicycles. But I like seeing them, and they always come to me to order new bikes or new gear. They are not so quick now, but you always see the club out on the road during the week.' He paused. 'A policeman, Frank. Of course, I'm not really surprised. Who was it?'

'Pieters. Know him?'

'A little bit. He's with that bastard Broussart.'

'Is there anyone in Ypres you don't know, Martin?'

De Groot gave a little "harrumph". 'Plenty of people. I expect it was about that explosion out towards Menen, or that dead guy at the Scottish Memorial. Broussart is ruthless, and he doesn't mind taking short cuts. Pieters is OK, though. I think you would say that he keeps Broussart honest. Yes?'

'Yeah, nicely put, Martin. And yes, they were asking me questions about this and that. At the station.' Sterling shrugged. 'But, here I am, and here's my passport. They've got some suspects, and I'm in the clear. They've got some good evidence, too. In fact, evidence that will interest you, if you can keep it to yourself. '

'Sure. Tell me. Don't leave me hanging.'

'Their forensic people found a T-shirt in the house near where the explosion was, and a bike in a shed behind it. The T-shirt had a spatter up the back of it – apparently pretty much in a vertical line up the middle. It was blood. And it matched some blood residue on the front tyre of the bike. And that matched the blood of the bloke whose head was bashed in at the Scottish memorial. One of the killers pedalled through a pool of blood.' Sterling sat back. 'You'll be able to use that as another selling point for your mudguards. If they hadn't found the T-shirt, they wouldn't have looked for the bike.'

De Groot perfected a new sales pitch. 'Mudguards aren't expensive. They're easy to fit. And if you happen to get involved in a messy blunt instrument murder by bike,' he said as if to a prospective customer, 'having mudguards will stop you getting blood on your clothes. Yes, useful. Thanks, Frank.'

They mulled things over for a few moments, smiling as they embellished the mudguard-selling scenario in their heads.

'Mudguards aside,' said De Groot. 'I have to say, Frank, you did well to get out of tangling with Broussart. He must have got a good case, or he'd never have let you have your passport back. He's not that concerned with the truth. Results are what interest him. There's a prison over behind the Reservoir Cemetery. It's not short of guys in there because of him – for things they did not do.'

They talked on about Broussart and the Ypres police, and about the recent dramas. De Groot had changed his strategy. He wasn't pushing Sterling to tell him what he was doing in Ypres and how he was involved. Like

Sterling, he could be a patient man. He sipped his coffee and they leaned back in their chairs, maybe waiting for the bell to ring to indicate another customer, or maybe just passing time, two blokes chewing the fat. The bell did ring once or twice, but each time De Groot returned relatively quickly.

'Tyres, puncture kits, helmets,' he said. 'Nobody much wants to buy a bicycle this time of year. Autumn is on the way. I do most of my bicycle business at Christmas and the start of spring.'

While he was in the shop, Sterling had been reflecting. He had taken the sheet of vellum out of his pocket, and now he was ready to ask about the photo.

'What do you make of this, Martin?' he said.

De Groot looked at the sheet, and then took it in his hands. From the breast pocket of his shirt, he took out a small pair of black reading glasses. On his face, they looked out of proportion to his large head and walrus moustache. When he first took the sheet and focused on it, he was relaxed, but he immediately became tense. He looked at Sterling over the glasses.

'Where did you get this, Frank? This is not good.'

Sterling shrugged. 'It doesn't really matter – somewhere in Ypres. It's part of the trail I'm following. What's the problem?'

'Look. Look closely at the lion.' He indicated the crest at the top of the sheet.

'The black lion of Flanders. So?'

'*A* black lion of Flanders. Not all the black lions are the same, and not all are what you call respectable. Just a second.'

He went back into the shop and came back with a pennant on a long thin flexible wire rod for putting on the back of a bike, with the black lion on the customary yellow background.

'Can you see the difference?'

Sterling looked from one to the other. The pennant lion had red claws and a red tongue. On his sheet of vellum, the lion was entirely black. He looked up at De Groot. 'OK, Martin. Tell me. I've got plenty of time. I reckon a coffee would be nice now. Keep me awake if it gets boring.'

As he gave him the cup and saucer, De Groot said, 'It's another history lesson, like the one the other day, but it will probably help you if you know all of it. If you think about flags in England and how they are used, that will help you understand.'

Getting Sterling to compare the flags showed that De Groot was a natural teacher, and as he talked, Sterling made the links as De Groot intended. For half an hour, he sipped his coffee and learnt about the origins of Belgium, about the Walloons in the south and west, and the Flemish in the north and east. Historically, Flanders and the Flemish were always second best to Brussels and the French speakers. That region used to be Belgium's industrial powerhouse, but now the roles had reversed and the historically more agricultural Flanders was wealthier. Walloon hegemony had extended to language. As an example, the principal language of the Belgian army had been French. Since the Great War, a Flemish separatist movement had gathered momentum. Having sketched the background, De Groot began to get more specific.

'Late in the last century, the Flanders nationalists and separatists were mainly in the *Vlaams Blok* – the Flemish Bloc. That changed its name a few years ago to *Vlaams*

Belang, which means Flemish Interest. They say it's not a racist party anymore.' De Groot tipped his head from side to side, as if weighing up the proposition. 'It's still kept out of local and national government (not that we have a national government right now) by what has come to be called the *cordon sanitaire*. Other parties refuse to form any coalition with it.'

'A couple of weeks ago, there was a kind of annual event up at Diksmuide, north of here, called *IJserbedevaart*, which means something like Pilgrimage of the Yser. The Yser is the river in Belgium where many Great War battles were fought. The event at the *IJsertoren*, the Yser tower, is meant to remember the Flemish soldiers who died, and as a reminder about peace. But it also became a political meeting for Flemish separatists, and for far-right groups across Europe, partly they say because the Germans organised the pilgrimages in the Second World War. The organisers have managed to clean it up so it's not so much about nationalism and neo-Fascism and more about peace and tolerance. The separatists and neo-Nazis have gone off somewhere else – started at *IJserwake* – I don't know the English for that – very near here at Zuidschote at about the same time. There's a memorial for two Flemish brothers there, soldiers in the Great War, Edward and Frans van Raemdonck.'

'Interesting, Martin. You seem very well informed.'

De Groot looked out of the window. 'AVV-VVK,' he said softly. '*Alles voor Vlaanderen; Vlaanderen voor Kristus*. All for Flanders; Flanders for Christ.' He pulled his focus back to Sterling. 'That's the battle cry of the Flemish nationalists. So we can speak Dutch and have our independence. I was brought up on that. My parents – my father a railway clerk, my mother a bookkeeper – were militant about it.'

'But not you?'

'Oh yes, Frank, I had my moments, as I think you say. But I escaped from that small world. It seemed stupid when I was racing, and in the same team as people from all over the world. It was stupid. You know, some people in the cycling clubs around here criticise me for selling pennants of the black lion with the red tongue and claws, as if I am betraying my nationality. To hell with them. I am Flemish. I am Belgian. I am European. I am human. The last is the most important.'

Sterling looked again at the sheet of vellum in front of them. 'So this black lion is the right wing, separatist one.'

'That's right. You could perhaps say that it's not very important, which lion. Like I said. In England, those St George's flags with the red cross come out everywhere at World Cups. People put them on their cars to support the England team. Nothing so very bad in that. It can be good. Brings people together. But when your British National Party changes them a bit, like our black lion, and flies them on its marches ... Well, that's very different. The paper is really good quality, Frank. This is about one of the far-right Flemish separatist groups – militant, racist, anti-gay. Not only that. Many of these groups have strong links to English groups like the BNP and the English Defence League. I said it's not good. You need to be careful. Very careful.'

Things had taken a darker turn. They both rocked in their chairs, as if to The Kinks' song. But that had long finished, and something else was playing. They quietly thought their separate thoughts.

'OK, Martin. You've been right about virtually everything so far. I certainly will be careful. Thanks for the lecture. The funny thing is though that I was more interested in the photo beneath the lion, rather than the lion itself.'

De Groot snorted softly, put his glasses back on his nose after he had pushed them above his hairline, and peered down at the photograph for a brief second. He tossed the sheet back towards Sterling. 'That's my bank,' he said casually. 'Fintro. See the name? Johan Hendrickx. He's the manager. Good chap. Those words. *Gaat ver, blijf dichtbij*. Go far, stay close. It's a few metres down Sint Jacobstraat. Just around the corner from your hotel.'

'The man who knows everything,' said Sterling admiringly.

A few minutes later, they finished their coffee.

'I'm off back home to England now, Martin. That's where the answer lies.'

At the door of the shop, De Groot put out his hand. 'Good luck, Frank. When you are next here in Ypres, come around and see me. Tell me the whole story when it's all over. Hire a bike. Maybe we could go for a ride together. I still don't know what you came for, but things got much more exciting while you were here. And remember, be careful. Those neo-Fascists are dangerous, whichever country they come from. Not always that clever. But certainly dangerous.'

Sterling passed a young man and woman in the doorway who went to look at the bicycles displayed in the racks. Newlyweds, perhaps, about to get his and hers machines and enrich, through cycle trips, the long journey of wedded bliss. 'Don't forget the mudguards,' he whispered to De Groot as he strolled back down the street towards the Grote Markt and beyond it, Sint Jacobstraat. He could hear De Groot's deep laughter as he went.

23

Sterling stood in the Grote Markt, next to the Peugeot. Without a mobile telephone, it seemed the best way. Mike emerged from an alleyway adjacent to Diksmuidsestraat. They stood silently together for a few moments, taking in the neo-medieval beauty of the square – dominated in one part by the Lakenhal, enhanced by the crenellated frontages on the other two sides and overlooked by the Stadhuis at the top.

As they stood, it became lighter, and the drizzle faded completely away. Sterling could see the sun as a dirty yellow orb above the cloud. A little while later, it came through completely, and was now too bright to look at. The day was changing for the better, and the square cast off its drab monochrome cloak like a piece of old black and white newsreel that segues into the multi-coloured present. It grew warmer by a degree or two.

'We're going home,' he said to Mike.

'I thought so.' Mike held up a small dark blue grip bag, as anonymous as he was himself. *Eurohike* was inscribed in small letters under the zip. 'I need to travel back with you, if that's OK.'

'Of course. What happened to the pick-up and all the … equipment?'

'You don't need to know that. Best you don't, actually. I know this area quite well. Becky and I used to come here a lot. Before the pub.' From Mike, this almost constituted a speech. 'Which way did you come? We could go back via a scenic route.'

'OK,' said Sterling. One of them had to be monosyllabic. 'Let's just get my bag from the hotel.'

In the weak sunlight, they stood in front of the Fintro bank. De Groot had been right. The frontage matched the photo. A sharply suited young man in highly polished black shoes went into the separate cash till area and up to a machine. Sterling thought about going into the bank himself, but what would he have said? And who would he have said it to? The bank was only half the answer he was looking for. The other half was in Sandley library. When he got back to the hotel to collect his bag, Mike waited patiently there, too, leaning against a lamp post as Sterling went in. Sterling rang the bell in the lobby, hoping for Christina. Her mother came out and smiled. She unlocked the door of the luggage room and retrieved his bag.

'Goodbye, Mr. Sterling,' she said. He was surprised when she offered a small pale hand. They shook, not a full handclasp but a delicate little half grip. Her hand was cool and dry. It felt like a post-tennis-match gesture, and he knew she did not consider him the winner.

'Goodbye, Mrs. Van de Velde. Thank you for your hospitality. All of it,' he added with what he hoped was a sort of cryptic irony. My regards to your daughter.'

As Sterling and Mike Strange drove out of Ypres in the dodgy Peugeot, the customary plume of dirty smoke trailing behind as the engine warmed up, Sterling felt a pang of homesickness for the town. He shook it off.

It was a ridiculous and illogical switch of allegiance, being homesick for a place he'd been in for barely more than a week on the way back to his proper home. But it was typical of his contradictory nature.

From Ypres, they did go back by a scenic route, aided by a map lying over Mike's knees. At Watou they smelled the yeasty aroma of the brewery that made Hommelbier, and crossed into France close by. They wound their way up the cobbles into the heart of Cassel, a kind of large bump in the middle of the Flanders plain, lunching late in a café in the small town square. Sterling discovered another thing he had not known: Mike's excellent if minimal French when they ordered. Then he took them up to a demolished radio station at the very top, where, by a windmill and a statue of Marshal Foch riding a horse, they looked out towards Calais in the far hazy distance, forearms resting comfortably on the enclosing wall.

'They say that this is the hill the grand old Duke of York marched his soldiers up and down,' Mike said.

'The Grand Old Duke of York, he had ten thousand men,' sang Sterling. 'He marched them up to the top of the hill, and he marched them down again. And when they were up, they were up....'

Mike had moved on. 'Flanders is not just the northern half of Belgium. We're still in Flanders now. French Flanders goes out to Dunkirk to the west and Lille and Douai in the east, in a band across the south of the Belgian border. There's even a Dutch area of Flanders to the north. It's only attached to Holland by a tunnel and a ferry. Don't know why that is.'

They walked across the garden to the eastern side. Way below them, roads stretched out in spokes from

Cassel to local villages and further off towns. A huge patchwork of fields in green and brown spread between the spokes in an ornate pie chart segment. It was a calm, timeless and orderly agricultural sight. Sterling thought of the Fenland journeys he and his father had made to see his paternal relations when he was young – the endless fields of rich black soil, the small towns in the flat landscape – March and Chatteris like Poperinghe and Watou, and Ely, a bump in the landscape like Cassel. Nationalists, separatists, racists: He could never understand the sheer petty-mindedness. Wanting to put the clock back, or at least, stop it going forward. The struggle for a spurious racial purity. But all this – Flanders in Belgium, France or Holland, was at least worth looking after; worth caring for.

On the road again, they criss-crossed the canal system again on their way to Calais, and sometimes drove down canal-side roads for many kilometres, passing barges on the way. At four o'clock, in the terminal, Mike's passport seemed to cause an interested flurry, and then they were on the ferry home. At six o'clock, they were drawing in to Sandley like two day-trippers after a successful foray for wine and cigarettes. They had said little. In the car, Sterling had just followed instructions. But all the while, he was wondering about the next piece of the jigsaw, and when Smithy was going to make his malign reappearance – when, not if.

Mike got out at the pub. He said he'd do a scout around Sterling's house. Sterling thanked him again and said he'd be in for a pint later. In return, he received a nod and perhaps a tiny smile – he could not be sure. From The Cinque Ports Arms, he drove over to Jack Cook's garage, and was surprised to find the doors open and Jack in it, bent over something at a workbench. The Peugeot's engine rattled and clattered loudly as Sterling drove it into the garage's enclosed space. When he turned it off, it died to a welcome silence. The smell of petrol fumes lingered in the close air.

'Return of the wanderer,' said Jack. 'Everything tickety-boo?'

'Well, I couldn't get fifth, as Mickey predicted. It was a bit rattly, as expected. But it was fine. I owe you at least a pint, Jack.'

'And how about the case, detective? All done and dusted? Perpetrators apprehended? Stolen jewellery retrieved? Murder solved?'

'See you later on, Jack.'

Sterling walked home through the town, through the small alleys and narrow streets he knew so well. The house smelled musty as he entered, and in the kitchen, he could see a layer of dust on a marmalade jar in the kitchen even in the fading light. He opened some windows, turned on the boiler for hot water and the kettle for a cup of tea. On the stereo, Dylan suited the mood. Sterling sat and sipped his drink. He'd missed home, his music, and properly made refreshments. He closed his eyes and sank back. In a little while, he was going to do something he should have done at the very outset of the case, but he'd enjoy the tea and the peace first.

A few moments later, he picked up the telephone in the hall and found the address book from the little table it rested on. He could hear the ringing tone of a mobile telephone, and hoped it wouldn't go through to voicemail. Just as he was going to give up, a voice came through.

'Andy Nolan.'

'Andy, it's Frank.'

'Frank. The shamus. The private dick.'

'Better a private dick than a … Oh, never mind. How are you doing, Andy?'

'Mustn't grumble, though I expect I will at some point. To what do I owe?'

'I'm on a case, and I'm thinking that you may be able to help. I've come a long way so far, but I think I should have had a word with you before.'

'A case. Astonishing. What case?'

'I've been hired by someone called Gloria Etchingham, and in connection with that, I've just come back from Belgium. I'm doing everything arsy-versy. I should have got a bit more background first. Are you still there, Andy?'

'Gloria Etchingham, eh? Well known in Kent Constabulary circles. I'm not involved in that case, of course, being in Canterbury and that.'

'But you know something about it?'

''Course. We all do in the legendary Criminal Investigation Department. Care to discuss it face to face? We can catch up on all the other stuff while we're about it.'

'That's what I was hoping, Andy. Are you around tomorrow?'

'I've got court in the afternoon, in Canterbury. I could slot you in about 10:30. Go for a coffee. Call in to the station and we'll make a break for freedom.'

'Thanks, Andy. I think I'll be owing you one.'

'Coffee for starters, Frank. Must stick to the guidelines. I am noted for my incorruptibility.'

Later on, Sterling strolled back through the town to the pub. His pint was waiting. Angela was in their corner with the crossword. Jack was talking to some other cronies leaning against the bar. Sterling nodded to Mike and Becky. He hugged Angela tightly, whispered a heartfelt thank you in her ear, and settled down to one across. They ignored the banter from the bar. As they worked through the clues, Sterling resisted all Jack's blandishments to tell him about the case.

'When it's over, Jack, I'll tell you everything. Until then, my professional code of conduct, etcetera....'

But Angela, research assistant, back-watcher and saviour, he told almost everything.

As he made his way home, he wondered what Andy Nolan had in store for him in the morning. And the Kent library service on Friday. Things were coming inexorably to a conclusion, and he loved the thrill of it.

24

You can catch a bus directly from Sandley to Canterbury, so that's what Sterling did, waiting at half past nine that Thursday morning at the Guildhall with his fellow travellers. But for two teenaged girls, a youngish couple and him, the crowd was mostly pensioners. As the bus wended through the villages on the way to the city, in a lulling rhythm of diversions off the main road and people getting on and off, the young couple in the seat in front looked at a racing page and discussed their bets. Sterling wondered about the teenagers. Today was a school day. But he wondered more, given his own reputation for bunking off, when he had become so puritanical.

The bus disgorged its passengers at the large bus station squeezed between the city wall and the Whitefriars shopping centre. The layout made it much easier to walk to the shops than the police station beyond the city wall, so Sterling made his way against the flow of the pedestrian throng. On the graffiti-scarred wall of the underpass, someone had written *Trop jeune pour mourir* – 'Too young to die' – a notch in quality above all the tiresome tags. He crossed the Dover Road at the crossing.

The Canterbury station was smaller than the one in Ypres, but when all is said and done, a police station is a police station. He announced that he had arrived to the civilian auxiliary and then took one of the hard plastic blue chairs near the door. A plump young woman with a pale, pasty face and small dark eyes rocked a grizzling baby in her arm, the baby's feet hitched over her hip. A toddler whinged softly next to her. The woman's right eye was almost closed, the skin around it yellow, turning to black. She looked exhausted and desperate.

From a side door, Andy Nolan emerged. Probably only the punch code was different from the door Sterling almost went through into the press throng in Ypres. He imagined a company called Bullingdon and Smith, makers of security glass doors to police forces the world over.

'Frank,' said Andy Nolan with his hand outstretched. 'Good to see you.'

'Detective Sergeant Nolan.'

'What about my fucking assault?' said the young woman. 'I've been here an hour already, and then he waltzes in.' She jerked a thumb at Sterling.

'Waltzed,' Sterling murmured. 'I hardly think so.'

'Whatever. But I need to see someone, and I don't like people pushing in.'

'My colleague will be out in a minute, Madam,' said Andy. 'She's taken all your details, hasn't she? I know she's working on it for you.' He took Sterling's arm and marched him out, rolling his eyes and grimacing as he did. 'She's got a point. Things are much slower. There are even fewer of us than when you were on the force. We'll pop into the university.'

'The university?'

'You need to get out of Sandley more, mate. Things are changing in Canterbury.'

Just next to the police station, a gleaming glass and steel frontage soared above them as the traffic roared around the ring road. That hadn't been there two years before. The university logo and title were etched next to the electric sliding doors. The two men stopped for a moment in front of the magnificent learning palace. They looked across at the stubby, shabby little police station.

'I think we might have made a wrong turn somewhere along the line,' said Sterling.

'Should have worked harder at school,' said Andy Nolan. He led them through the sliding doors. 'I come in here quite a lot. I helped them sort out some illegal downloading. There's a café on the third floor. Follow me.'

He nodded to the desk staff, and they made their way upwards through a vast atrium. Sterling looked askance at his friend, the man who had shared a patrol car with him in the early years. He was a little shorter than Sterling's five feet eleven. His light brown hair was beginning to go at the temples, but he did not sweep it back, so only a scalp connoisseur scared of losing his own fair locks would notice. He wasn't the skinny young police officer Sterling used to know. He wasn't fat, but he had filled out. Being a detective was not as active as being an ordinary plod. Sterling knew that himself.

Andy Nolan's suit was smart, but not football-pundit fashionable. Sterling knew he couldn't be bothered with all that. There was no change to the shoes, which were dull and scuffed, but just the right side of acceptable. My father made us polish our shoes daily, Andy Nolan had once said on a long night of vigil, so I can't stand doing it now. He still walked in a kind of splay-footed amble. Sterling remembered what a good officer he had been.

He had an easy manner, communicated well, calmed things down, moved things on – the perfect foil for the hothead Sterling had been. But he was implacable, as well. His shrewd brain had got him to the top of the league tables for convictions. And he was a politician. Sterling couldn't be bothered, and that was why things were as they were now.

In the café, students were sprawled around drinking and talking. Nearby, a boy with dark, swept forward hair curved around his forehead tapped frenziedly at his laptop. Sterling found them a place to sit in the glass, chrome and plastic bubble looking out across the medieval city wall and into the park beyond it. The tall, white stuccoed Georgian mansions at the far side of the park looked as gracious as he remembered them – as gracious as the building he was sitting in was brash and modern.

'Thanks, Andy,' said Sterling as his coffee appeared.

'Since I'm the one with the regular income….'

They sipped their coffee for a few moments. It was quiet in the café. One of the benefits of being in the library was avoiding the noise that passed as modern music. They small-talked for a while. Long ago, they had shared evenings out with their wives, as well as in the squad car. Andy Nolan was still married and had two children. Sterling's wife was long gone.

'So, Gloria and Keith Etchingham,' he said, getting them down to business.

'Yeah, the Etchinghams. Dover office is looking at it. As we say, "pursuing various promising lines of enquiry".'

'So they're stuck.'

'I think that's a fair summary. There hasn't been much progress since it all kicked off in late June. Or rather, some progress, but it's all come pretty much down to nothing. Funny case. As in funny peculiar. Keith Etchingham was an entrepreneur. He did a bit of this and a bit of that, built things up in profitable directions. He was a wheeler-dealer and from all I've heard, a charmer. He and Gloria lived in a Georgian house near Martin Mill. She's still there, of course.'

Sterling nodded. More than ever, he wished that he had had this conversation just after Gloria Etchingham had visited his office.

'Gloria Etchingham called our Dover lot when her husband had been gone for about a day. At the beginning, they just said the usual. A day's not enough. He could have just gone on a visit. Had they had a row? As I said, the usual. But she was insistent. He'd gone and something was up. His car was still outside the house when she got in from the weekly shop, but he was nowhere. So they sent a couple of blokes in a squad car to have a look around. In the garage, which Keith Etchingham used as a workshop rather than a place for the cars, and which Gloria rarely went into, they found blood. A lot of blood. And signs of a struggle. So then Dover took it more seriously. They got Etchingham's DNA from wherever – toothbrush or hairbrush, can't remember which – and compared it to the blood in the garage. It was a match. So someone had bashed Etchingham, maybe killed him, and borne him off.'

'Borne him off, Andy?'

'In effect. I can't bear the jargon sometimes.'

'But you're looking for person or persons unknown.'

'Well, perhaps not persons entirely unknown. What do you know about Keith Etchingham?'

'Nothing directly. Alive or dead, he's been sending me messages – but with a difference. He's a bit of joker, a practical joker. I've been traipsing around in Belgium and in the end, here I am back almost to my front door. I found out he was charming. He took a Flemish chocolatier on a pub crawl, if you can imagine that.'

Andy smiled. Then he said, 'Heard of PEDU, Frank?'

'PEDU....' Sterling rarely kept up with the news or current affairs. 'Vaguely familiar, unpleasant con-notations if it's what I'm thinking of. Pan-English something-or-other.'

'Every police force's nightmare. As you know, we don't care who does the marching and demonstrating. We'd just prefer if no one did it. But the Pan-English Defence Union is about the worst. Speciality: marches in ethnic and religious minority communities, with racist sloganising and flags. It's got all the European far right connections. It's eclipsing the BNP and all the other wacky groups. Credit to the Dover people – do you remember Tim Jones and Freddie Foxhill? – they dug up all that. And more. Etchingham was involved somehow. Apart from that, as I said, he was something of an entrepreneur. The marriage was meant to be good, though both of them apparently had their moments. They had all the trappings.'

'So your blokes in Dover, among other things, they're thinking that there might be a PEDU connection.'

'Yup. But that's where it gets difficult. They're getting nothing from the PEDU leadership, and it's all gone to the lawyers. Anyway, that's one line of enquiry. The biggest, I think. The anti-fascist groups have been helpful – for once. They reckon they've heard rumours of stuff gone missing, feuds, vendettas; power struggles. What those far right groups are best at, I reckon.'

'What about Gloria? Where do Jones and Foxhill think she fits in to all of this?'

'Gloria … I've never met her, but she's made her mark with my Kent Constabulary colleagues. Beautiful. Sexy. Knows what she wants and how to get it. Quite the femme fatale. Indisputably, according to the Andy Nolan classification system you know so well, a man's woman.'

Sterling shifted uncomfortably, looked down, sipped some more of his coffee. Part of him knew exactly what Andy was saying. The stupid part thought that Gloria was charmed exclusively by some mysterious qualities found only in him. When he looked up, Andy was looking at him with a little smile.

'Same old Frank,' he said, but kindly rather than mocking. 'So, I've laid the force's cards on the table. Your turn.'

Sterling knew it was coming and was just about ready. The boy at the keyboard had stopped and was sprawling over a banquette. All that tapping had exhausted him. 'Your Dover colleagues. Do they know we're having this meeting?'

'They know some of it, Frank. They don't know all you've been up to, any more than I do. But they, and I, for that matter, are interested in solving the case. It's murder or abduction, and you can't hold up a police enquiry. You know that. And – this will interest you – they have been contacted by our Belgian counterparts. Perkins, Pikestaff, Peters – some name like that, but Belgian.'

Pieters had been efficient.

Sterling wondered how long he had known Andy Nolan – ten, twelve years. They'd had some good and bad times together. They had stuck up and covered for each other. They'd shared all those greasy kebabs at godforsaken hours. There was no one he trusted more. He told him almost everything.

At the end, Andy said, 'We can help each other.'

And Sterling said, 'All I ask is, let me work out how best.'

25

It was irksome. Even private investigators have to grapple with the mundane. Somewhere in Sandley, or Woodnesborough, or Eastry, or Felderland, or Worth, or one of the other surrounding villages, an aficionado of Westerns had the library book that Sterling needed. The borrower, most likely a man (it was a Western, after all) was probably sitting in a favourite chair, enjoying the sunshine and a cup of coffee, finishing it off before tomorrow, oblivious to its true importance.

In the lull back in Sandley, Sterling caught up with domestic duties and shopping, walking to and from the Co-op in the sunshine with his bags of provisions. Inside the front door at the bottom of the stairs to his office, no one apart from Gloria Etchingham was making an old-fashioned request for the services of Frank Sterling Investigations. Amongst the bumf and junk, people offered him two-for-one pizzas, but only on Tuesday evenings, cavity wall insulation, solar panels, distance-learning accountancy modules and cut-price tanning sessions. As he screwed up and tossed the last flyer into the waste bin, the bin teetered and toppled over. He switched on his computer. No one was requesting his services by electronic means, either, but there were plenty of e-mail offers for cut-price sofas or rail journeys to York and places beyond. That reminded him. He should tot up his expenses charges for presentation to Gloria Etchingham.

He telephoned her, but there was no reply. That suited him. He left a message asking her to call at the office at four tomorrow afternoon. The book would be back by then, and he would have news for her. On his way home, he popped in to the library to see Angela. After that, there was nothing to do with the Etchingham case until tomorrow. The Grateful Dead were playing when he fell asleep near midnight. He dreamed he was driving a High Speed 1 train down a lane just outside Ramsgate until it was too narrow to go any further. He phoned Andy Nolan for help, but he just talked about family. Then Christina was visiting him again in his room at Hotel Sultan. He dreamed of Norway, though he had never been.

He was in his office and at his desk early, earlier even than Angela. There was nothing to do except wait. He looked out over the square. A mother cycled through with her two children beneath his window on the way to the primary school through the passageway just beyond. Their cycle helmets bobbed as they pedalled. He saw Jack Cook open the café. A waitress turned up a few moments afterwards. Downstairs in the library, he heard sounds of movement – a key in the latch, the hum of a fan.

Sterling got out his best Delft blue cups and saucers, brewed the tea and added the milk. He paid attention. The tea could not be too dark or too milky. Then he gathered his documents and the Mehrtens chocolates, wedged them under his arm, picked up cups and saucers in each hand and tottered precariously downstairs. The saucers rattled. At all costs, he wanted to avoid spillage. At the bottom of the stairs, he nudged open the door with his hip. Angela was quick to get organised. He was banking that she had not already brewed up.

There was no one at the reception desk.

'Angela,' he called. 'Tea.'

She appeared from the side office. Seeing the cups and saucers, she smiled with pleasure.

'Good timing, Frank. Tea was going to be my next job. The Delft, too. The Sandley-Low Countries connection. To what do I owe this privilege?'

'I think you know already. You've helped me so much.' He offered the chocolates. 'A small token. And I wonder if you have a library registration form?'

'You're really wanting to make it right, aren't you?' She smiled again. 'And of course, you charming devil, you're succeeding. But we can enrol you online these days. Have you got....?' He flipped his driving licence and a gas bill onto the desk. 'Impressive,' she said in response. 'You seem to know the ropes from the last time, circa 1985.'

'*Meet Lemon Kelly*,' he said. 'Can I reserve it?'

Angela rolled her eyes as she completed the registration. 'We updated the children's section years ago. But you might want to try *Appaloosa*.' Then, more seriously, she said, 'We close at five, Frank. You might have a long wait. The borrower might not even bring it in today. Thirty five per cent of our customers overall return late and pay fines.'

'Impressive county-wide analysis, Angie.' He swallowed nervously. 'I expect you also have the capacity to analyse individual borrower patterns and rates of prompt return. Now that everything is computerised. Not, of course, that I would want to be party to any results involving names.'

Angela gave him the long, hard bureaucratic look. It reminded him of their contretemps on the telephone a few days ago. He shifted uncomfortably in his seat and looked away. Then she turned to her computer screen. Her black fingers darted over the keyboard.

She gave a small smile. 'There's a very strong chance, not far off 100%, that you'll have the book in your hot little hands by midday.'

Sterling had more questions. After all, he was a PI. But in the gap between Angela preparing for business and actually opening, they sat comfortably together and sipped their tea. Angela worked open the chocolates, and they had one or two as a breakfast supplement. Sterling was used to waiting, and he knew when he was pushing his luck.

He was doodling in his office, sketching theories and scenarios in the Etchingham case and thinking of Smithy, when the call came. It was 11:51. He scuttled downstairs. As he went through the library door, a shorter man in his late 40s or early 50s was coming the other way. He and Sterling feinted this way and that, blocking each other's path for a moment. 'So sorry,' he murmured with a smile. He wore luminescent cycle clips and carried a cycle helmet. Sterling noticed a standard hearing aid in one ear and a more complicated device near the other – a small, dark blue disc above it attached by wire to another dark blue aid tucked behind it. Angela nodded at his back and looked at Sterling. *Appaloosa*'s returner had been his statistically reliable self.

Sterling was worried that another eager borrower would pounce on the book he coveted so much. He quickly had Angela scan it and his card, so that he was the new loanee. He wanted to go to a nearby table to examine it on his own, but without Angela he would have had nothing, and perhaps he would have been nothing – a discarded body in some lonely corner of West Flanders.

'May I come around and sit at your desk with you, Angela – so we can look at the book together?'

'Be my guest,' she smiled. He could tell she was pleased.

He placed the book in front of them, square and parallel against the edges of the otherwise almost empty desk, as if symmetry would help. He splayed his fingers each side of it. It felt that this was the moment. *Appaloosa*, by Robert B. Parker. There was a formulaic picture of a wild stallion and a tall cowboy on the front. He never read westerns.

'Parker is very good,' said Angela. 'He writes crime novels, mainly, but his westerns are a popular sideline. We've got a lot of his stuff across the county. I think *Appaloosa* has been made into a film.'

Sterling nodded, but barely listened to what she was saying. He thought she might be saying it because she was nervous, too.

'Where's the ISBN?'

'Somewhere in the first couple of pages.'

He opened the book and leafed through. He quickly found the page with all the details of publication, and there it was – except that the ISBN had been neatly crossed through and replaced in small, neat black letters and numbers – a/c 000111769.

Angela turned to him. 'That's IT?' she said incredulously. 'That's what you've been schlepping around western Belgium this last week for? That's what all this is about?'

He shrugged, feeling the same sense of anti-climax but convinced as well that the journey was just about over. 'It looks like it. I'm seeing Gloria Etchingham this afternoon. This is an account number. It goes with a photograph I've got. I think she's going to be pleased. Do you think it's time for another cuppa, Angela?'

As she smiled again and moved away to the kettle in her office, he thought that Gloria would be very pleased. He'd solved her case, but that did not prepare him for the twists and turns that followed.

26

Gloria Etchingham was the kind of woman for whom opportunities open up. That's what Sterling thought when the parking space just below his window became available as the black BMW eased into the square, just as it had when they first met. She didn't even need to back in. The Red Sea couldn't have done better for Moses and the Israelites. Today, she was in a simple satin electric blue frock and matching heels. Her arms were bare, and her earrings looked like sapphires. The frock ended just above her knees, and although the neckline described a simple line across her shoulders and she wore no belt, she had a way of wearing and moving that fixed eyes on her, including Sterling's. As she closed the driver's door, she looked up at and smiled. She knew he'd be looking down. She did not disguise the little shimmy she needed to perform in order to have the dress settle. The indicator lights on the car winked orange as it locked, as if in appreciation of her little performance.

As she reached the door to the library and the office, she leaned over to adjust a heel, her leg bent behind her. It was the same Gloria Etchingham and Sterling felt the same frisson. Then he heard the clicking as she climbed the stairs, and waited with the door open at the top. Sense and sensibility conducted their usual battle in his head.

His resolution to be the embodiment of professionalism in this case always crumbled in Gloria Etchingham's presence.

'Frank, nice to see you,' she said as they shook fingers delicately.

He gestured her to the visitor's chair and went around behind his desk. He tried not to look as she sat down and crossed her legs, the shimmy downstairs already redundant as her frock rode up.

His voice sounded hoarse and he had to clear his throat. He sipped at the water on his desk. 'Well, Gloria. I'll say this. It's been an adventure. But I think it's got a good ending.'

She clasped her hands around her knees and leaned forward. 'Tell me,' she said.

So Sterling told the story – all of it except for some editing in key places. When he got to the body at the Scottish Memorial at Frezenburg, he stopped.

'In one of the earlier messages I left on your voicemail, I mentioned Thomas Jackson. I asked if you knew him.'

'Tommy … I haven't seen him for a few days. I haven't spoken to him, either.'

'So you know him.'

Gloria raised her eyes to his. 'He's my brother.'

Sterling sat back, shocked, knowing what he needed to say, but not knowing how. It was the same when he was a policeman. You never got used to it.

'Gloria, there's no easy way … I'm sorry to have to tell you….'

'What? What?'

'I'm afraid he's dead.'

'Dead? Dead?' Her eyes had an unfocused look. 'He can't be.'

Sterling passed over a box of tissues from a drawer in his desk. He waited for a few minutes as she struggled to compose herself. A tearful Gloria Etchingham seemed more genuine than the actor he'd come to know. She accepted the cup of tea he made for her.

'So,' he said finally, 'I identified the bank in the photo – Fintro in Sint Jacobstraat in Ypres – and what I strongly believe is an account number. Gloria, this was never about your husband's ancestors in the Great War and his family honour. It's about money. The mystery is why he had someone – me, as it's turned out – gallivanting around Belgium on some treasure hunt. Still, that's not really my concern. I've done what you asked. For me, the case is over.'

'Frank, that can't be it. You can't....' – there was a catch in her throat – 'abandon me now.'

'Abandon … That's a bit dramatic. You gave me a slip of paper and some background. I followed the trail. It led back here to Sandley, via – in no particular order – my abduction, a sustained brush with the Belgian police, sundry other episodes of danger and intimidation and a couple of beatings up. I'm really so sorry – but your brother is dead – murdered by some English gang while following me about. The trail itself seems to have stopped with the photo and the account details I've just given you. I've racked up lots of expenses and a large bill for my services. I don't think there's anything more I can do for you. Actually, I don't think it's safe to do anything more for you. I told you, remember, that one of the gang is still around somewhere.'

Her shoulders slumped. 'What do you think I should do?' she said in a small voice.

'Go and make arrangements with the Belgian authorities about your brother, Gloria. Concentrate on him and your family. When you're ready, go and see what's in the account. It's probably in Keith's name. I expect you'd need your passport and proof of marriage and so on. Presumably there's a lot of red tape to get through as Keith's … status is not really certain. At least you'd be able to find out what cash from that source you might be in line for. You might be able to have a preliminary conversation with the bank manager. I've got his details here – Johan Hendrickx. You don't really need me anymore.'

'Perhaps you could come with me. I'd pay you. I need the support, Frank. Especially with Tommy gone.'

'I'd need to think about it. But I'm afraid I've got to give you the bill for what I've done so far.' He opened the drawer again and slid it over.

Gloria looked carefully at all the items. Sterling had expected some quibbles on the basis of past behaviour, but she reached into her bag. 'Will a cheque be OK?' As she handed it over and he reached to take it she tightened her grip. 'You will think about it, won't you, Frank? You've done so well for me so far. I've come to rely on you.'

When she had gone, a light clatter down the stairs and back to the car in the street below, he leaned back in his chair and rocked a little. He looked at the cheque. The price was good and the timing was welcome. But another instalment would be a bonus. At the same time, he was troubled. Her brother was dead, but it didn't take her long to recover. Somehow, Sterling knew the case wasn't over.

—⁓—

He paid in the cheque at opening time the next day, Saturday. He didn't know the cashier. He went into the bank too rarely. The young man looked as if he wasn't yet old enough to have left Sandley Academy. If a human being had been monitoring his account, rather than an automated programme in a super-computer on an industrial estate in an anonymous corner of England, she or he might have been pleased. His savings had been diminishing rapidly, and this halted the trend. He went over to the office, thinking about Gloria's offer. On the floor was a small, white envelope that someone had slipped under the door, addressed to him.

He sat at his desk and turned the envelope over in his hands. His name was printed using a black biro. The envelope was one of hundreds of thousands, millions for all he knew, for sale anywhere. He was no Sherlock Holmes, but even Sherlock Holmes would have struggled to elicit any clues. Sterling slit the envelope open and extracted a small square of plain paper. He thought he'd finished with all this, but there in front of him was another cryptic message:

O Lord, help me to be pure, but not yet; X; 1509122300

He went downstairs to Angela. Today was her busy day, and he reckoned he'd had enough practice to tackle it himself. But it was his morale that needed attention. There was a bustle around the doors and a queue at the desk. Kerry, Angela's Saturday assistant, was in. All the computer terminals were occupied. He was just about to turn around and return upstairs when Angela spotted him. She indicated her little side office and undid the catch to the desk top flap so he could slip through. Her computer hummed and the screen glowed. It felt good to start the search amongst the bustle that swirled around him, rather than in the silent isolation of his office.

Through Google, the quote was easy. Sterling thought it was familiar, anyway. X could have been anything, and he wondered if the numbers could be another bank account. He leaned around from the screen and looked at the desk. The early rush was easing. It was still busy, but it looked as though Kerry might be able to manage for a while by herself. He filled the kettle and turned it on. Angela came in almost straight away.

'Are you making one for Kerry?

'Awaiting instructions.'

'She has it like me, but with one sugar.'

'Did you hear the kettle or smell the tea?'

'Sensed it. My antennae for tea never fail. So, what now?'

'Another clue. Look.'

'I thought you'd finished. Closed the case. Hopefully, cashed the cheque. Said goodbye to Mrs. E. Moved on.'

'I thought so too, but this was posted under my door this morning.' He showed Angela the small sheet of paper. 'The quote's easy. The rest of it's still puzzling me.'

They looked together at the square of paper. Under the quote he had written, 'St Augustine'.

'If it wasn't for the semi-colon,' said Angela, 'I'd think that the 'X' meant 'not St Augustine' – St Augustine wrong. Something like that. Is it an 'X' or is it something else?'

'This is St Augustine country, in a way,' said Sterling. 'He founded the cathedral at Canterbury, didn't he? Didn't he convert one of the Saxon kings? What's that place in Canterbury – St Augustine's Abbey.'

Angela's dark eyes were shining. 'Ethelbert. He converted Ethelbert. In the 6th century. Ethelbert's wife Bertha was already a Christian. But I don't think it's the Abbey, and it's not about them. The 'X' is a cross.'

Then Sterling saw it too. 'St Augustine's Cross over at Cliffsend. Of course. So what about the rest of it, the numbers?'

At that moment, they heard Kerry answer the phone. She tapped on the computer keyboard as she cradled the phone between shoulder and ear. 'It's due back on the 15th. Yes, the 15th of the 9th 2012. Correct, yes, that is today, but if you want, you can renew now, over the telephone.'

Angela and Sterling turned from listening back to each other.

'2300, then, is the time of day,' he said. 'And it's got to be a rendezvous.'

As he left to go back to the office, he called out his thanks to Kerry.

'For what?' she said.

Angela touched his arm. 'Best take Mike,' she said.

27

When Sterling was drinking coffee and eating cakes in Jack Cook's in the mid-afternoon, he didn't even have to ask for the Peugeot.

'You can have the car anytime,' Jack had said. 'If I'm not around, Mickey will sort it out for you.'

He'd stopped asking about the case, too. Perhaps all the knock-backs had sapped his will.

Sterling picked the car up early, after he had been back to his office to make some phone calls. There was no room for parking by his house, so he put it in the cattle market car park. The pub was open all day on Saturday. He thought he'd go in for a pint and see if he could book Mike. Becky was at the bar. When he asked if Mike could come out with him later on – around closing time – she frowned.

'Sorry, Frank. Mike's not around at all this evening. I've got some help coming shortly, but I'm holding the fort by myself at the moment.'

Sterling sipped at his beer. It would be OK, he thought. Only he and the message sender knew of the rendezvous. But there was no doubt that Mike was handy in a crisis.

Becky looked at him. 'Do you want me to pass on a message, just in case? I'd be happy to do that.'

He looked into his beer. There was no answer there, but he made a quick decision. 'I'm going to St Augustine's Cross – that little space between Cliffsend and the golf club along the Minster road – at 11 o'clock tonight. I've had a mystery summons. If Mike's back, I wouldn't mind him in the vicinity, like before.'

'OK. I'll give him the message. He'll know where it is.'

Being married to Mike Strange clearly taught Becky to take everything in her stride. But there was something else about her. Sterling had known her for some while, and they were close. He tried to identify exactly what it was. She was competent and attractive. She had a good sense of humour and an open, modest way about her. All those things were important. But then he realised what it was. Above all, she was utterly reliable.

Later on at home, as the witching hour approached, the adrenaline started to flow and his mouth had the familiar dryness, he left a voicemail message at Dover police station, for insurance. The cryptic summons had not stipulated that he should come alone.

—∞—

Sandley was a pretty town. That was why Sterling liked living there. But when you got to the quay from where the sea had long receded and where all that was left was the sluggish river, and cross northwards over the old toll bridge to the other side, it all changed. The old military married quarters were not so bad – individualised and altered now they were in private hands – but then there were the old printing works, The Press on the Lake, the tatty Waterside garage and Falcon Sheds, whose products lined up randomly behind the fence by the roadside.

On the other side of the road and further up, Clarksons and Co. hired and sold industrial generators from dilapidated hangars. Beyond that was pharmatown, the huge glass and steel daytime rival to Sandley itself, and the locality's biggest employer - the one that called the shots with the district and county councils. Sterling liked to believe that the tiny enterprises dwarfed by the pharmaceutical company existed in defiance of it, but more likely they lived off the host organism.

Further on, the landscape reverted to shabby type. The paper recycling plant's corrugated iron shed had stark holes where panels had fallen out and never been replaced. Huge cubes of compacted paper lay scattered around. On the other side there was a large compound of cars for auction, a household waste site and a metal fabrication workshop where a firework manufacturing company had once been.

A Kentish miner sculpted in dark metal still crouched on one knee outside the decommissioned power station, headlamp attached to helmet and pick in hand. The control block of the power station beyond the gates gaped with broken windows and the cooling towers loomed from behind, red warning lights blinking warnings to passing aircraft.

Sterling had not been this way for some time, beyond the desolation old and new. At the petrol stations on each side of the road beyond the power station, they were adding some kind of new arterial road. The road he intended to use to get to the Cross was closed – forever, according to the sign, though it didn't express it so dramatically. He'd have to go the long way around the bay and through Cliffsend itself, and so he did, sea to his right and golf course to his left.

He turned left into Cliffsend and left again towards the entrance to the golf club, doubling back on himself. At five to eleven on the dark, cloudy night, a little later than he intended because of the detour, he pulled into the lay-by in front of St Augustine's Cross, switched off the engine, turned out the lights and tried to control his quick breaths and fluttering heartbeat.

The silence was heavy as he climbed over the stile in front of the monument. Behind it, he could just make out the railway line and the concrete bridge of the unfinished new road. Up close, the cross looked like just what it was – a stone cross, not very ancient, not in very good condition; the conceit of a local Victorian dignitary. The saints carved into the base were fading back into history, worn away by wind and rain over 140 or so years, just like the lettering. Sterling was thinking that he and Angela had got something wrong – the date or time, or maybe even the location – when a figure stepped out of the shadows behind the cross.

'Frank Sterling,' said the figure's voice. 'Did you come alone?'

'Yes,' said Sterling, and as far as he knew it was true. He would have preferred to have Mike Strange somewhere close by, and he was expecting more company later. 'And my guess is that you are Keith Etchingham.'

The figure approached. A match flared in the darkness, and Sterling made out for a moment a handsome, weathered face with a few days' growth of beard and longish dark hair, wavy and expensively cut, but due for another visit to the barber's. He caught the pungent smell of tobacco smoke as Etchingham pulled at his newly lit cigarette so that it would take. The smell hung on the damp evening air. They faced each other in front of the cross. Sterling waved away the cigarette packet offered out to him.

'I had given up smoking until all this.' Etchingham gave another deep pull, blowing the smoke upwards. 'But then it got stressful. I expect you've got a lot of questions. How did you like my little treasure hunt?'

'It had its droll moments, Keith. It had its hairy moments, too.' Sterling rubbed at the little burn scar on his neck.

'Yeah, I imagine you had those. Sorry about that,' he said. The apology seemed sincere, and Sterling remembered the charismatic effect Etchingham had had on Mehrtens the chocolatier. 'In the end, I was running out of ideas for packaging the clues.'

'It was getting a bit ragged. But if this is a question and answer session, my first question is, why are we meeting? What's this all about?'

'That's two questions, Frank. Anyway, I suppose it's about information exchange. Did you give Gloria the number and the Fintro bank photo?'

'Yup. She's paid me for what I've done and technically, my involvement is over.'

Etchingham seemed to mull over that information. Then he said, 'But you're here, so you must be curious.'

'Yes, I am curious in this specific case,' Sterling said cautiously.

'So am I, Frank, from my end. Gloria and I didn't choose you randomly. You were recommended. You had the exact skills set, as the recruitment people say, that we were looking for.'

'You and Gloria? You planned it together?'

'I think you probably deserve the whole story, given those hairy moments. I feel bad about the way things have turned out.' Seeing the impatience in Sterling's face and the shuffle of his feet, Etchingham put up his hand. 'Just hear me out, Frank. Let me give you some background. Then you can decide what you want to do next.'

He leaned against the monument and the tip of his cigarette glowed red-orange as he took another pull. 'In the course of your … investigations, I expect you heard a few things about me. I've run a few businesses, successfully most of the time, but that's never been my main interest. My main interest, as you've probably found out, is how this country has been going to the dogs over the whole of the last century, and how it's still going on. We all owe money. We don't make anything. We open our borders to all and sundry. We have stupid, bureaucratic rules. We have millions of welfare scroungers. I don't even really know where to start, to be honest. So I got myself involved in politics.'

'PEDU is politics? I don't think so, Keith.'

'Well, I got involved, anyway. A bloke like me was an asset to them. I understood money and could read balance sheets. They decided that I'd be most useful looking after party finances. That suited me. I was using my skills to achieve what I thought was right. I was younger then – and a bloke with extreme views. We were going to save the country from itself – and from all its enemies. I wasn't scared of what it would mean, either. People bashing people, the ends justifying the means, all that.'

Sterling said nothing. He could see better as his eyes got used to the dark.

'It was alright for a few years. But then something happened. I got older for one thing. Have you ever been to a demo or a political meeting? God, the abuse, the hostility. The things we got pelted with. The Socialist Workers and the Anarchists can be just as bad as we are. Even our own private get-togethers were depressing. PEDU used to go mob-handed over to Belgium for an annual solidarity jamboree with other far right groups from all over Europe. That's why I had you running around Ypres. I came to know it well. All those blokes, and their wives and girlfriends, were milling around muddy canal-side fields in August.

Have you heard of the van Raemdonck memorial? It was there. We laid wreaths at the pillbox and plans for mayhem Europe-wide. We were going to cleanse our nations and put everything right. But what do you call it when you have a sudden change of heart? An epiphany. I had an epiphany, that's what I had. Those blokes with swastikas tattooed on their bald scalps, the stupid posturing, the marches and chanting, the cock-eyed policies, the hatred and bile against anyone who disagreed – I fell right out of love with all that. It wasn't me anymore, and it wasn't the life for me. The reds talk about wallowing in a slough of false consciousness – that's how I came to feel about PEDU.'

'What about Gloria?' said Sterling.

'Ah, Gloria.' Etchingham gave him a sly, sideways look. 'She's sexy, isn't she? I really fell for her, like any man would. But I was the one who got to marry her. The thing with Gloria, though, is she has no interest in politics; no interest in what's going on around her. I don't know if I've met anyone with less political awareness. Apart from sex, of course, the only thing Gloria is interested in is money. Always was. Always will be. And there's another thing about Gloria that I only found out about later … I was scared of her. Scared of what she's capable of.'

'So you see where this is going. I was going up in PEDU, but my businesses were going down, and so was my belief. You don't get much competence in fringe groups. Most sensible and competent people gravitate more to the mainstream. It wasn't hard to divert PEDU cash somewhere else. So that's what I did. It worked well for a while. PEDU was propping Gloria and me up. I enjoyed the irony of it all. But when James MacNade came on the scene, it all started falling apart.'

'James MacNade?'

'MacNade. Bastard. He's one of those rare combinations, a financially competent fanatic. A bit like I used to be, perhaps.' He stopped and reflected for a moment, as if this thought had never occurred to him before. 'When PEDU's national executive committee wanted an independent look at the books, he was the one they turned to. From that moment, the writing was on the wall. It wasn't going to involve the Fraud Squad, either. PEDU has its own little branch of enforcers, and they haven't heard of the rule of law. I had to think quickly. Since everything was going belly-up, the best thing to do was disappear. I'd have to start again.'

'Yes, the disappearance,' said Sterling. 'That must have taken some planning.'

'It was painful, the way we did it, I'll say that. The police found a lot of my blood. We splashed that around. I was weak from the blood-letting for days afterwards. But it achieved its purpose. Up to that point, the point where PEDU were asking questions but not getting much in the way of answers, Gloria didn't know anything. But when she knew that the car would have to go, the house, the clothes, the whole lot, she agreed to do whatever she had to do. And what that meant was getting MacNade into the open. Gloria and I made a kind of pact. The trouble was, and still is, that I don't trust her. It's funny. I love her, but trust – that's a very different thing. I had to plan everything so that she still needed me – you know, a kind of half a sixpence thing. So long as she needs me, I've got a bit of security. We're finished, Gloria and I, but she's not going to get all the cash.'

'Well, this is all very interesting,' said Sterling. It felt as if Keith Etchingham had wanted to make a confession, and he'd chosen to make it to Sterling. 'It's making a bit more sense now, although it all seems a bit long-winded. But I've got my fee and expenses from Gloria. She's got the account number and the bank, so I expect she's got all the jigsaw pieces. She's even offered me a contract extension to go to Belgium with her to get the cash. So why are we meeting, you and me?'

'I've got a counter-offer, Frank,' said Etchingham.

Sterling put his hands in his pockets and rocked on his heels. He was getting tired of the whole business. It was about was a cache of money stolen from a worthless, vicious organisation, a bit of which might come to him. It wasn't a thrilling prospect from any angle. Even the money Gloria had given him was tainted.

He might have listened to Etchingham's proposal to get more of an understanding of what he had been through, but he didn't get the chance.

'This is cosy,' said a voice from towards the road. Sterling recognised it straight away. Smithy emerged from the shadows with four others.

Etchingham began to look a lot smaller. 'MacNade,' he said – a statement, not a question. To Sterling, he said softly, 'I thought you came alone.'

'So did I,' Sterling whispered back. 'This has nothing to do with me.'

MacNade walked forward, flanked by another set of thugs, although they looked very like the ones he'd left to their fate in Belgium. For the moment, he seemed to be ignoring Sterling. 'We thought you were dead, Keith. You steal from us, you hide from us, you try to cheat us. One way or another, you've caused PEDU an awful lot of trouble. We've had enough. Where's our money?'

Sterling remembered poor Tommy Jackson lying battered and dead next to the Scottish Memorial in Frezenburg. He and Keith Etchingham were facing a similar outcome. Without Christina to bolster his courage with her own, Sterling looked for ways to slip out of the danger.

'Look, this isn't my business. You need to sort things out among yourselves. I'm off home.'

One of the henchmen put his palm against Sterling's chest. He said nothing. He didn't need to. Sterling thought he saw a metallic blue-grey glint from somewhere else in the entourage.

'I'm waiting, Keith, and as both you and Mr Sterling here know, I am not a patient man,' said MacNade.

Sterling's prospects were looking dire again. He felt a wave of fear, or more accurately terror. This couldn't end well. Then things started happening in rapid slow motion. He and his police mates used to discuss the phenomenon in the canteen after the Saturday night rumbles and riots – how, when there was danger and confusion all around, running and fighting and missiles and fire and broken glass and shouting and the very stench of fear, everything seemed to slow down.

It started at the monument when another of MacNade's entourage sank to his knees and pitched wordlessly forward into the damp grass in front of the cross. It looked for a moment as if he had seen the light and was saying a prayer. Uncertainty replaced menace in the eyes of the men around him. One of them fumbled in his jacket to draw a gun from a shoulder holster. As it came out, a gloved hand appeared from behind in a chopping motion on his wrist. He shouted and doubled over as his good hand grabbed the wrist and the sole of a boot was propelled into his back. He, too, pitched forward, his face smashing into the ground. Now the rest of the group was in disarray in the darkness.

Sterling turned sideways to see Etchingham's reaction, but he was gone. Sterling still had the advantage of night eyes. He just saw Etchingham's foot and the bottom half of a leg disappear into the foliage beyond the grassy area at the back of the monument. The slow motion effect was rapidly wearing off. Sterling pitched after him, hearing the crack, crack, crack of an automatic pistol and a rush of air close to his arm and head. Fear added seconds to his speed. He dived into the hedge, banging his head on a tree stump. He could smell leafy decay all around. As he lay panting and terrified in the dampness, St Augustine's Cross was flooded with light. A shrill voice screeched, 'Stop, armed police'. Christ, he thought, that'll be a sergeant from an armed response vehicle. Behind him, he could hear more shouting and then sirens. The area around the cross could not have witnessed such excitement since Augustine himself landed, or maybe the Saxon invaders Hengist and Horsa at Ebbsfleet, just down the road.

A few seconds later, he had got a little breath back. He began to follow what he was sure was Etchingham's path through the dense undergrowth. He knew he had the advantage. As the trailblazer, Etchingham would be slower. Through the leaves Sterling could make out the lights of the golf clubhouse. He emerged from the undergrowth in the driveway. In front of him, an embankment bulged out of the darkness. Etchingham had prepared himself well. His tracks led up to the fence protecting the uncompleted new arterial road. Sterling didn't doubt that this was the way he had come down, too. As he scrambled up the embankment, he saw the neatly cut square hole in the fence. He slipped through, his chest heaving, and then over the gleaming new crash barrier. Beneath him, he felt the deep rumble of a train and a sudden piercing two-pitch klaxon blare. In front of him thirty metres away in the gloom, Etchingham was frantically trying to kick-start an old Honda moped. Sterling could hear the 'cough', 'cough' at each unsuccessful attempt.

He bent over and put his hands on his knees, still heaving. He needed to get fit. Seeing Sterling start to lurch forward, Etchingham abandoned the kick-start, slipped the moped into gear and began pushing. He let the clutch out and the machine finally spluttered into life. If an inanimate object could be reluctant, that was it. He jumped on, the machine veering and swerving as he fought for control. Sterling wanted to sprint forward, but it was just a shamble. His arm stretched out to catch Etchingham's jacket but he leaned desperately forward as the moped inched away. Something Sterling barely registered flew off the machine or Etchingham himself and flashed past, dislodged by the turbulence.

As the moon emerged from the cloud, Sterling saw Etchingham's wan face turn back, a mixture of triumph and regret. The moped puttered into the empty distance along the almost-finished new road in the silver light. It was a long time before Etchingham became just a pinpoint and then disappeared. Only a faint smell of petrol and oil mix remained.

Next to him, Sterling sensed a black presence, breathing lightly. The slight figure, face obscured by a balaclava, was holding a small leather satchel.

'Well, you lost him, Frank. But he dropped this.'

He recognised the voice straight away. 'Holy Mary mother of God, Becky,' he said. 'Where in the deep pits of hell did you come from?'

28

Sterling caught the white gleam of Becky's teeth in the moonlight. Then she peeled the balaclava from her head and shook her hair loose. He was still short of breath and his shoulders were heaving, but she looked as cool as she might have been pulling a pint.

'As Mike wasn't available,' she said, 'I took it on myself to provide the back-up.'

Sterling wondered if he would ever again be able to look at any husband-wife publican team in a casual way. She handed him the satchel, which turned out to be more of a leather handbag popular with a certain type of man. They stood on the unfinished road and leaned over the contents. There was just an envelope addressed to F. Sterling. Perhaps it had something to do with Etchingham's counter-offer. He slipped the envelope into his pocket.

'Can we keep this to ourselves for the moment, Becky?' he said.

'Sure,' she said.

'Good. Maybe we'd better see what's happening back at the cross.'

'It's probably best if you go alone. It will just get unnecessarily complicated if I turn up as well, and of course, I don't really want to blow my cover.'

'Of course, Becky. I didn't think. I expect the police will want to ask me a few questions.'

'Come over to the pub tomorrow evening. I'd be keen on an update.'

'Fair enough. One thing before I do rejoin the party, Becky,' he said, putting his hand lightly on her arm. 'I didn't know your talents stretched so far beyond running a pub. If you hadn't been there, it would have ended very badly.'

Again, he saw her teeth gleam in the darkness. 'Where do you think Mike and I met?' She saw the light of understanding come into his eyes. 'Yep, in the SIS. Specifically doing one-to-one combat training for the Belgian Intelligence Services. And where do you think he got that pick-up? There's an old house and walled garden in Sint Jacobstraat in Ypres – near the Grote Markt. We've still got friends there.'

'Of course. Obvious,' he said, though really it didn't seem obvious at all. He clasped her hand to his chest. 'Thank you.' A moment later, she had gone, out over the marshes beyond the commotion behind them.

Sterling scrambled back the way he had come through the hole in the fence and down the track to the golf club. He thought his story to the police would be straightforward enough. He could tell the truth, but not quite the whole truth. Perhaps it was because he was preoccupied with the tweaks and planned omissions that he did not immediately notice the movement in the undergrowth next to the railway track. But he knew the stumpy figure that emerged straight away. Some trick of the light combining the bulk and shadow into one mass made him loom large.

'It's time we had a tête-à-tête, Sterling, just the two of us – now that Etchingham and your little helper have vacated the scene,' said James MacNade. 'I'll get Etchingham some other time, but he dropped something. Give it to me,' he said, holding out his hand.

'You delegate too much, Smithy. Other people to do the torturing. Other people to hold the guns. Other people to do the beatings. It must be a bit of a shock to have to do your own dirty work.'

'I should have had Jason get rid of you on the ferry, Sterling, when I had the chance. But I'm perfectly competent when needs must,' he said, gesturing for the envelope with his fingers. 'You really don't want to find out just how much.'

As he spoke, MacNade squared up in a curiously old-fashioned boxing stance, crouching forward with his fists bunched. If he had not seemed so determined, it would have looked faintly ridiculous. Sterling, on the other hand, knew nothing of Queensberry rules. The only ones he knew were Margate rules, which generally apply on drunken summer Saturday nights along the seafront. In addition, he was fuelled by a rage at all the double-crossing and manipulation he had suffered. When he launched himself at the figure in front of him, they were a potent combination. The head butt, launched over a hopelessly inadequate guard, instantly gave him the initiative, and in the two minutes the fight lasted, MacNade was never close to wresting it back. The daze of that first blow seemed to numb him, and then Sterling was punching, kicking, biting, clawing, banging, kneeing and elbowing in a furious, frenetic onslaught. Expecting a kind of traditional fisticuffs, MacNade wilted after the first flurry. He never got over his surprise.

Sterling remembered a kid in his road when he was a boy still in primary school – Freddie Pell. He was a big kid and a bully, and when he got two pairs of boxing gloves one birthday, he got into the habit of challenging other kids, the same age or younger, to fights. When Sterling finally had to fight, he learned a lesson he never forgot. Up to the fourth round, he had only just managed to hold his own. But in that round, the momentum shifted. At the end, Sterling hadn't cared that the other boys judged Freddie the winner. He and Freddie knew different. The bloody nose he got was worth it. The boxing gloves were put away and Freddie never hassled him again.

When MacNade scrabbled away, his coat torn, a red weal on his forehead, an eye beginning to close, one arm holding the other, Sterling recognised that Freddie Pell moment. MacNade was no longer the cocky bully who had lolled on a sofa in a farmhouse in Flanders, clicking his fingers and calling the shots.

Sterling leaned back, panting, and gathered himself for the next assault. He read fear in MacNade's eyes, and a kind of flickering doubt. Sterling was ready for the rock that hurled at his head, and dodged it easily, but that gave MacNade a second to scramble away back into the undergrowth. From the direction of the golf club and St Augustine's Cross, there were sounds of people moving across the driveway, and Sterling could see the beams of torches like mini-searchlights getting closer. He did not think MacNade could get far, but he wanted to be the one to stop him. He plunged into the undergrowth after him.

A bridge carrying the new road towered over the railway track. Sterling saw MacNade twenty-five metres ahead, just in front of a self-closing pedestrian gate across the track. It was remote enough not to have the panoply of warning lights and signs there was at urban sites. All you had to do was stop, look, listen. And that is exactly what was too much for MacNade. Sterling saw his white face turn back to see how far he was behind. He saw him dart through the gate. He heard the gate clang as it rested back in its original position. He heard the horn of the train braying 'Dooo-derrrr' into the night. As he reached the gate, the train, a white and yellow brightly lit blur, rattled past. All that was left of MacNade after that was a blood-soaked leg on the track.

A figure materialised at the gate next to him. 'What's happened now, Frank, for God's sake?' said Andy Nolan.

'Better get the Transport Police, Andy,' he said. 'See the train stopping along there? There'll be a mess to clean up. Good job you turned up when you did. The perfect alibi.'

Later on, when there was nothing more to do on the track and the Transport Police were supervising the grisly clear-up, Sterling and Andy Nolan re-emerged at Saint Augustine's Cross into the bustle of a building site. The ARV was in the lay-by in front of the monument. It had been joined by an ambulance and two squad cars. The glare of spotlights, the moonlight and the flashing blue lights on the vehicles created a theatrical atmosphere. The road had been closed and little knots of police officers were standing around. There was no sign of the men who had been with MacNade. The ARV sergeant spotted Sterling, and for a moment it looked as if she was just about to restart her operation. Then Andy Nolan came into the light from behind him and put his hand on her arm.

'It's OK, Clare, I know him,' he said. 'Frank, you need to tell us what's been going on. We know about MacNade. Where's Etchingham?'

'He got away.' But Sterling wanted an update of his own. 'Where's the rest of MacNade's lot?'

'Jones and Foxhill have taken them down to Dover for questioning, except for one who's going to hospital,' said the ARV sergeant. 'We shot him in the leg. Resisting arrest. They'd already been in the wars. If I was guessing, I'd say that someone used some kind of martial arts on them.'

Andy Nolan gave Sterling an odd sideways look. 'Have you taken up karate since the old days?' he said.

'No. I just got fed up with being pushed around.'

'Whatever. We'll get back to that. You'll have to come down to the station anyway. We need a full statement.'

'Yeah, yeah,' said Sterling tiredly. 'I know the drill.'

Down at Dover, Jones and Foxhill were good. They let Andy Nolan do the questions and they were ready with Keith Etchingham's file and photograph. Sterling looked at his dark, handsome face. There was no beard and his hair was beautifully cut. He stared at the camera with a puckish, challenging look. It was easy to see this man devising the clues and riddles Sterling had been following in Flanders and Kent.

'Yes, that's him, Keith Etchingham. That's the man who met me at St. Augustine's Cross earlier. He slipped away when Smithy and his mob turned up.'

'Yes, the man Smithy,' said Andy Nolan, reaching for another file. 'Is this him?'

Sterling looked closely at the determined, steely face. His fingers went to his neck. 'Yes, that certainly is him. Pieters and Broussart would have wanted him in Belgium. It's too late now.'

Andy Nolan finished taking the statement. He had accepted that MacNade had run onto the tracks before Sterling had reached the crossing gate. Even if it was different, Sterling guessed he would have come down on his side.

'So you reckon Etchingham was going to give you the final bit of the jigsaw, but couldn't because you were interrupted. Right?'

'Right,' said Sterling, but it was hard to meet his gaze. 'And there's nothing else, Frank.'

'Not so far,' he said, and it was easier this time, because that bit was true. He could feel the envelope in his jacket pocket chafing against the lining.

As he and Andy Nolan were in the corridor waiting for a patrol car to take Sterling back to the Peugeot at St. Augustine's Cross, the ARV sergeant came through.

'Clare James, Frank Sterling,' Andy Nolan said solemnly as he introduced them, formally this time. Sterling made a quick decision.

'Why don't we meet tomorrow night in my local and talk everything over? Get some things clear. It will be more comfortable there,' he said to them both. They could join him and Becky, and maybe Mike and Angela.

'That's a bit unorthodox,' said Clare James.

'Better than the nick,' said Andy Nolan. He could be patient, too.

Sterling got back home at half past five when dawn was still far off. He should have been drained, but the prospect of opening the envelope that Keith Etchingham had dropped on the unfinished road kept him alert. He sat at the kitchen table in the still house, took it from his pocket and tore it open. There were two sheets of paper. On one was a list in Etchingham's precise hand: passport, power of attorney sheet, the account number Sterling recognised from the library book, the name and address of a bank in Ypres, the name of its bank manager and a password or security clearance code. But the name and address of the bank and its manager were not the same as the bank in the photo. He wondered why it was Dexia and not Fintro. Keith Etchingham did not make such obvious errors.

Sterling turned to the second sheet, which was written in French and Dutch. It looked very much like a power of attorney document. He started when he saw his own name and office address on it, and, if his school French was correct, permission to withdraw 100,000 euros every three months. Etchingham had been serious about his 'counter-offer'. Later, in bed, Sterling was exhausted but he could not sleep.

—⁂—

Clare James was a character. She had a squeaky voice when she shouted, but she was drinking port and lemon with Andy Nolan, Becky and Sterling in the snug, her Kevlar jacket hung on a coat hook, and she'd entered into the spirit of the debrief. She had more flexibility than some of them.

'All I know,' she said, 'is that we were called out to Cliffsend for 11:15 to assist in the arrest of a fugitive. When we finally found the place, it was already kicking off.'

'Armed response,' said Sterling. 'Bloody late as usual.'

'Sarky,' said the sergeant, but she seemed amused rather than irritated.

'That was Dover's fault, I'm afraid, Frank,' said Andy Nolan. 'Your message got picked up late.'

Sterling sipped his Scotch. He had not been entirely disadvantaged by the way events had unfolded.

'To summarise, Clare,' he said, 'you and your blokes got involved in my case. I thought it was about a long-buried family secret but it turns out it involved embezzlement of European neo-fascist funds. There was a murder too – in Belgium. I was meeting the embezzler whom your colleagues were preparing to arrest. They reckoned he was dangerous enough for Armed Response to be involved. But the embezzler, and me, for that matter, were being followed by his former comrades, who wanted to get their money back. In all the confusion the embezzler, Keith Etchingham, slipped away – on a moped, of all things. He'd planned well – only a bike or a moped could get on and off that new road. I expect he dumped the moped and got in a car at the other end.'

'Embezzler'. said Clare. 'Lovely word.' She rolled the zeds around her tongue.

'You were right about Etchingham's getaway,' said Andy Nolan. 'We found the moped at the new roundabout near Richborough Power Station. We're still looking for him.'

'MacNade had followed me up to the new road. We had an … altercation, and while he was trying to get away from me, he got hit by that train. But you lot,' Sterling said, nodding at Andy and Clare, 'missed the big fish.'

'We got MacNade's associates, though, Frank,' said Andy Nolan. 'That, and MacNade getting killed, will set PEDU back a few years.'

'Yeah, good news. They're all off my back, too. The thing I don't understand is how Smithy – MacNade – and those other blokes knew that I was meeting Etchingham. He wouldn't have told them. He was terrified when they turned up at the cross. I only told you and Becky.'

Andy Nolan and Becky Strange saw him shift and the doubt come into the eyes. 'Come on, Frank,' Andy Nolan said, affronted.

Becky got up abruptly, went behind the bar and came back with a small rectangular device caked with mud. She was quivering as she slapped it on the table. 'It was underneath the Peugeot,' she said. 'It probably explains more than just what happened tonight.'

Sterling put his hands up, palms outward. 'Sorry, sorry. Becky, Andy. Just a joke – poor taste, rubbish timing. And I've had a rough fortnight all in all. But Becky, how did Mike miss that?'

'I'll be having a word,' she said.

Becky was a trouper. So was Andy Nolan, for that matter. They recovered quickly from the slur. Clare sat back with her port and lemon. Everything seemed to amuse her.

'All these police hours and resources,' she mused, looking at Andy Nolan. 'When everything's tied up, who's going to be done for what? From what I've heard, PEDU, or whatever it's called, haven't said a thing about their missing money, so we can't do anything about that. Where does that leave Etchingham?'

'Fair point,' said Sterling, looking at Andy Nolan too.

'It's not really my case. Jones and Foxhill, and their superiors, will decide what to do and take it to the CPS. I'm trying to think what crimes have been committed and then take it from there. Etchingham disappeared of his own accord, so he's wasted police time and his wife aided and abetted him in that. It looks as though he stole lots of PEDU money. Whether PEDU want it pursued or not, that's fraud. Who knows what that might also turn up? Gloria Etchingham's brother was murdered in Belgium. MacNade and his gang did that, it looks like. But MacNade is dead, so only his thugs will cop that. That's a job for the Belgians. Then there's the kidnapping of the hotel receptionist. That's for the Belgians. The St Augustine's Cross thing ... Well, where's the crime? Maybe a bit of intimidation of you and Etchingham, Frank. Maybe our arrival with Clare's armed response unit prevented something really bad happening. But we were there to arrest Etchingham, and he got away. The PEDU people had weapons, so there's something in that. MacNade on the railway line – accidental death. That will help his mates in Belgium, because they can say he killed Tommy Jackson and they were too scared to do anything but keep shtum. The same with the kidnapping.'

They all stared at the table in front of them, lost in their own thoughts. Sterling knew why Andy Nolan was getting promotions in the Kent police. Analytical minds like his were not so common on the force.

'So Gloria Etchingham,' he said. 'She's just going to be done for helping Keith disappear, after all my trekking around western Belgium and all that other hassle.'

'Even then, Frank, where's the proof? It's only what Keith Etchingham told you. So don't hold your breath that she'll get charged. And there was nothing illegal in what she asked you to do. Anyway,' Andy Nolan continued, mainly to Clare, 'look on the bright side – a murder and a kidnapping solved, a suspected kidnapping or murder solved, and a case of embezzlement likely to be solved. We can't have the first two – the Belgians will get those, unless we can fiddle something – but the others are ours. It's going to be good for our clear-up stats.'

Sterling took a long pull of his pint. Andy Nolan was the same as Pieters. Tying up the loose ends didn't matter to him. But it wasn't as neat and tidy for Sterling as it was for the Kent Police. He still had plans.

29

Gloria Etchingham was as keen to meet Sterling as he was to meet her, but he had the feeling that their reasons were very different. On Monday, they arranged an 11 o'clock rendezvous at the tearoom of the Secret Gardens. It felt right – somewhere away from the office on neutral ground. Their interests had been diverging for some days. He had been to the bank, and reassuringly the fee and expenses had moved into his account. He emerged from St Peter's Church and Holy Ghost Alley into Sandley High Street and turned left down to the tollhouse and quay. He realised he was whistling softly, but more from unease than lightness of spirit.

At the quay were a few sailing boats, too small to be yachts, too large to be dinghies, and one or two cruisers, sea going if they hugged the coastline. The Sandley Boat Company, consisting of one little riverboat beneath an awning that was faded and tatty, was still offering trips up the small river to Great Stonar. Sterling wondered what the guide's patter might consist of. It was just a grey bit of water in marsh and flatland. He had lived in Sandley for years but was never curious to find out.

A Mr Whippy ice-cream van had still not been laid up for the season, and its generator hummed faintly. A couple of hikers were buying cones before their expedition across the paths and golf course to the coast at Sandley Bay. Sterling's walk was shorter: a right hand turn off the quay into Knightrider Street and then through the gates into the Salutation, the Lutyens house which the Secret Gardens enclosed.

He neared the gate and scanned the small car park. Gloria had arrived. There was the BMW. The tearoom was on a wooden decked platform to the left of the house. You could get tea there without going through the turnstile into the gardens. The tearoom abutted the wall against Knightrider Street, and an outside seating area ran around it on three sides. Gloria was in a corner where the teashop dais backed on to the wall, which itself backed on to the quay.

Although he was some distance away, Sterling could see her fingers drumming on the table. She cast frequent glances at the mobile device next to her teacup. In his limited experience of encounters with her, she had been intent on creating an impression. Now, she had no thoughts for that. This was about business, and business conducted unobtrusively. Her jeans were stylish, though, and her navy top a plain but expensive-looking cashmere. He knew she would look up towards the gates and see him.

He started walking towards the steps of the tearoom as if he hadn't been watching her. As he went up the steps, he saw a robin foraging for crumbs on the wooden floor and the railing. Its eyes, tiny, glittering black dots, focused single-mindedly. Gloria didn't see the bird at all. On the way to the table, Sterling buttonholed the waitress for a pot of tea and checked that there would be enough for Gloria to have a refill.

She had no time for preliminaries. She didn't even say his name. The words came out in a torrent. 'I went to Belgium. I found the bank in Ypres, but they hadn't got the account number. They hadn't heard of me or Keith. Something's gone wrong. I paid you good money. I need it sorted out.'

Sterling put his hand up. 'Whoa, Gloria. The other day you were pleased with what I'd done. I did everything you wanted. I can't help it if the information I got was inaccurate. That's someone else's fault.' He chose not to mention the satchel and the envelope that Keith Etchingham had dropped, and the information it contained. That might come later.

Her hand kept drumming. He did not think she even noticed she was doing it. They sat in uneasy silence as the waitress brought a new cup and saucer and a new pot of tea.

'Anyway,' he said, 'I've got my own beefs. I'm tired of listening to you. It's time you listened to me.' He poured his own tea and without asking, topped up Gloria's. She looked chastened enough to fall silent.

'While you were away, I met your Keith.' Gloria was listening now. 'He summoned me to a meeting and we had a chat. He was very much alive and kicking. I've been used, Gloria. You used me and I'm really pissed off. Keith didn't tell me everything, but here's what I think happened.

'You know when I thought something wasn't quite right? That first time you came to see me. It wasn't just how you found me irresistibly attractive. It was that sense of relief I think you felt when I agreed to take on your case. I thought it might be because you couldn't think of any other way to get things going, but now

I know that you and Keith set me up. He told me as much. Someone recommended me, and I took the bait. It set things in motion, as you planned. You set me running, you and Keith, like a hare.

'Yep, that's a good way of looking at it. I was your hare. Keith knew that someone was after him because he was stealing money – MacNade – and I reckon my job was to flush MacNade out. But I was also your hound. Keith laid the trail, and my job was to follow it. You were in it together, but he didn't trust you, and I guess you didn't trust him, so neither of you could get the cash without the other. We don't have to pretend about Keith's family honour anymore, do we? It's always been about money stashed away secretly somewhere, though not the Fintro Bank branch in Ypres, as it turns out.'

Gloria was very quiet. She stirred her tea and looked at the table. Occasionally, she'd look at Sterling and then back down.

'So, you and Keith. In it together. I believe what he told me. He seemed desperate enough to be telling the truth. You decided that things were so hot that he'd have to disappear. It would be even better if it looked as though he'd been bumped off. You did a realistic job on that. Poor bloke, recovering from all that lost blood. It must have been a bit sad that you were planning all this, but for a future apart. Keith said that the marriage was over. Maybe he wasn't being quite honest there. He still seems very fond of you.'

'So far so good. But I think you added some embellishments, we could call them, of your own, some deviations from the plan. I don't think Keith knew about them. Tommy was the first one. I saw him in the square outside my office that time you first came up there. You and Keith did a bit of research on me beforehand. I think Tommy attacked me in my home to get my dander up. It worked, too. And then Tommy's job was to keep an eye on me and make sure I did what I was meant to do. He tracked me too, using the tracking device on the Peugeot I borrowed.'

'I met Tommy, you know. He came and sat with me one evening in Ypres when I was having my dinner. He was scared by then. He was in the open and was going to disrupt MacNade's plans. I reckon your embellishments got out of hand. You got in touch with Smithy, or MacNade or whatever he was called. Maybe you thought you could do him enough of a favour to share some of the money Keith stole and get him off your back. He saw me as a threat on the ferry. I was almost killed, you know, tossed off that boat.'

'I'm struggling to think all this through,' he said. 'The trouble with involving MacNade is that you lost control. He wasn't an easy man to manipulate. He became a loose cannon. He realised that it was me who was the key to tracking down the PEDU cash and when he knew that, Tommy was in trouble. Tommy must have known from you about the clue at the Scottish Memorial. Maybe MacNade and his gang didn't mean to kill him, but things got out of hand. MacNade wanted access to the tracking device on the Peugeot. Tommy wouldn't give it up. I think that MacNade also realised that he didn't need you anymore. He could get everything he needed by kidnapping and torturing me.'

'You really did muddy the waters, Gloria. MacNade was after Tommy, and not me. He had me attacked as a rival pursuing Tommy. Then he switched to me. That seems to make sense.' Sterling leaned back and closed his eyes. He could feel the beginnings of a headache, a slight throbbing in his skull. He massaged his temples. 'When it all started falling apart for MacNade in Belgium, maybe he teamed up with you again. You must have needed each other more than ever by then. The tracker on the Peugeot – that's how MacNade knew I was going to meet Keith.'

Gloria leaned forward. There were no heated denials. 'What do the details matter? Keith underestimated you, Frank,' she said softly. 'He thought you'd do what we needed you to do. I went along with it. Things had got very difficult. But when I met you, I really liked you. I still do. I knew Keith wouldn't make things easy for me, but everything got out of control. Poor Tommy. I'll never get over that.' She dabbed her eyes with the corner of a small white handkerchief.

She looked off into the distance. 'We grew up in a council flat in Coombe Valley in Dover. Do you know it? Up one of those awful valleys out of the town. Dad left when I was three. Mum was a cleaner. We never had anything, Frank. Our clothes were from charity shops. Holidays were in a caravan over at Camber Sands. I never had a new dress till I was 14. Treats were fish and chips every other Friday night. I swore I wasn't going to live like that when I grew up. I can't go back to it. When I met Keith, that was my way out. I loved him, too. He had energy and confidence. He was going places. He made money. I had to support him when things went bad.' As she spoke, she clasped her hands over Sterling's. 'There are millions of euros in a bank account in Ypres, just waiting.'

'No, Gloria,' he said angrily, pulling away. 'Let's get this all straight. In the end, Keith didn't trust you, any more than you trusted him. So you double-crossed him and he's on the run. You used Tommy, and he got his head bashed in. You double-crossed MacNade, and he got squashed by a train. Worst of all, from my point of view, you used and double-crossed me, and you're still trying. What a piece of work you are.'

He understood then where Keith Etchingham's fear had come from. Gloria drew back and folded her arms. 'Suit yourself, Frank. I don't think you'll ever amount to anything but a small time, hick-town private detective, if that,' she said with a sneer. 'You could have had so much more. Anyway, you can't prove anything. No one's going to say anything – not Tommy, not MacNade, not Keith. I've done nothing illegal.'

Sterling got up, putting a few coins on the table to pay for the tea. 'I expect the police are dredging up something as we speak, Gloria. PEDU will probably still be on your back, too. I don't reckon any of it matters much, though. It looks to me like you are on course for a council flat in Buckland, without the car and all the trimmings. Just like in the old days. You and Keith must have been living on borrowed time for years.'

As he left the tearoom dais and walked to the gate of the Salutation, he looked back. The beautiful woman who had stepped out of the black BMW and into his office two weeks ago, making him feel the only important man in the locality, had gone. The woman sitting fingering a teaspoon radiated anger. He felt Gloria Etchingham's malevolent eyes on his back. In Knightrider Street, with the high brick wall of the secret gardens between them, it was as though a beam boring into his back had been cut off.

30

Sterling plunged down Strand Street towards the High Street. There was no time for a detour around by the Quay. Crossing the road, he slipped back through the alleys and lanes into Market Street. He needed an antidote, and only Angela would do. If he remembered correctly, Monday was half-day closing for the library. He had one thing to do before he might catch her locking up.

The windows of the café were steamed up. It was just after midday, and the lunchtime rush was beginning. A woman and her daughter were going through the door with their shopping bags. People already sat at some of the tables, looking through the menus. Sterling could hear the hiss and roar of the coffee machine, or perhaps it was the internal roar in his ears.

'Is Jack about?' he said to one of the waitresses. Her eyes gestured towards the kitchen beyond the counter and he strode on through, noting the 'In' sign on the serving door just in time. Jack was hunched over a table talking with Mickey and his chef. As he rose, Sterling grabbed his lapels, swung him around and pinned him back to the wall. He was a big man, a little taller than Sterling and a lot wider, but Sterling had the advantage of anger and surprise. He could smell coffee on his breath, and a dried rivulet of sweat streaked down his temple on to his cheek. The chef Sterling had never seen before. He withdrew, startled and shocked to the far end of the kitchen, a culinary Pontius Pilate. Mickey looked on impassively, as if this sort of thing happened every day.

'Frank, for God's sake. What's going on?'

'You bastard. You set me up. You're the one who put the Etchinghams on to me. You're the one who put the tracker on the Peugeot so I could be followed. That's why you never asked for money. That's why you stopped asking questions. You already knew what was going on. I fucking trusted you. I drink with you. You bastard. Why?'

At first, Jack's eyes had pretended a kind of genial bewilderment. There had to be some mistake. What on earth are you doing bursting into my kitchen and pinning me against the wall? Are you insane? But he could tell there was no way out. He relaxed against Sterling's hands, feigned confusion replaced in his eyes by a look Sterling did not quite recognise. Not defiance. Something else.

'Naïve, Frank. Very naïve. You think someone like Gloria Etchingham would ever have heard of Frank Sterling Investigations without input from someone like me? You think a woman like that would look at someone like you? I was doing you a favour, mate. You got a case. You got paid. So what's a little GPS between friends? Anyway, it was my car.' He took Sterling's hands from his jacket and brushed it down in a studied kind of fashion. 'You need to grow up, Frank. It's a nasty old world out there.'

'What did you get out of it, Jack? What did she promise you?'

'Well, now, mate, what makes the world go round?' He winked. 'More than the pint and the few quid you'd give me for a favour. And the rest is between me and the lady.'

'Keep out of my way, Jack, or I'll fucking kill you.'

'Yeah, yeah,' he said. 'Noted. Do you mind if I get on with the lunch rush?' He turned back to the table.

Sterling stumbled, still shaking, out of the café and over the road to the library. As he went through the door, Angela called from inside her office. 'Sorry, we're just closing.'

He leaned against the counter, breathing heavily. 'It's me,' he called back.

Angela's head appeared from behind the office door. 'Frank. You look dreadful. What's happened? Come through.' She opened the counter and led him through to her office. 'Sit down. I'll finish closing up and lock the door. Then we can have some peace and quiet.'

A minute or two later, they were facing each other across the small table. 'In a nutshell, I've been used and double-crossed,' said Sterling.

'I know what that's like,' said Angela softly. 'From London.'

'I never really knew about that. We thought there might have been something. You know, the pub crowd. But we thought you just wanted to spend some time out of the big city and in the provinces.'

'Well, there's a story to be told sometime. After you've told me yours,' she said.

Sterling left little out, and ended by telling her about Jack Cook and the tracker on the Peugeot. 'Almost from the beginning, while I was investigating, I felt as though there was a parallel operation going on. And I was right.'

'And now the puppet's cut his strings,' said Angela. 'I feel a bit bad about Jack. I could have reminded you how dubious he is. It's not as though he didn't have form. Good company but chronically unreliable. Hard wired to do a friend down for a quick buck. Talking of which, were you ever tempted to take up Gloria or Keith Etchingham's offers?'

'What, go back to Ypres and get the money? 'Course I was. A dodgy journey for dodgy money. Just up my street,' he joked. 'Lucky I didn't get the chance to explore any details with Keith, what with Smithy turning up.'

Then he could see that Angela had thought of something. 'Hang on a minute. The Etchinghams sent you off on this wild goose chase to Belgium. The idea was to flush out the PEDU thugs, who were after Keith. Keith didn't really trust Gloria. The information you were finding was what she needed to get hold of the money, but he changed one of the details – the identity of the bank. She did her own double-crossing by involving Tommy and doing some deal with Smithy. Right. But as things turn out, surely the Etchinghams can get just what they had planned to get. Everything's even better than they could ever have dreamed. Between them, they've got everything they need to access that bank account. Smithy and PEDU are out of the picture. I bet they're still in contact with each other. What's to stop them going to Ypres and picking up the first tranche of the cash?'

Sterling gave her a little hug. 'Don't worry, girl,' he said. 'I've thought of that. After all, I'm a private investigator.'

———※———

By late afternoon the next day, the balmy sunny weather that had enveloped Sandley and Ypres for most of the last fortnight had moved away. Sterling put the telephone down and looked out over the square. A dark cloud appeared over ahead and made the day even gloomier, and shops and businesses were turning on their lights for the last stretch of the day. Rain spat at the window, the drops getting progressively larger. A man and woman in their early sixties emerged in their raincoats from the Spar shop with grocery bags in each hand. Seeing the swift decline in the weather, they put on plastic rain hats and tied the strands beneath their chins. At that age, practicality was clearly trumping ridicule, whereas the young girl who walked past them ignored the water that frayed the bottoms of her jeans and seeped through the thin cotton hood of her top, plastering her fine hair to her forehead.

The wind squalled around the square, rustling the damp leaves. Sterling put on his coat and picked up his umbrella. He couldn't wait for the weather to ease. He was meeting Angela in the pub, and he had news.

Holy Ghost Alley was dark. The streetlights had not yet come on. He walked through the wind tunnel into the High Street and ducked into the cosy warmth of the pub. Angela was already in the snug. He didn't see Mike Strange straight away, but a pint appeared in front of him when he sat down. He went back to the bar and leaned right over into the serving area, looking from right to left.

'Mike, Mike, where are you?' He appeared suddenly from around the corner from the opposite direction from the one Sterling had been looking in. Sterling started and recovered. 'I've got a bit of an update. Do you or Becky want to come over? I'll buy you a drink.'

It was Becky who joined them. 'I'll tell Mike later,' she said, 'but to be honest, it's the bish-bash-boff he likes, not the boring details.' They smiled into their glasses. In the other bar, Sterling could see Jack Cook drinking with his other cronies. He had acquired a defiant air. He'd probably be coming in here less often now, to the dubious benefit of the George and Dragon. Everything might settle down between them in time, but there would be no rapprochement, only accommodation.

Angela put her hand on his sleeve. 'What were you going to tell us, Frank?'

He dragged his eyes back. 'I just got a call from Andy Nolan before I left the office. He'd got a call from Belgium. My mate Pieters and his boss, Broussart, have just arrested Keith Etchingham as he was coming out of the Dexia Bank in Ypres. They picked up Gloria at a nearby café. Andy Nolan said the Fraud Squad, HMRC and Interpol are all involved. It looks like the Etchinghams are going to be extradited back here.'

'That's if Gloria doesn't get some clever lapdog Flemish lawyer,' said Angela.

'It doesn't really matter. The point is, she's not getting the money. That's the worst thing for her. It's funny. I've done the right thing, but in a way I've done my own bit of dirty work – with the Etchinghams, and Andy Nolan. I'm more worried about Andy. He wasn't best pleased when I finally told him about Keith Etchingham's offer to me – 'Obstructing police business,' in his words. He called me some names I couldn't repeat in any company. But at least he didn't mess about. He got on to Belgium straight away. He's a clever bloke. He knows my interests are different now that I've left the job. I hope so, anyway. He's not the kind of friend you want to lose.' He looked back over to the public bar.

When Becky had drifted away, Angela got out the crossword.

'Got any dreams for me, before we get going?' she said.

'So many, Angie, that I don't know where to start. Maybe when we've done the crossword. You know, I've got to think some things through after this case. I still can't believe how badly I got played.'

'Yes, well,' said Angela. 'I couldn't say it before, not when you were so agitated, but it was partly your fault – with Gloria Etchingham at least.'

'How come?' said Sterling.

'Well, to be blunt, not enough thinking from what's in your head, and too much from what's in your trousers. Remember, I saw her little performance when she came to your office the first time. And I saw her the second time as well. That blue dress. That shimmy. That preposterous little heel adjustment. I bet you were salivating up there in your office.'

'Salivating? That's a bit extreme.'

'You know what I mean. You agree with me too, when you're being sensible.'

'Then there's the homesickness,' said Sterling. Thinking about Gloria Etchingham, his stupid naivety and the waspish accuracy of Angela's assessment was too uncomfortable. 'A few days away and I'm homesick. What's that about? He punched her lightly on the arm. 'Now you're laughing at me. Stop it. And can I do the job without a car? I really don't want to go down that route. And my moral compass. I worried that that went haywire.'

'Your moral compass? Where did that come from?' Angela was really laughing now. Then she paused. 'Welcome to the 21st century,' she said. 'It's not a game, is it?'

'No. It's real. It's life.'